Once More the Hawks

ONCE MORE THE HAWKS

MAX HENNESSY

CANELO

First published in Great Britain in 1984 by Hamish Hamilton

This edition published in the United Kingdom in 2019 by

Canelo Digital Publishing Limited
57 Shepherds Lane
Beaconsfield, Bucks HP9 2DU
United Kingdom

A CIP catalogue record for this book is available from the British Library.

Print ISBN 978 1 78863 594 3
Ebook ISBN 978 1 78863 451 9

Look for more great books at www.canelo.co

Printed and bound in Great Britain by Clays Ltd, Elcograf S.p.A.

Part One

One

To Dicken Quinney, the junction of the Rhine and the Mosel at Koblenz had always seemed a point of separation in Germany. North of Koblenz it was harsh; the south belonged to the Black Forest and a softer climate. Staring down from the cockpit of the big American Lockheed 12a at the two rivers, one the jugular vein of Germany, the other heading straight for the heart of its traditional enemy, France, he reflected that of all the European countries, he knew Germany better than any. He had fought in France between 1914 and 1918 but as part of a huge army with only brief contacts with the French people. There had been a spell in Italy during 1918, a spell as attaché in Holland, and a spell in Greece as instructor, until one of the political upsets in that country had changed its policy and he had been withdrawn. But all these appointments had lasted only long enough for him to pick up some of the language and little else, while he had visited Germany many times, firstly as pilot to a newspaper proprietor flying regularly to Berlin, later in the insecure period of the Thirties as attaché at the embassy. Now, on the verge of retirement from the RAF, he was back again, this time working for a man called Sidney Cotton, who, like himself, had flown 1½-Strutters in France in 1916 and 1917. Tall, bespectacled, ebullient and a well-known figure in aviation, in recent years Cotton had become involved in colour photography and was now selling film in quantity to the Germans. He was selling it in other countries, too, but it was the Germans, with their increasing interest in it, who had long since begun to arouse suspicion among the more probing minds in the RAF.

The gloomy Gothic pile of a ruined castle passed slowly beneath the wing of the Lockheed. Round it, the Rhine turned and twisted like a moving snake. Down there, Dicken reflected, barges were carrying goods from the industrial Ruhr through Holland to the sea, and at the moment, in the heat of the late summer, the Rhine ferries were full of holidaymakers, the German drinking songs filling the night with tunes that sounded almost like military music.

'Mannheim coming up,' a voice behind him called out.

His navigator, Frank Babington, recently retired from the RAF as a flight-sergeant and recruited by Cotton for his skill with cameras, was watching the route carefully. As they passed over the double kink in the river at Mainz and Wiesbaden, Dicken could see the haze ahead that indicated the factories for the making of electrical equipment, chemicals and motor cars. He knew Wiesbaden well, with its Imperial palace, its state theatre and its wide gardens, and he found himself wondering how many more times he'd be looking down on it from the air, because his time as an active airman was almost finished and he couldn't imagine himself having the money to possess an aircraft of his own when he left the service. Despite his record, he was still no more than a wing commander, thanks chiefly to the fact that barring his path to senior rank had always been the implacable form of Cecil Arthur Diplock.

Diplock had married Annys Toshack, the girl Dicken had been in love with in 1914, and joining the Royal Flying Corps late in 1916, had, despite his poor showing as an airman, contrived by the cultivation of the people who mattered, to pass him in rank and now finally sat across his route to promotion. A desk officer at RAF Headquarters, under the patronage of his old Wing Colonel, now Air Vice-Marshal George Macclesfield St Aubyn, a man of the same breed, he had influenced the whole of Dicken's career. Dicken's skill, his knowledge of flying, had meant that he could never hold him back completely, but he had managed to prevent any swift rise, so that now the only alternative seemed to be to retire and seek employment elsewhere.

At the thought, Dicken frowned. His retirement was due within days now and he didn't look forward to leaving the RAF. The job with Cotton was only a temporary one, replacing one of Cotton's men who was sick, and he had no one with whom to share his retirement. His wife, Zoë, sister to Diplock's wife, had died in 1930, and he didn't fancy growing old alone. But merely flying from one place to another without any purpose seemed an empty pastime. Which was why he was now flying for Cotton.

Because of the growing German threat, even at the time of the Munich agreement when Chamberlain, the British Prime Minister, had been obliged to kowtow to the German dictator, since information about German fortifications, airfields and military establishments were necessary while there was still time, Cotton had been recruited by the British Government to acquire it by clandestine methods. As the private owner of aircraft and well-known throughout European aviation circles, he had already worked for the French Deuxième Bureau and had finally set up an independent unit of his own. A determined and ingenious man on intimate terms with the senior Nazis in Berlin, he had found a dozen ways of satisfying the requirements, though the official RAF attitude to him – largely conceived, Dicken knew, in the department of Air Vice-Marshal St Aubyn and Group Captain Cecil Arthur Diplock – had always remained one of ambiguity and jealousy.

'Mannheim below.' Babington's voice came again.

Dicken lifted his hand in acknowledgement. He and Babington had flown together many times, in Iraq, India and England, and there was a rapport between them that made them easy companions despite their difference in rank.

'New airfield down there, sir, by the look of it.'

'Got it?'

'Without question.'

Babington's smile came, a cheerful, confident smile. He trusted Dicken in the way that Dicken trusted him. He had been working with the Cotton organisation for some time and it had been Babington who had involved Dicken in Cotton's work.

'It's a good job, sir,' he had pointed out. 'And not without its measure of excitement.'

In that Babington was right because, known only to its crew, to Cotton, and a few others, the belly of the twin-tailed Lockheed contained secret RAF F24 Leica cameras of German manufacture. The sleek all-metal machine had been painted a pale duck-egg green because

Cotton had discovered that colour tended to make it invisible from below when flying at height, and the cameras were smuggled aboard in ordinary suitcases covered with travel labels. Holes had been cut for them in the floor of the cabin and three of them, mounted one behind the other – the front one tilted to the right, the rear one to the left, the centre one pointing straight down – could produce overlapping pictures and at a height of 20,000 feet could cover a strip of country ten miles wide.

They were operated by a button under the pilot's seat which activated a motor that opened secret sliding panels; and the aircraft, maintaining a straight course, aroused no concern in the minds of the suspicious Germans as they built up their installations for the conflict which everybody in Europe knew was on its way. Already the system had been used to photograph Italian installations in the Dodecanese and on the North African coast.

The present trip was officially to fly film to Berlin but Dicken knew that if the Germans found the cameras, they could be treated as spies, and since the film was being sent at a German company's invitation, there was always the possibility that the Germans suspected what they were up to and they were flying into a trap. In any case, with hostilities likely within the next few weeks or even days, the hazard of being trapped by an outbreak of fighting on a German airfield was a real possibility and, as a precaution, it had been arranged that if things grew worse a telegram would be sent to Dicken in Berlin, saying his mother was ill and urging his return. Similar messages had been arranged for Cotton and others of his men in the danger zone.

As the machine lost height and touched down, Dicken taxied slowly to the parking area. To enable Babington to dismantle the cameras and hide them in their luggage, he pretended to check his engines. As Babington signalled that everything was done, he switched them off and turned. Babington was pointing.

'Trouble,' he said.

It seemed as if their fears of German suspicions were only too true because a squad of jackbooted, helmeted soldiers armed with rifles was doubling towards them. But, as they opened the door and began to climb out, the soldiers lined up in two ranks and the sergeant slammed to attention.

'Heil Hitler!'

The barked command, part of the elaborate choreography of the dictatorship, came with clicking heels and raised arms.

Dicken responded briskly. Britain was not yet at war and it was of vital importance that he should be looked on as friendly. Then, as they started to walk between the lines, a familiar stocky figure appeared, its raised arm distinctly lacking in enthusiasm.

'Erni Udet, by all that's holy!'

Dicken's face broke into a smile at once. He had flown more than once with Ernst Udet, the best of the German pilots who had survived the 1914 war. It had been Udet's circus which had shot him out of the sky late in 1918 and, at the time, limping around half-blind and full of holes and believing he would never fly again, he had cursed the fact that he had ever met him. But, meeting again in America, England and Germany since the war, they had become fast friends because Udet, much preferring carousing to fighting, had more than once dragged Dicken round the night spots of Berlin in a shattering pub crawl. He was an uncomplicated happy-go-lucky soul who had made and lost more than one fortune and more than one woman, and Dicken had first met him in person as an unemployed young air ace restless in the peace of 1920, juggling plates and driving a motorcycle round a night club near the Budapestherstrasse. He was a shallow, cheerful individual who hated the politicians of the iron-fisted dictatorship that was now stringing the streets of Germany with red swastika banners, crowding its squares and street corners with brown-shirted thugs, and filling the hours of darkness with torments for intellectuals, Socialists and Jews. But Udet was a German, too, and he had been trapped. Because he was international, as well known as an aviator in America as in Europe, he had resisted for years the blandishments of Hermann Goering, the head of Hitler's newly-born air force, but it was as an aviator that Goering had finally ensnared him and now he carried the rank of a major-general. He had, Dicken reflected, done better than Dicken himself.

He was in full uniform and was beaming with pleasure. 'I thought you vould like a guard of honour,' he said cheerfully in his accented English. 'And now I am a general I can order you one. Tonight, Dicko, there will be a magnificent *grossstadtbummel* – the best pub crawl we've ever had.'

Two

'What about Customs?'

As Dicken spoke, Udet gestured at a large black Mercedes and shook his head. 'All that is arranged,' he said.

They were driven to the Adlon Hotel where a private room had been set aside. It seemed full of uniformed men but Udet himself didn't seem to have changed much. Despite his brilliant record between 1914 and 1918, he was an unwarlike man and his smile was as friendly as ever.

'We've arranged a special suite,' he said. 'Goering vants to meet you. He's boss of all industry in Germany now, of course, and in addition, he's an old flier like us.' He passed over a long flute of German Sekt, the sparkling Rhine wine the Germans drank as champagne. 'How are you enjoying being a civilian?'

Dicken shrugged and Udet smiled. 'About as much as I am enjoying being back in uniform,' he said. 'They got me in the end, you see. They said my name was needed to boost German aviation so I couldn't say no because I've always insisted aviation's the only thing I'm interested in.' He gestured with his glass. 'But I'm not a major-general, Dicko. I'm a flier pure and simple.' He held up his hands. 'These are my antennae. I feel an aeroplane. I'm part of it when I fly. I am a seat of the pants flier. I can make an aeroplane talk. And what have they done? Put me in charge of Luftwaffe production of which I know nothing. I think I have put my head in a noose. I persuaded them to build dive bombers.'

Dicken frowned. Dive bombing was a new concept of aerial warfare. First tried in 1914 against Zeppelin sheds at Friedrichshafen, it had been developed by the RAF to a fine art by the trench strafing of 1918. They had used SE5s then, because they were strong and could pull out of a dive without leaving their wings behind; but most of it had been done with Camels, because they went down like a stone and, if they didn't fly out of their wings, went up again like a lift. The American Marines had improved on the method against Nicaraguan rebels with great success in the Twenties and had later demonstrated their skill at air displays across the States where Dicken and Udet had first seen it used. Since then it had been developed by a number of nations including the French and the Swedes, but the RAF had become obsessed with long range heavy bombers and, though there had been a lot of disagreement, they were still only toying with the idea.

'The flying artillery we saw in the States?' Dicken said. Udet gestured. 'It will work, Dicko.'

'Will it have to, Knägges?'

Udet grinned at his old nickname because it was odd to call a German general Titch. Then his smile died. 'Would the British fight, Dicko?' he asked. 'If it came to a fight?'

'They don't want war, Erni, but they've put up with a lot: Sudetenland. Czechoslovakia. Albania. Does your Führer intend to go into Poland?'

Udet's face was bleak. 'He might.'

'Then I think we would.'

There was still no certainty that they hadn't run into a specially prepared trap. Dicken was certain that Udet wasn't part of any plot against him, but he'd let it drop that the hangar into which the big all-metal Lockheed had been pushed belonged to the Gestapo and they knew it would be thoroughly searched. There was nothing to indicate they had carried cameras because they were safely in Babington's luggage, but there was always the possibility of the moving panels being discovered and questioned.

The dinner that had been arranged for the evening seemed to include half the top brass of the Luftwaffe. In addition to Udet there was Sperrle, one of its leaders; Milch, Goering's deputy; Bruno Loerzer, one of Udet's contemporaries in the Imperial German Air Service of 1918; Bodenschatz, the great Baron von Richthofen's old adjutant, who was now Goering's chief of staff; and Wolfram von Richthofen, the baron's younger cousin, who now commanded one of the Luftwaffe Fliegerkorps. This time the uniforms all belonged to the Luftwaffe and the wearers had all spotted the Lockheed and were eager to talk about it.

'I would like a flight in it,' Udet remarked. 'To see how it works. To see what the United States are producing.'

Goering arrived late and once again there was the complicated choreography of Nazism, with everybody clicking heels and raising their arms. Though his large head was handsome, Goering's appearance was spoiled by his stomach and double chins and the decorations that appeared to have been hung all over his person like wassail balls on a Christmas tree. 'Chest trouble.' Udet whispered. 'Too many medals.'

The Reichsmarschall greeted Dicken warmly as an old opponent but there was a calculating look in the pale blue eyes. 'I have been looking at your aircraft,' he said. 'It compares well with our German Junkers. Have the British abandoned biplanes yet? There seems to have been a fixation about biplanes in England.'

Dicken forced a smile. 'Oh, we have the other kind now, Herr Reichsmarschall.'

Goering smiled back but he hurriedly changed the subject as if he had no wish to hear of the potential of any power but Germany. 'I'm having my home, Karinhalle, photographed,' he said. 'We're using your film.'

As he turned away, Udet's voice came in a murmur. 'He doesn't want war,' he said. 'But he's having a private air raid shelter built just in case. He thought England wouldn't fight but now I've told him what you said he's not so sure. He says Ribbentrop, our Foreign Minister, is in Moscow, trying to line up the Russians on our side.'

'Think he will?'

Udet shrugged. 'It doesn't seem to follow our Party line, nor theirs either, but if half Poland's the prize, then it's a possibility.'

The following morning, they took off from the Tempelhof with Udet alongside Dicken and Babington in the rear of the machine. From 2000 feet it was quite easy to see the new airfields that were springing up and they duly recorded them by the simple procedure, while Udet admired the view or commented on the layout of the instrument panel and the handling of the machine, of Dicken reaching casually under his seat and pressing the hidden button.

Beneath them they could see the whole layout of the German capital and, finding themselves over what was clearly a new airfield, Dicken pretended to shield his eyes from the view.

Udet laughed heartily. 'Berlin's a splendid city,' he said. 'Built on the formation of the German Empire in 1870 to become the capital of a great European nation. It's a symbol of German pride.'

'It would be a pity to see it all destroyed, Erni.'

'That would be impossible.' Udet's voice carried conviction. 'Berlin's too far from any enemy airfield.'

The city seemed to be full of uniforms. Germany had always enjoyed smart tunics and caps and even the most junior officials wore them, but at that moment every hotel seemed crammed with them and they were obvious in every street. Another party was held in the evening at which Udet produced half a dozen wartime fliers, one of them a man Dicken had shot down during his last desperate fight with Udet's Staffel. He was plump and balding with a deep scar on his face, acquired as his machine had crash-landed. But there was no apparent resentment and the atmosphere was cheerful, though the next morning as Dicken and Babington waited to pick up the receipts for the film they had brought the city seemed to have changed. The newspapers were full of fabricated insults to Germany by Poland and tension seemed to have mounted. From the front of the hotel, they could see squads of troops marching by, the sound of their feet ominous and loud. Staff cars carrying the Nazi swastika kept passing.

'Faster than yesterday, don't you think, Bab?' Dicken said.

Babington's face was grim. 'It's a bit like sitting on a gunpowder barrel with the fuse burning,' he agreed.

That evening the city was plunged into darkness as blackout exercises were carried out but inside the hotel little seemed to have changed except for the fact that the uniforms seemed suddenly fewer and the men wearing those they saw were edgy and worried. When Udet arrived he was in civilian clothes and looked depressed. 'We've signed a non-aggression pact with Russia,' he said immediately. 'They wouldn't sign anything like that unless they intended to use it. I've been told to stand by. They didn't say what for but it seems pretty obvious to me.'

Dicken frowned. 'It'll mean war, Erni.'

Udet's shrug seemed defeated. 'Ribbentrop doesn't think so,' he said. 'He says Britain's too decadent to go to war over Poland.'

'Tell him not to be too sure.'

Udet gestured. 'For the love of God, Dicko, you can't get at Poland except through Germany! How *can* you help her?'

There was considerably less friendliness in the hotel by this time and even a few overt sneers, and the following evening the expected telegram arrived – 'Mother ill.'

That it was time to leave became obvious the next day when Udet arrived once more.

'I think you'd better go, Dicko,' he said. 'I can tell you now in strict confidence if you give your word of honour not to pass it on, that orders have been prepared for the march into Poland. I've just learned.' His eyes were watching every face as if he felt people might read his lips. 'It was due to take place in forty-eight hours but I've just heard the order might have to be withdrawn. Some

14

problem over that oaf, Mussolini. You'd better disappear while you can.'

'What about you, Knägges? What will you do?'

Udet frowned. 'There's a lot to do,' he said. 'Too much for old Knägges.' His frown deepened. 'Dicken, tell your people that all our dive bomber units have been re-equipped with Stukas. They're rugged aircraft. They're accurate and can pinpoint their targets. We have a lot of them and they'll be difficult to stop because their crews learned their job in the Spanish Civil War. They come down like a cartload of bricks. *Wie ein Klavier aus dem fünfsten Stock*. Like a piano falling from a fifth-floor window. What have you got?'

Not much, Dicken thought. The heavy bombers the RAF was banking on weren't yet ready and so far there wasn't much else. Even the Cooper bombs that were still being used might as well have been made by the Dundee marmalade factory of the same name for all the use they were. Since their puff went upwards, they were more danger to the crew which dropped them than to their intended victim.

'Oh, we've got a few,' he said.

'Hawker Harts?'

Dicken gave the German a quick look. Nazi intelligence was known to be good and it was true that up to February that year dive bomber training was still being carried out in the old adapted biplanes. They could achieve good groupings but the pilots had to cheat by going as low as they dared, a habit that might exact a nasty penalty under war conditions.

Another cable arrived later that evening, indicating that 'Mother's health' was failing rapidly, but when they drove out to Tempelhof the following morning they found it impossible to unearth anyone who could give the authority to let them leave, while the officials they approached were noticeably hostile.

'The VIP treatment's beginning to wear a bit thin,' Babington commented.

Would anybody miss him if he didn't make it, Dicken wondered. There was no one dependent on him, no one who would be concerned if he failed to appear.

As he thought about his dead wife, he frowned. His had never been an easy marriage, because Zoë Toshack, as she had always preferred to call herself rather than use her married name, had been an airwoman very nearly in the same class as Amelia Earhart and Amy Johnson. Nearly, but never quite, and her last desperate attempt to reach the ranks of the immortals had been her undoing. Dicken had learned of her death while in India. As if it were a token of atonement for the years of misery she had caused him, with the exception of the house at Deane in Sussex where she had been born, she had left him all her wealth. He still hadn't managed to touch it.

As he thought of his wife, he began to wonder what had happened to Marie-Gabrielle Aubrey. He had met her first in Italy in 1918 when she was nine years old and childishly eager to marry him. At the time he had thought he was in love with her older sister, but the sister had married an American and Marie-Gabrielle, turning up in Rezhanistan where Dicken had been sent to organise the evacuation of a besieged Legation staff, had coolly informed him that she *still* hoped to marry him. Because he was still married to Zoë Toshack, he hadn't even thought seriously about her suggestion, though he'd not

16

been unaware of her beauty, intelligence and courage. After the siege he'd discovered that the wife who didn't want him was dead and that the girl who did had vanished, and he had never since been able to track her down.

He tried to brush the thoughts away but they refused to go. He still had a house which he had acquired for Zoë at Lensbury near Northolt. They had lived in it together for a matter of weeks only, then, while he had gone to Iraq, Zoë had disappeared to the States. They had never occupied it again, meeting only in hotels while the house was let to Service couples forced to live the usual gypsy life in other people's houses, the husband always disappearing to the ends of the earth while his wife was left behind to pack and follow. Pack and follow. It was a motto by which Zoë had never been prepared to live. Determined from the day he first met her to follow her two ambitions – to fly and be independent – she had managed to fly but had never been able to be entirely independent, and even when she had fled from Dicken's side she had always seemed to need his affection.

Since her death, he had refurnished the house, half-hoping that someone would come along to occupy it with him. But, though a few had tried, no one had. At least, he thought dryly, people of his age didn't rush into marriage just for sex.

There was still no sign of any permission to leave. Udet sent a message to say he was trying to obtain it but while other English tourists in Germany were bolting for the frontiers and the ports, because Dicken's exit involved an aeroplane, permission had to come from Goering. By afternoon, they were beginning to grow suspicious.

'Think it might be worth taking off and chancing it?' Babington suggested.

Climbing into the Lockheed and starting the engines, they taxied to the holding area near the runway. Immediately a red light flashed from the control tower.

'Think we could do it?' Dicken asked.

Babington's eyes were flickering over the field. 'There are a lot of new planes on this field,' he said. 'Fighters by the look of them.'

As they watched, a Luftwaffe machine, two engined and crewed by two or three men, taxied in front of them so they couldn't move. They studied it carefully, noticing its armament.

'Daimler-Benz engines,' Dicken observed. 'Must be the new Messerschmitt Zerstorer.' Glancing at the map, he looked about him. 'The shortest route out of this place,' he went on, 'is east to Poland, then north to Sweden. Unfortunately, if the Germans are massing on that frontier, that could be hazardous to say the least.'

'Could we head for London for a few minutes as a feint, then bolt for Italy?'

Dicken eyed the sky. 'There's hardly a cloud about.' He indicated the fighters. 'And, fast as this job is, I dare bet that lot are faster. They'd have us in no time. If there's no permission or any sign of them bringing us back to the hangars by evening we'll chance it and bolt at ground level for the Netherlands. The sun'll be low then and in their eyes.'

'What'll happen if we don't manage it?'

'Internment, I suppose.'

'And if we do?'

'Home, of course.'

'I meant if the war came.'

'Back into uniform. They'll want everybody they can get. I saw them calling up the reservists in 1914. Boozy old men, a lot of them. They weren't a scrap of good. The good ones all disappeared at Mons and First Ypres. The others – they slung them out or gave them jobs at base where they started the usual fiddles and made themselves comfortable for the rest of the war.'

'There'll be a few like that if it happens again,' Babington said slowly. 'What'll *you* do?'

'Desk job, I expect. Bit old now for fighting. How about you? Why don't you go for a commission? If this war comes, it'll be a big one and on the law of averages could take five or six years. And because we're about as unprepared as we were in 1914, I reckon they'd be glad of experienced men, and there's nobody more experienced than you Halton apprentices.'

A car approached them. It was Udet again, in the full panoply of uniform this time. 'All flying's banned,' he explained unhappily. 'I'm still trying to get permission for you to leave.' He looked worried and his face was moist with perspiration. 'But it's difficult,' he went on. 'Everybody's on edge.' He lit a cigarette with uncertain fingers. 'There's been a hell of a disaster. To the Stukas.'

'I thought they were unsurpassable.'

Udet shook his head, as if he were dazed. 'They are. They are. It's not that.' He gestured. 'Wolfram von Richthofen, the Master's cousin – you'll remember meeting him – he laid on a demonstration at the Neuhammer training ground for Sperrle and Loerzer. He didn't like dive bombers but he's got used to them and wanted to show what they could do. There was to be a mass attack using smoke bombs, by two groups.' He dragged nervously at the cigarette. 'They were instructed to approach, from about four thousand metres and dive through a cloud layer that had been reported at between eight hundred and two thousand metres, and release their bombs at three hundred metres. But there was ground fog near Cotbus and only one group recognised it for what it was. Gruppe G76 thought it was the cloud and the whole formation tore through it into the earth at full speed. Not one piano from the fifth floor. A whole lot.' He drew a deep breath before continuing. 'Only a few realised what had happened and pulled up, but they were hitting the trees and in seconds the ground was littered with debris. They're trying to push the blame on to me. But it wasn't my fault. I only supplied the damned machines. Somebody failed to tell them about the fog, but those bastards will try to wriggle out of things in case it loses them prestige with the Party.'

He was obviously badly shaken and Babington, who had bought a bottle of German brandy to take home, opened it and offered it.

Udet took a good swallow. 'First time I ever thought of conducting a *grossstadtbummel* inside an aeroplane,' he said glumly.

He soon disappeared again but his car had hardly vanished from sight when they saw it returning.

'Made it!' Udet climbed out, grinning his relief. 'I got my people to see Bodenschatz personally. You're all right. And the disaster wasn't as bad as we thought. It only affected one group and some of them escaped. There were only thirteen. But, hell, that's bad enough.' He lit a cigarette and frowned. 'They've accused some controller who failed to warn about the fog. I expect the poor bastard's for the chop. As for you, you can go. Anti-aircraft batteries have been advised. You're to fly south at a height of three hundred metres.'

'So they can hit us if they have to?'

Udet handed over a sheet of paper containing their flight instructions. 'For the love of God stick to the courses and heights shown,' he said. 'I don't want your death on my hands, Dicko.'

There was a pause, then Udet extended his hand. Dicken took it warmly.

'*Auf Wiedersehen*, Erni. Until next time.'

There was a trace of Udet's old smile. 'If there is one,' he said.

'You'll never win, Knägges,' Dicken said earnestly. 'And it'll mean the end of Germany and the end of Hitler and the Nazis.'

Udet shrugged. '*Besser ein Ende mit Schrecken als ein Schrecken ohne Ende,*' he said with a wry grin. 'Better an end with horror than a horror without end.'

They flew south towards Switzerland, the cameras working all the way, and hit the Swiss border north of Zurich. The sky seemed to be empty of fighters but there were a lot of bombers of various types heading east – towards the invasion of Poland, they assumed. Their camouflage was dark and as they passed beneath it was hard to see them against the ground. Crossing into Switzerland, they flew on into France and landed near Dijon for fuel. Heading north-west again, they hit the English coastline at Portsmouth.

'Wonder if they'll pick us up on the Sound Locator System,' Babington said, and they smiled because they both knew that the Sound Locator System was the name given to disguise a new radio scheme which worked on a system of bouncing waves from a ground station to identify friendly aircraft from hostiles. Turning east, they landed eventually at Heston.

The Customs Officer greeted them with the usual laconic question. 'Where from?'

'Berlin,' Dicken said.

The Customs man eyed them as if he didn't believe them. 'Left it a bit late, haven't you?' he said.

Three

To Dicken's surprise, the German invasion of Poland did not take place. Goering was believed to be sceptical of Ribbentrop's claim that the British would never go to war over Poland and it even began to look as if Dicken's talks with Udet had had their effect.

His service career finished, Dicken headed for his house at Lensbury, and for the next two days worked about the garden, wondering what he was going to do now that he was no longer in a position to fly. He was not happy and considered writing letters to everyone he could think of who might be interested in him. There were firms producing instructors who were now turning out pilots for the newly-formed Air Force Reserve, but he didn't try too hard to attract their attention because, despite the reassurances of the more self-satisfied daily newspapers that there would be no war, he had long since decided there would and found himself thanking God for the short service commission scheme that had been introduced and the eager young pilots who were willing to train at weekends.

The country had been saved by the skin of its teeth. Before the Munich meeting between Hitler and Chamberlain the previous year, the RAF's front-line fighters had been Fury biplanes, machines with slow twin

Vickers whose performance was purely academic, anyway, because everybody knew perfectly well that the aircraft that carried them would never get close enough to the German Heinkels and Dorniers to fire at them. The atmosphere had been heavy with depression and even the Super-Furies and Gladiators, which had four guns and a top speed of 245mph, were Stone Age machines by comparison with what the Germans flew. Of the 750 fighters Fighter Command had possessed only ninety were Hurricane monoplanes.

They had been in the presence of a disaster of the first magnitude and only the constant threats from Hitler had stirred things up until the squadrons were at last being re-equipped. Even so, the Hurricanes, intolerant of faulty handling and possessing a Merlin engine that was still giving problems, were far from popular.

Staying up late on the last day of August to listen to the late news on the BBC, Dicken woke at five o'clock the following morning from a deep dream of marching feet to realise the sound came from a heavy knocking on his front door. Sitting bolt upright, he hurried to the window. Below, in the grey morning light he could see the postman standing on the porch with the village policeman.

The policeman looked up. 'Are you Wing Commander ND Quinney, DSO, MC, DFC, MM?' he asked solemnly.

'You know damn well I am, Fred,' Dicken snorted.

The policeman didn't even blink. 'Will you please come down to the door, sir. The postman 'as an important letter for you.'

Putting on his dressing gown, Dicken opened the door. The postman handed him the letter.

'Since when have you needed an escort to deliver a letter?' Dicken asked.

The postman gave a sheepish smile, then for the first time the policeman showed signs of being human. His face split in a wide grin. 'You've got to put your uniform back on, sir,' he said, 'and go and shoot down some more of them old 'Uns. You've been called back.'

Dicken stared at him for a moment, then wrenched at the envelope. The letter instructed him to report to Training Command, Shawbury, Shropshire, as chief signals officer. 'God damn and blast it to everlasting hell!' he shouted. The policeman looked alarmed. 'Ain't it that, sir?'

'Yes, it is.'

'Then what's the trouble? Don't you want to go?'

Dicken glared. As an under-aged youth wanting to go to sea in 1914 he had become a fully qualified radio operator, though his mother, fearful of him being drowned, had refused to give her consent and he had gone into the RFC instead. But that first class certificate had dogged him throughout his career and at all sorts of odd moments he had found himself in charge of signals stations or groups in which, because he had long since lost this enthusiasm for wireless, he hadn't the slightest interest. He was still trying to work out some means of avoiding the posting when the telephone rang. It was Willie Hatto.

Like Dicken a veteran of the earlier war, Group Captain William Wymarck Wombwell Hatto had also had his career blighted by Diplock. With an American, Walt Foote, they had formed an anarchical trio that existed chiefly for the derision of pompous or downright bad senior officers, chiefly Diplock and his mentor, St Aubyn.

Because his father, Lord Hooe, sat in the House of Lords and he had brothers in the Foreign Office and the Church, Hatto had been harder to hold down but even he had only recently managed to struggle up to group captain.

'The balloon's due to go up,' he said at once. 'The Germans have gone into Poland. Have you heard?'

'I guessed. I've just received a letter telling me to report to Shawbury. As a bloody signals officer!'

Hatto gave a hoot of laughter. 'That old wireless certificate of yours!'

'I've been on the telephone to the Air Ministry and asked for a squadron. The bastards informed me that owing to my advanced age and the new techniques of fighting, such a posting's out of the question and I have to be a good boy and attend to the job they've picked out for me.'

Hatto laughed. 'Don't worry,' he said. 'The CO at Shawbury's Cuthbert Orr and he's all right. And, look, I'm at the Air Ministry at the moment with my own department. I'll find you a job. We could do with someone with some sense. The place's in a panic because the bloody politicians are delaying carrying out their promise to declare war and while we're sitting with our thumbs in our bums the Germans are wiping the floor with the Poles. If they don't wake up, the Luftwaffe will be first off the mark and bomb us in the first minute after the declaration and the navy's worried sick that the German fleet will nip out while we're still at peace and place its ships across our trade routes.'

-

Almost the first person Dicken met at Shawbury was Flight-Sergeant Handiside, who as a corporal had first welcomed Dicken to the RFC in 1915. He was wearing civvies and looked stouter than Dicken remembered.

'Hello, sir,' he said with a grin. 'They recalled you, too?'

Cuthbert Orr, who had been Dicken's CO in India and China, was as burly and ebullient as ever. His moustache and eyebrows were sprinkled with grey now but he was itching to get into the fighting and he welcomed Dicken warmly. He, too, had crossed the path of what he called the Unholy Duo.

'I see that pill, St Aubyn, and his lapdog, Diplock, have sorted themselves out a couple of cushy jobs at the Air House,' he said at once. 'Still, they never produced much between them in the way of guts.'

To man the station's ground defence weapons – mostly ancient Lewis guns on tripods – were a large number of recalled soldiers who had rushed after the Munich fiasco and Chamberlain's promise of 'Peace in our time' to take advantage of the government's offer of increased pensions, never dreaming that they'd ever be called up. They were mostly in their late fifties and sixties and moved torpidly about, some of them even using sticks, one actually using *two* sticks. They wore ungaitered trousers and khaki side-caps unadorned by any badge so that they looked like elderly convicts and they had long since forgotten what they'd ever learned and were mostly already trying to wangle their discharge.

'Just another example of the government's hurried thinking,' Orr pointed out dryly. 'Now that the weather's turning cold, the poor old buggers are going down like flies.'

The war started officially for Britain two days later. It was a Sunday and, as he listened to the Prime Minister's gloomy tones, Dicken found his attitude was less one of worry than of relief, a feeling that 'Oh, well, now at least we can get on with it.'

'From now on,' Orr said, 'I suppose everybody had better wear steel helmets.'

Two minutes later, getting into his car to view his outposts, his helmet hit the roof with a clang and he fell back as if pole-axed.

'God damn!' he said. 'The first British casualty of the war!'

They had all expected the fighting to start at once but, apart from a little skirmishing along the Franco-German frontier, nothing happened and the British Expeditionary Force landed on the Continent without difficulty and moved to positions along the frontier. Poland vanished beneath the German attack, Udet's Stukas proved to be all he had claimed, and a new word, *Blitzkrieg*, entered everyone's vocabulary.

England didn't change much, however. Nobody seemed to be doing any fighting or, for that matter, making any preparations for doing any fighting. The government was refusing to allow the RAF to drop bombs anywhere near German civilians, which meant that targets were severely restricted, and a suggestion that they set the Black Forest on fire with incendiaries was turned down indignantly with the fatuous comment that it was private property. They were trying to fight the war with one hand tied behind their backs.

Shawbury was far enough away from the coast to be even less involved and the major interest there was the complaints of the older of the old soldiers recruited for ground defence. They were billeted in sergeants' quarters, two to a room, each with its little stove, and when coal was delivered to them and dumped between the huts, the older men were shoved aside by the younger of their comrades and got nothing, so that they were having to endure the increasing cold without any means of keeping warm.

The signals job didn't last long. Because there had been no real fighting yet, nobody was taking the war very seriously and communications were still amateurish. Radar stations had been built ten to fifteen miles apart along the south coast of England which, with posts of the Royal Observer Corps, were linked with the filter room and Observer Corps Plotting Room at Fighter Command Headquarters at Stanmore. Still plagued by his 1914 radio certificate, it became Dicken's job to make the communications function properly.

It was a harsh winter, with RAF stations snowed up and, heading towards Norfolk over a road covered with icy slush, his car skidded into a ditch full of muddy water. A breakdown truck hauled it back on to the road but, because he was wet through, Dicken was given a lift to a nearby operational training unit to spend the night there. The commanding officer turned out to be Tom Howarth, who had flown with him in Italy in 1918, and the signals officer turned out to be Babington, beaming and already resplendent in a brand new pilot's officer's uniform. Howarth lent him a tunic and trousers and Babington a mackintosh and a cap which sat on his head like a tit on a mountain.

'Fancy seeing what happens here, sir?' Babington asked. 'They do circuits and bumps through the hours of darkness to get them used to night flying.'

Collected from the operations room by a wireless operator who had just finished his course and was awaiting a posting to a squadron, Dicken immediately found himself the subject of condescension by the trainee, a fresh-faced young man by the name of Fisher with a large moustache and Volunteer Reserve badges on his shoulders. At first it didn't occur to Dicken why, then he remembered that on all training stations there were large numbers of teachers of physics and chemistry of his own age who had been given commissions to teach radio and electricity to the masses of volunteers and conscripts who were pouring into the service and, because they were desperately needed, their basic training had been rushed and they still had hands full of thumbs and were uncertain how or when to salute, still civilians despite their uniforms and regarded with a measure of contempt by the young men – for the most part just as new to the service themselves – who were training to become aircrew. It was clear that, because he was wearing Babington's brand new mackintosh and side hat, Fisher was assuming he was one, too.

They walked to the end of the flare path, a line of goose-necked paraffin flares, which reminded Dicken how far behind the Americans the RAF's airfield lighting was.

'Better stand over there,' Fisher said briskly.

'You seem to know the ropes,' Dicken said mildly. 'Have you done much flying?'

'About a thousand hours,' Fisher said casually. 'It begins to grow boring when you get that many in.'

Dicken smiled. 'I'm sure it does. Night flying?'

'Plenty of that.' Fisher picked up the Aldis lamp and flashed green to an aeroplane at the end of the runway that was anxiously giving its letter as it sought permission to land. 'It's in France where you learn to fly, you know. That's why I'm here. Rest. Crashed. You wouldn't know about that, of course.'

The chatter went on all evening, Dicken thoroughly enjoying himself. The following day, he accepted Tom Howarth's invitation to give a talk to the new aircrews.

'Gives them a bit of a kick to see someone they've actually read about in magazines,' he said. 'Mind, you'll very soon find out that they know who's going to be fighting this war – *them*. And—' Howarth smiled '—bless 'em, they're dead right, of course.'

The talk was short but for Dicken the most entertaining part by a long way was the sight of young Fisher sitting below him in the front row full of his own importance. By this time, Dicken's uniform had been cleaned and dried and when he rose he was in the full fig of a wing commander's rank with two rows of medal ribbons beneath his wings.

Afterwards, he saw Fisher waiting by the door. He looked very hot under the collar.

'Permission to speak to you, sir,' he said. 'I think I've been a bloody fool.'

Dicken laughed. 'Yes, you have a bit,' he agreed. 'But I shouldn't let it worry you. It's something we all suffer from at your age.'

'I never dreamed, sir—'

'Especially in that hat I was wearing.'

Fisher managed a nervous smile. 'I've just discovered who you are, sir. I've read about you. I owe you an apology.'

'I don't think you do,' Dicken said. 'But I expect you've discovered something I discovered very early in *my* career. When you shoot a line, it's a good idea first to find out who it is you're shooting it to.'

–

The communications job lasted two more boring months before Dicken received a call from Hatto to report to the Air Ministry. He found Hatto in a bad temper.

'Usual trouble,' he said. 'Somebody isn't pulling his finger out. The navy's complaining that unidentified aircraft are flying over Chatham and Portsmouth and that our Sound Locator System isn't giving them the proper warning. "Sound Locator System", as you well know, is the name we give to this radar device of Watson–Watt's. It isn't working as the navy wants it to, but they can't get a satisfactory answer from the Air Staff. I'm going over there now. Your first job with this department, therefore, is to look after the shop till I come back.'

When Hatto returned his face was grave. Even his monocle looked subdued.

'Something wrong?'

Hatto frowned. 'Not half there isn't. The navy's getting no satisfaction at all. Every time they claim somebody's flying over them all they get is a snotty letter complaining about the number of times they bring the subject up and insisting that the system's reliable. And you know who signs the letters?'

'I'll have a guess. Diplock.'

'Diplock. Chief of Staff to St Aubyn. And it fits the half-baked attitude at the top at the moment. After all, if all we're doing is bombing the Germans with leaflets, why not this? If I can persuade the navy to lend us an observer would you be willing to nip out and come back in over Portsmouth? We can lay on Cotton's Lockheed again and they won't be able to argue if we have photographs.'

The following day when Dicken reported at Heston it was warm with woolly clouds at 5000 feet. With a naval commander in the co-pilot's seat, they took off without submitting a flight plan, flew west and climbed to 14,000 feet, then started the cameras and, heading south, came in over the coast at Portsmouth which they circled for fifteen to twenty minutes to give the warning system plenty of time to become aware of them. It only required one flight across the naval base to photograph everything that was happening and the pictures demonstrated not only all the installations but also the route of the flight. When he saw them Hatto thumped the table in delight.

'This,' he snapped, 'ought to put a cork in that bastard Diplock's ear!'

Two days later Hatto arrived back from the Admiralty with a grim face, and produced a copy of a letter from the Air Staff. Signed by Diplock, it complained in a fretful tone about what it considered the navy's persistence with something that didn't exist. 'Not only,' it concluded, 'were no enemy aircraft flying in the area referred to on the day in question, but no British aircraft were in the vicinity either.'

'The ammunition the Admiralty want,' Hatto said. 'We've got the bastard.'

They were summoned to the Admiralty the following day. From the number of gold-encrusted light blue hats hanging in the corridor it was obvious that a great many senior air force officers were present. From beyond the closed doors the murmur of voices rose angrily. Summoned inside, they saw Air Vice-Marshal St Aubyn bent over the table staring furiously at the photographs Dicken had taken.

'There but for the grace of God,' Hatto murmured, 'goes God. I suppose it's only by the contemplation of the incompetent that we can appreciate the competent.'

As the door closed St Aubyn looked round and then, at the other side of the table, they saw Diplock.

'You two!' he snapped.

He had grown fatter since Dicken had last seen him, and his high protruding ears made him look more than ever like the Morane Parasol aircraft after which he had been nicknamed as long ago as 1916. The name had stuck and with the approach of war and the interest by the newspapers in the services, to Diplock's fury the name, Parasol Percy, had even started appearing in the columns of the popular press.

There was an immediate hubbub of voices, with the sailors smug and the airmen indignant and angry. But there was no getting away from the fact that the navy had proved its point. And it didn't take long before the backlash arrived, and Hatto and Dicken were summoned to the office of Air Vice-Marshal St Aubyn, who met them angrily.

'You are air force officers,' he snapped at them immediately. 'You flaunted authority. You've given us a great deal of trouble.'

'I beg to submit, sir,' Hatto snapped, 'that the one who's giving us trouble is Hitler.'

Though they defended themselves strongly it didn't help much. St Aubyn and Diplock had had their casual attitude to their job shown up and they were in a spiteful mood.

'I'm buggered if I can understand,' Hatto said as they returned to their office, 'why the battle between the Air Ministry and the Admiralty is of such importance that people like those two can take risks. It seems to me it might be better if they directed their energy into defeating Hitler.'

There was some sympathy among other senior officers.

'Like all services,' Sholto Douglas said, 'the RAF's full of regulations thought up by people with nothing better to do. You have to learn how the machine works to beat it. In the meantime, you'd better start looking for a new job.'

–

Everybody was still working much as they had before the war, with Wednesday and Saturday afternoons for football and Sundays off altogether. Sometimes it was hard to believe the war was on, especially in the areas away from the Channel where the peace seemed deeper even than in peacetime. Landing a Blenheim at a small aerodrome in the West Country with a dud port engine and therefore no flaps or undercarriage, as Dicken touched down there was a bang; one wheel collapsed and a wingtip scraped. He climbed out to find there was no sign of life anywhere.

Everybody was clearly at lunch and, since it was a warm day, he sat down alongside the aircraft. When still no one appeared, he stretched out in the sun. Eventually an airman on a bicycle came past and out of the corner of his eye Dicken saw his jaw drop as he saw the lopsided aircraft and the prostrate figure, neither of which had been there when he had gone for his meal. Hauling his bicycle round, he pedalled off at full speed.

Soon afterwards Dicken heard the fire engine and the ambulance screeching to a stop alongside him, followed by other vehicles and finally the car of the squadron leader in command. Dicken didn't move until everybody had worked themselves up into a state of panic, then he came violently to life. 'Is this how you usually run your bloody station?' he demanded.

The incident symbolised the whole attitude to the war. Although it had started, nothing much was happening, and apart from the odd skirmish there were few signs of hostility. After the first violent attack on Poland it seemed as if Hitler had gone to sleep.

There were a few sinkings, and a naval battle in the South Atlantic when a trapped German battleship was scuttled in the River Plate, but nothing on the ground and little in the air except for patrols across the frontier in France and odd sneak raiders slipping over Scapa Flow to look at the navy. With transatlantic appositeness, the American correspondents christened what was happening as the Phoney War.

And that was how it seemed, with the newspapers even beginning to talk about a negotiated peace.

It was in this atmosphere that Hatto appeared in Dicken's office with a rueful grin on his face. 'The bastards are after us,' he announced. 'St Aubyn wants Cotton's recce and photographic unit taken out of his hands and put in the hands of a regular RAF officer, while I'm for the north of Scotland, where nothing's happening.'

That evening, Dicken went round to Hatto's flat for a farewell drink. Hatto's wife greeted him with a kiss.

'I suppose eventually things *will* begin to happen?' Dicken said.

'For me they're happening now,' Hatto's wife retorted. 'They're taking Willie away.'

Hatto's family were growing up and it was obvious that she had realised long since that if the war lasted more than a year or two, they would be involved.

'At least,' Dicken pointed out, 'they're girls.'

She wasn't deluded. 'Girls marry soldiers and sailors and airmen, Dicken,' she said soberly. Then she smiled and patted his arm. 'Don't be afraid to call while Willie's away. We might be glad to have a man around the house.'

Dicken said nothing because he had a feeling that now that Hatto had been disposed of, he would be the next to go.

He wasn't far wrong. The following week he was ordered to report to RAF HQ in France.

Four

The RAF in France consisted of four Hurricane squadrons, four squadrons of obsolescent Blenheims, and four army co-operation squadrons flying the small single-engined Lysanders whose chief claim to fame was that, because of the forward sweep of their wings, they always appeared to be flying backwards. In addition there were ten light bomber squadrons of the Advanced Air Striking Force flying Battles which had passed beyond obsolescence and were definitely obsolete. Carrying a three-man crew, they were heavy machines powered with the same engine as the lightweight Hurricane and they were said to be so slow the observers had to stick out their arms and paddle. Nobody gave much for their chances.

Crossing the Channel in an Anson, another of the RAF's obsolete machines that looked like a greenhouse and, according to its crews, flew like a London bus, Dicken found the pilot gesturing at the interior which was cross-strutted with what looked like bicycle frames.

'Wouldn't advise moving about much, sir,' he suggested. 'It's a bit gusty today and those things are just the right height to hit you in the face if the plane lurches.'

They became airborne at a speed at which most other aircraft were just getting going, and the wings began to flap up and down like a bird's.

'We leave the undercarriage down, sir,' the pilot explained. 'It's easier. Unless of course you fancy turning that rather stiff wheel there a hundred and eighty-six times.'

The Anson floated badly as they came into land and the pilot grinned. 'I'm told,' he said cheerfully, 'that if everybody jumps up and down it helps to push her earthwards.'

Air Marshal Sir Arthur Barratt, who was running the RAF in France, was a balding man with a good reputation but it seemed he was being very badly advised. With the approach of spring it was clear something was bound to happen in the only place other than the sea where the opposing forces faced each other; but there seemed no sense of urgency anywhere among the French who were running the show. Even when the balloon went up, they felt, there would be ten to fourteen days to prepare their defences.

The feeling expressed by the Prime Minister that the Germans had missed the bus appeared to have seeped through all ranks down to the very bottom and, to Dicken's eyes, every unit seemed overloaded with the sports gear and wireless sets they had gathered round them during the winter. They all seemed more concerned with sleuthing after spies than battle and the technical wing commander went out every night looking for lights which he was convinced were being directed towards Germany to attract bombers. Certainly, there were a few odd personalities about, one of them a blind professor who, despite his affliction, somehow needed to rush into the road to peer after every RAF convoy that passed. Strange fires were reported in the middle of woods and occasionally a man complained that he had been shot at, while rumours came in that four RAF officers had been found with their throats cut. When Dicken investigated, he could find nobody who knew anything about them.

It was a strange eerie period when, despite the self-satisfaction of the politicians in London, it was obvious to everybody that the Germans weren't merely sitting still. Remembering Udet's faith in his Stukas and the way they had finished the Polish campaign in record time, Dicken could imagine their crews practising, practising, practising, knowing perfectly well that when the day came they would be needed. It had been found that ground troops couldn't stand up to them and that anti-aircraft fire was virtually useless once they started their dives, and he knew that German efficiency wouldn't allow their skills to deteriorate.

When the invasion of Norway started, everybody with any sense started hitching at his sleeves, knowing that when the holocaust had swept Norway it would arrive in France. Dicken's duties were vague and he was used as dogsbody for anything that required doing. When the Hurricane squadrons complained they weren't shooting down the enemy aircraft they should, he was sent to investigate, and found they had been instructed to harmonise their guns for 400 yards to compensate for aiming error.

'Try two hundred and fifty,' he suggested. 'We found in the last war that the ranges suggested as suitable were put up by people who knew nothing about it.'

Almost immediately the squadrons reported success and they were so pleased they were even encouraged to complain about the painting of their aircraft.

'One wing black, one white,' the CO said. 'It makes us stick out like a sore thumb. Whose idea was it?'

'I can guess,' Dicken said, thinking of Diplock. 'Why not try duck-egg green like Sidney Cotton. He's found it makes them virtually invisible.'

They were also worried about the lack of back armour and when the Air Ministry experts had maintained it would affect the Hurricane's centre of gravity and lead to difficulties of flying, they had simply stolen a plate from a written-off Battle and, fitting it into a Hurricane, had found it made no difference at all.

As far as the intentions of the Germans were concerned, nobody seemed to know very much, chiefly because the concept of air reconnaissance was that the Lysander would look after the short range work at low level while longer range cover would be supplied by Blenheims flying at 12,000 feet, the maximum height at which it was believed cameras could give acceptable pictures. The Blenheims, in fact, were suffering casualties in their attempts to get information.

Barratt was at a loss. He was being pressured by the Commander-in-Chief of the British Expeditionary Force for photographs because he didn't agree with the French, who, assuming that their Maginot Line defences would present an impassable obstacle, were convinced that the German attack would come across the Belgian Plain between Namur and Antwerp. Fortunately, at that moment Cotton turned up, a huge bespectacled man full of Australian self-confidence, and when Barratt asked for proof of his suspicions that the Germans planned to use a southern approach, he immediately offered a Spitfire he had made faster by replacing the thick dope with a hard semi-gloss.

'With all the holes blocked up and all projections streamlined,' he said. 'We can push the speed up by thirty or forty miles an hour The Germans won't ever catch it. Especially with the guns out.'

A fortnight later, with the weather improving, the Spitfire arrived. When Dicken wanted to mount the camera behind the pilot's seat, the engineer officer promptly objected that it would upset the balance of the machine.

'You'd better see Number One Squadron,' Dicken said dryly. '*They* were refused back armour because one of you lot said it would affect the flying qualities so they fitted it anyway, and it made no difference at all. Besides, in case you haven't noticed, to compensate for the heaviness of the new three-bladed steel propellers we're fitting, lead weights have been let into the tail.'

The red-faced engineer officer had to admit this was true and the camera was mounted in place of the weights and, at the beginning of May, with the weather improving all the time, Dicken flew along the wooded country of the Belgian-Luxembourg-German border.

Taking the photographs into Barratt, he indicated what they had picked up. 'Tanks,' he pointed out. 'Hiding among the trees in the Ardennes.'

Barratt frowned. 'The French regard the Ardennes as impassable for armoured troops,' he pointed out. 'Allied strategy's based on that assumption. It's the whole basis of the French plan. When they come, we're to advance to the River Dyle to cover Brussels and Antwerp. I think we'd better have a low-level for confirmation.'

The following day was bright as Dicken climbed into his seat. The Merlin engine's crackling roar filled his ears as it started up in a cloud of dust and streams of white smoke from the exhaust stubs. The Spit was a difficult machine to taxi and oversensitive to fore and aft control so that lifting the tail tended to dig in the prop while a correction tended to dig in the tail.

As he howled over the ground at low level he saw faces turned up to watch him, so that woods that had appeared to be empty were suddenly sprinkled with white spots. The forests of the Ardennes were in full leaf but it soon became obvious that there were army units hiding there and he could see men running for cover and occasionally lorries lurching out of sight. It seemed worth taking a risk to double check so, heading beyond the German frontier, he swung round in a wide arc and headed south just inside the German border. At once he saw tents, lorries and tanks. As he swung round for a second look, he spotted two dots in the sky and realised that the Germans had picked him up. The machines were 109s and he pushed the boost through the barrier so that the stripped-down Spitfire leapt away from the Germans as if they were standing still.

Barratt was delighted with his report. 'I'll send a man to London at once and ask for Bomber Command's help,' he said.

The following day, with the Spitfire on its way back to England, Dicken was called to Barratt's office. French attachés in Switzerland were saying that the German attack would come near Sedan sometime between May 7th and May 10th. Barratt had also discovered that, despite what the French claimed, it was felt by the British that the Ardennes would *not* present the barrier to an armoured force that had been thought.

Nevertheless, Bomber Command could offer no help. 'They get their orders from the Air Staff after they've been approved by the War Cabinet,' Barratt said. 'And their plans are laid days, weeks and even months ahead. They expect to be bombing the Ruhr, not targets along the border.'

The countryside was gay in the full bloom of spring. Trees were in blossom and the grass wore the young yellow-green of its first appearance. The French villages were bright and clean in the sunshine and the only fly in the ointment was the arrival at headquarters of Diplock. His duties seemed to be nebulous but he seemed to have furnished himself with the authority to interfere as he liked, and his interest in aerial photography soon convinced Dicken that he was there to check on Cotton's activities. Cotton was only a reserve squadron leader with the temporary rank of wing commander but, with his natural Australian bounce, was running his own show and it was obvious that Diplock was watching for any misdemeanours which would enable him to be put in his place.

On May 9th, Dicken was sent to talk to the French commander in Metz. Despite the reaction in London, Barratt was still worried and felt the local commanders should be warned of what they had discovered. It was a warm day with a soft breeze and the city was full of soldiers. The little lime trees towards the Ile de Saulcy showed glimpses of the tall steep-roofed mansions on the wooded slopes beyond the Ban St Martin, and the lace-like stonework of the cathedral spire stood out against a blue cloud-flecked sky.

Sitting at a pavement table under a gaily-striped awning in the Place de la République, it was pleasant to relax in the sunshine. Booted and spurred French officers strolled by, with pilots of the Armée de l'Air and Troupes de Forteresse from the Maginot Line.

Dicken watched them with interest. He had heard disquieting rumours that, despite their supposed élan, they were not what they seemed and, while some of the regular units were excellent, many reservists were indifferently equipped and badly led. Like the British, they had spent all the years between the two wars being ruled by the same old political gang and they seemed curiously apathetic and not very impressed by the posters he saw everywhere, '*Nous vaincrons parce que nous sommes les plus forts.*' We shall win because we are stronger. It seemed a curiously uninspired way of putting the point across.

As he left the city in the evening, the setting sun was touching the turrets and spires with golden fingers. As the car climbed the hill from the Porte Serpenoise, Dicken stopped it and turned to the driver.

'Can you hear anything?' he asked. The sound was faint, a mere murmur from the east.

'There's something, sir.'

As they listened, the sound came again, more distinct, and they looked at each other. Then it came a third time and this time it sounded like distant thunder.

'Guns,' the driver said.

'And big ones at that! Let's go!'

-

It was a perfect night and when he reached base Dicken strolled towards the airfield. The stars were bright and sharp and there were a lot of aircraft about overhead. This was nothing unusual because there was always activity along the frontier, but this time he could hear the whango-whango-whango of French anti-aircraft guns, and a piece of shrapnel struck the ground nearby. In the early hours of the morning he woke with a start to see his batman standing in the doorway, his hand on the light switch.

'You're wanted at headquarters immediately, sir.'

'What's happening?'

'I think it's started, sir. Number One Squadron's already in the air, patrolling towards Metz. The Germans are coming through Holland, Belgium and Luxembourg. There are plots all over the board!'

Five

Already the panic messages were arriving. The uncanny quiet of the previous day was sharply contrasted by the reports that were coming in now of the most modern army in the world on the move. By evening, the airfields at Lille and Nancy had been bombed and Barratt had lost a lot of precious aeroplanes.

The Allied army's plan to swing north through Belgium was already in operation but there were reports of a gigantic phalanx of armour breaking through the Ardennes, just as they had suspected they would. Within forty-eight hours they were all involved.

The Germans seemed to be everywhere, both on the ground and in the air, and the Advanced Air Striking Force with its pathetic Battles had lost half its numbers. The Dutch army was collapsing and they all knew that the Belgian army would go the same way. Their machines, Fiat biplanes with a single machine gun firing through the propeller, were worse than the RAF's and the replacements were even older. As attrition wiped away their squadrons, the Battles took over from them the attempt to destroy the Maastricht bridges, but four out of the five that were sent were shot down and the fifth crashed on the way home. Within two days the AASF had shrunk to seventy-two machines.

'I wish to God we'd developed a few of Udet's dive bombers,' Barratt growled, 'instead of concentrating on those wretched Battles.'

The Stukas were everywhere. To capitalise on the natural scream of an aircraft diving at speed, the Germans had added sirens to the undercarriages. They called them Jericho trombones and the name had somehow crossed the frontier, and it was found that the sound was numbing to unseasoned troops.

They had shattered the morale of the French second-class reservists on the Meuse and were paralysing the French artillery, whose gunners stopped firing and went to ground as soon as they started their dives, while the infantry cowered in trenches, dazed by the crash of bombs and the shriek of the bombers.

Leading the German armour, they were pile-driving their way into France and it seemed that nothing could stop them. The first attacks had been against front line positions and airfields, wiping out the opposition air strength, and, unlike the Allies, the Germans were using their machines in large numbers, not scattering them all over the front. The long-cherished illusion that the Battle was a worthwhile aircraft had vanished in the attacks on the Meuse bridges when whole squadrons were wiped out without registering a single hit, and on May 13th, the Germans put 700 machines into the air over Sedan, 200 of them Stukas. The French simply threw away their rifles and ran and, after an attempt to help by attacking the bridgehead, the AASF was as good as finished.

Within days the whole front was beginning to crumble and the army was withdrawing to the line of the Escaut because the French First Army had collapsed. There was now no question in the morning of fighting to throw off the deep sleep that came with spending all day in the open air. Everybody came awake in a flash to buckle on tunic and revolver and within a week had forgotten what sleep was like.

There were reports of German spies everywhere and no one was certain where the front was because the recce machines that were sent to find out never seemed to come back. Frantic requests for more British fighters to be sent to France had been turned down by Hugh Dowding, commanding Fighter Command, whose view was that the Battle of France was already lost and that the Battle of Britain would follow shortly. There was a lot of bitterness, but it was clear to anyone with intelligence that the battle in France *was* lost and that Dowding was right.

Diplock was already making indignant noises about wishing to return to England. He seemed satisfied that he could nail Cotton to the mast whenever he wished – and he probably could, because Cotton acknowledged nobody as his master – but Barratt refused to allow him to go. He was desperately in need of senior officers to deal with the constantly changing circumstances, and Diplock, who had never had a fierce obsession about risking his neck, had that sort of experience in abundance. His whole career in the RAF had been spent behind a desk, and he sulked about the place complaining constantly that he was of more use in England.

When the situation became so confused no one knew where the front line was, Dicken offered to find out. Flying a borrowed Hurricane, something that wasn't easy to obtain because they were already desperately short, he was aware of the tension as he climbed into the cockpit.

The faces of the fitter and rigger and the Intelligence Officer all wore bleak expressions and as the engine warmed up a Roman Catholic padre appeared.

'I'm here to give absolution to one or two of the pilots,' he said. 'Some of them are Catholics and want to confess. Do you wish to?'

'I'm not a Catholic, Padre,' Dicken said.

'It can never do much harm,' the padre smiled.

He was a big man and reminded Dicken of Father O'Buhilly, the American priest he had so admired. Somehow, religious toleration went with big men, particularly in service padres who had to deal with every kind of human being imaginable, including a few of the King's Hard Bargains, so Dicken nodded, wondering as he did so where Father O'Buhilly was at that moment and what had happened to him, because they had once shared the very uncomfortable jail of a Chinese warlord called Lee Tse-liu.

He found the front line and just had time to identify the area when he was attacked by three Messerschmitt 110s. One of them was across his route to safety so, picking the nearest, he manoeuvred on to its tail as it turned. As he fired, he was surprised to see pieces fly into the air. As he passed the stricken machine, it was still turning and he watched in fascinated horror as the turn became a spin that trailed a curling stream of smoke before the machine blew apart in a shower of debris.

Almost immediately there was a tremendous explosion in front of him and he became aware that the Hurricane was limp on the controls. Black smoke was pouring from the nose, and he could feel the blast of heat and see the flicker of flame. Pulling the pin of his parachute harness, he tried to jettison the hood but it was stuck. In a panic, by thumping at it with his fist he managed to dislodge it and, swinging the aircraft on to its back, he fell free. He was lower than he had realised because he seemed to hit the ground almost at once and almost immediately a French gendarme appeared and stuck a pistol in his face.

'*Haut les mains!*'

It took a minute or two to convince the Frenchman of his nationality and immediately the gendarme became full of comradely hatred for the Germans. '*Merde à ces cochons d'Hitler,*' he snarled. 'We will have our work cut out.'

Dicken arrived on an RAF base just as its fighters returned, the pilots hungry, exhausted and strung up. They had been flying ever since the balloon had gone up, never changing their clothes, never sleeping in a bed, their beards days old, their hair matted by the constant wearing of their flying helmets. Sprawled on the grass under the shade of a tree, they were waiting for a petrol tanker to arrive and, wondering if it had been misdirected by some fifth columnist, were nervous about being caught on the ground. With no idea of Dicken's rank because he had no hat and his borrowed overalls covered his badges, they were spitting out their bitterness against inefficiency in a way that reminded him of his own youth and his own hatred of the staff in the last war. They were angry because the replacement aircraft being flown from England had not had their guns harmonised and in some cases were not even fitted with sights. The previous day they had been reduced to four serviceable machines and the technical officer was in tears of fury.

They were watching a bunch of young thrushes making their first flights, their absorption hiding the tension they felt.

'These sprog sparrows get the knack amazin' quick,' one of them said. 'You never see 'em crash-land. Fine pitch and plenty of flap and off they go. Wonder if they use a link trainer.'

One of them, who had had to twist and turn through trees to throw off a gaggle of 109s, was still shaking. 'Christ knows what state my poor bloody flogged machine's in,' he said.

He had lost his kit and his trousers were covered with sticky glycol that had drenched him as his engine was hit. A lot of it had got into his eyes and they were still red-rimmed and sore-looking.

'I'm scared stiff,' he admitted. 'And I keep wondering if I've gone yellow and I'm losing my nerve. But when you see the Jerries you find there's something to get hold of and you get a grip on yourself and everything's all right.'

Because of the shifting of the front, wounded pilots had been sent to a hospital in Paris. The feeling was that there they would have a chance to recover, but it was already beginning to seem that the fight was lost because it was possible now to hear the thunder of guns quite clearly. Despite the impact of war, however, in the next field a French peasant was still following a harrow pulled by two huge Percherons. With him was a labourer and a small boy and, with the sky a brilliant blue, it seemed hard at that moment to believe there was a war on.

Dicken's report was telephoned to Intelligence; then, as he tried to organise transport again, the war suddenly woke up. They became aware of silver dots in the sky and the faint clatter of machine guns, then one of the dots detached itself and began to fall, spinning like a leaf, while they all watched hypnotised. It was trailing a column of smoke that curled and swerved through the sky as the machine descended. Half expecting a parachute to appear, they continued to watch, but nothing happened except for that quiet spinning lower and lower, leaving the crooked trail of smoke to mark its descent.

'That's one of the bastards, anyway,' someone said.

'Except,' another pilot replied in a flat voice, 'that it looks uncommonly like one of ours.'

Then they saw it was a Hurricane, falling against a backdrop of towering pink cumulus, and eventually it disappeared behind a hill. There was no explosion, no thump, just silence and smoke rising slowly to join the curling column that coiled down from above.

The farmer with the horses had stopped to watch and he and his son and the labourer were silhouetted against the sky. As they stared, the sound of aeroplanes grew louder and the watching pilots saw the puffballs of anti-aircraft fire appear in the sky beyond the hill.

'There they are!' The man with the glycol-covered trousers pointed. 'One of them's coming this way! I'm for the shelter!'

But nobody moved and he halted uncertainly, anxious not to show nervousness. The German aircraft vanished behind the rise, and they thought he had gone but then they heard the engine again in an increasing howl, and the next moment a Heinkel leapt over the hill. As they flung themselves flat on their faces, Dicken found himself crouching behind a lorry which seemed to bounce on its tyres with each bang. There were six explosions, one after the other, and someone yelled. 'The stupid bugger's blown himself up with his own bombs!'

The German pilot had dropped his salvo from too low and one of them had removed his tail surfaces so that the machine flew on in a wavery line until it vanished into a clump of trees. Everybody started running but the aeroplane had already started to burn and as they broke through the undergrowth they found themselves looking directly into its nose where two men were struggling to open the hatch. Even as they arrived, the flames roared up and the Germans' clothes started to smoulder then caught fire and the pilot's hair started to blaze. The faces grew redder and redder then turned black and the screaming stopped. Finally the port wing tank exploded in a shower of blazing petrol and popping ammunition.

They were still watching the blazing machine when they became aware of the farmer who had been harrowing his field stumbling towards them. His clothes were torn and he was hardly able to stand.

'*Ils sont morts,*' he croaked. '*Mon fils! Mon fils et Alois!*'

They found the bodies near a bomb crater. The boy was unrecognisable as a human being and of the labourer they found nothing but his cap and one hand. The horses lay bleeding alongside the smashed harrow and the air was full of the reek of high explosive.

The farmer stared at the bloody flesh and burst out weeping, then he lifted his fist and shook it at the air. '*Salaud de Boche,*' he yelled. '*Je te casse la gueule, toi!*'

–

Still eager to return to England, Diplock, growing more shrill and more indignant by the day, was finally given instructions to go via Paris, pick up all the wounded RAF pilots on his way, and see them safely to England.

By this time the roads were full of refugees and what had originally been a trickle from the frontier villages had now become a flood. The sky was full of smoke and the noise of engines and explosions never seemed to cease.

But the weather remained perfect and the wretched refugees could do nothing to hide as the German aeroplanes came over. Riding with a driver in a borrowed army car, trying to find out what was happening, Dicken was trapped in a small village called La Motte. There was a smell of blossom in the air and old women in black were enjoying the sunshine, but the road ahead was clogged by refugees who eddied into gardens and back streets like water from a burst dam.

There were thousands of them, all pressing against the military vehicles trying to get past. Then Dicken noticed a Fieseler recce plane hovering overhead, humming like a dragonfly in the bright blue sky, and with a sudden horrifying awareness, he realised what was going to happen. A Heinkel flew over but its bomb dropped outside the town and a soldier in a Bren gun carrier yelled his contempt. 'They couldn't 'it a pig in a passage,' he roared.

It was still impossible to move because the refugees, who had bolted for the fields, had already begun to swarm back on to the road, and Dicken was just watching a line of cars loaded with people and their possessions passing ahead when he saw the Stukas arrive, 10,000 feet up, in a formation like an arrowhead. Even as he saw the point of the arrow disintegrate, the refugees started to run again.

The sky was alive with bursting shells as the leading plane dived. It came down at a terrific speed, filling the air with a maniac scream so that impulsively everybody flung themselves from their vehicles and hugged the earth. To Dicken, cowering in a ditch with his driver, it was as if he'd been singled out individually and that nothing on earth could stop the diving plane. For the first time he began to realise why the Germans had backed Udet's dive bomber tactics.

As the first salvo of bombs struck, the ground seemed to heave as if in a heavy swell. Almost immediately a second plane came down, followed by a third and a fourth, and Dicken felt the earth moving beneath him as their bombs landed. A house collapsed with a roar and tiles sliced viciously over his head through the yellow smoke lit by tongues of flame that eddied about him.

The horror appeared to go on for a lifetime while they clawed at the earth, their mouths hanging open, their eyes blinking at every shower of debris. Dimly, they could hear the incoherent cries of women and children, then the last bomb fell only a few yards away in an ear-shattering crash and, as suddenly as it had begun, the bombing stopped and the world was full of silence, an uncanny silence. Dicken lifted his head, breathing painfully, his face blackened by dust. La Motte seemed to have been blown off the face of the earth.

There was nothing now of the village but piles of rubble, and the air was filled with a wailing which rose and fell in an eerie cadence that was broken immediately by the shouts of stretcher bearers, as soldiers ran to do what they could for the injured. The black-clad old ladies had vanished beneath the debris of their houses and the road junction ahead was completely blocked by the wreckage of vehicles and human beings.

It took an hour to get past. Though it was hard to press on through the misery, it was pointless to try to help. There were already too many helpers and nowhere to put the injured. Beyond La Motte there were still more refugees, waiting limply by the roadside, exhausted and grey-faced with fear, staring mutely as if they were too tired to care at a company of Senegalese troops who were marching past with impassive faces.

They hadn't gone more than a mile when the aeroplanes came again, strafing the road to complete the confusion. As they heard the howl of engines, the driver braked and yelled to Dicken to take cover and, as the bombs came screaming down, a wail went up from the refugees. Flinging himself down a bank into a ditch, Dicken found himself shouting at them to lie flat. But, bewildered and shocked, they simply stood gaping at the sky, and scrambling from the ditch, he went among them, pushing at them, sending them flying into the ditch one after another, then finally tossed a baby down to its mother, pushchair and all, as the bombs struck. He saw flashes and people falling like toppled ninepins, then something like a huge soft fist hit him in the back and flung him into the ditch on top of the driver.

As the aeroplanes returned, he saw the Senegalese form up in a group and fire their rifles. By some miracle they hit the leading machine, which was only thirty or forty feet up, and it came lower and lower and finally hit the surface of the field ahead at an angle. It bounced once or twice, sending up showers of dust and clods of earth before finally coming to a stop.

Heads lifted from the ditch but as other machines howled past stick after stick of bombs whistled down to explode with cracking roars along the side of the road. As the scream of the engines finally faded, Dicken scrambled to the road. There had been no casualties in their immediate neighbourhood but up ahead they could hear piercing shrieks from a group surrounding a farm cart that lay on its side, its wheels still spinning, the horse struggling to drag itself out of the ditch, its hind legs trailing like those of a dog run over in the street. The cart had been full of children and small bodies were scattered all over the road.

The Heinkel which had crashed had caught fire now and the crew, struggling free, started to run. But the Senegalese soldiers started firing and, as one of them went down, the others stopped dead and raised their hands. As the Senegalese advanced on them, one of the Germans reached for a pistol. There was another fusillade of shots and he fell backwards, and the Senegalese, without a change of expression, picked up the other two by their arms and legs and tossed them into the flames of their stricken aeroplane. As their screams came, the Senegalese, with the same unmoved expression, picked up the bodies of the remaining two, and flung them after their comrades. Then they formed up again and marched back to the road to continue their westward trudge.

By this time the confusion was appalling and the air was alive with rumours of parachutists and motorcyclists across the path of the retreat. It was Dicken's opinion that they *were* just rumours because most of them appeared to be hearsay and the damage was being done entirely by fear and lack of knowledge. But there was no question of standing and fighting. The French army had collapsed. Some regiments had fought to the last man but the

conscription system had produced poor regiments offi-
cered by middle-aged men, and the German intelligence
had been good. The Stukas had smashed a colossal hole
in the French front through which their armour was now
pouring en masse and, fanning out behind, were creating
chaos by the spreading of alarmist stories.

Still undefeated but feeling they were surrounded, the
French had fallen back to try to establish a line of the sort
their generals remembered from the last war. But there
was no line and they went on searching until the Germans
rounded them up in groups. The British army was already
pinned against the coast at Dunkirk and it was obvious
they were about to get out of the Continent. But the
Stukas were taking a tremendous toll of ships and there
was already a horrifying loss among the destroyers.

All the lines of communications troops had long since
gone with every scrap of equipment that could be got
away, followed by the experienced soldiers who had
fought against the Germans and knew their tricks. But
there was no longer time to pick and choose. It was now
a case of every man for himself, and it was with the crisis
at its worst that they learned from an agitated telephone
call from a British attaché in Paris that the wounded pilots
there were still awaiting transportation to the coast. Frantic
contacts with London showed that Diplock had already
reached home.

Barratt gestured. 'Get off there, Dick,' he said. 'Round
'em up. Get 'em away. Most of them will be able to fight
again and we're going to need them. Get them to Dieppe
or out via the Gironde.'

Driving to Paris, Dicken found its inhabitants already
leaving for the Mediterranean coast, Bordeaux and

Brittany, and, rounding up a fleet of ambulances and cars, he stuffed them with men in blue wearing bandages and plasters and set them on the road south. By the time he had finished, it was possible to hear anti-aircraft firing and the sound of aeroplane engines. Crumps, bangs and whistles were followed by the clink and clatter of falling splinters and the rush of tumbling brickwork. Great billows of black smoke were rolling across the city from St Denis, the Seine and St Germain to the west.

The following day he learned that nearly 300 people had been killed and there had been a lot of damage at the Citroën Works, city aerodromes and the French Air Ministry. People were still cramming the stations for the south and west and heading in streams for the Porte d'Italie, their cars laden with household goods, mattresses draped across the roofs in the hope of keeping out the bullets of strafing German aeroplanes.

There were still a few British service personnel about the city and, since Dicken had started the exodus south, they began to approach him for instructions. Commandeering service and private vehicles, he sent them after the others. It was clear by this time that the Germans would occupy Paris before long, but there were still a few people around who refused to be hurried. The American Ambulance Corps was still busy about the city, and, searching for a wounded sergeant, Dicken saw one of them, a woman with a sweet face and a low voice, holding the hand of a boy of about nineteen, who clutched his bloodstained flying helmet as if it were a talisman.

'God bless America,' he muttered as he passed and the woman turned and looked up, startled.

A French tank captain he talked to who had knocked out three German panzers insisted that his tanks had been superior all along the line to the German machines, but that the Germans were winning because the French politicians were a lot of craven-hearted cowards who had bolted for Bordeaux at the first alarm.

It was obvious there weren't many days left before the Germans arrived. They were already coming up the Seine and their aircraft were over the city daily. Caught near the Champs Elysées by the thud of bombs that came even before the sirens sounded, Dicken started to look around him for a shelter.

The aeroplanes were appearing overhead now and, standing in the doorway of a shop nearby, he saw a woman in the uniform of the American Ambulance Corps. He recognised her at once as the woman he'd seen holding the hand of the wounded pilot. She looked bewildered, so he grabbed her arm and dragged her with him. Ahead of him he could see the sign, ABRI – shelter – and he pushed her in front of him down the steps just as the first bomb landed in the street. There was a tremendous crash and the air seemed to be sucked out of their lungs, then a cloud of dust filled the shelter to make them all start coughing. The American woman hid her face in Dicken's shoulder, and, without thinking, he put his arm around her and pulled her closer.

The raid didn't last long and after a while the American woman lifted her head. 'Thank you,' she said.

'Perhaps a drink would help,' Dicken suggested, but she shook her head.

'I'm sorry. I'd love to, but under the circumstances I'd better get back. There'll be work to do.'

News arrived that the Germans had reached Rouen and it was clearly time to go. With no kit to pack, nothing but the revolver round his waist, Dicken called at the American hospital to thank them for all they had done. He had half hoped to bump into the woman he had met in the shelter but nobody could identify her from his description and time was hurrying by so he had to leave without finding her. He decided to travel by train to Blois where the headquarters of the Advanced Air Striking Force had moved. But it was impossible to get near the Gare de Lyon for the crowds of people trying to escape. The Gare d'Austerlitz was similarly crowded and he found out that the lines were being bombed, anyway, and in the end decided to leave by road.

That evening he wandered round the streets which were empty except for an occasional car. The cafes and restaurants were all boarded up, the pavements deserted and devoid of the famous *flâneurs*, and the atmosphere was one of desolation. Walking up the Champs Elysées to the Etoile, he stood by the Tomb of the Unknown Soldier for a while, watched by a silent gendarme, and stared at the words on the tomb – *Ici repose un soldat français mort pour la patrie* – remembering bitterly how after the last lot the politicians had promised it had been the war to end all wars.

As they moved off the next morning, there was a strange mist over the city and a strong smell of burning. The rumble of gunfire in the distance seemed to reach him through the bones of the earth. He had acquired a car and a truck filled with fifteen RAF policemen and their baggage and was escorted by two RAF despatch riders, who worked wonders as they reached the crowded country roads. Looking back he saw a shroud of black smoke hanging over the city and the smuts from the fires settled on their clothes and made the faces of the despatch riders as black as negroes'.

Châteaudun came up and they moved on to Blois which was as crowded as every other town, then they began to follow the Loire until they came to Nantes. They had been unable to find food because of the horde of refugees moving ahead of them and were forced further south to Poitiers where they knew of an airfield where there might be aircraft going to England. Aircraft were moving all right but they were all packed to suffocation and, beginning to grow angry, Dicken found an abandoned Bristol Bombay. It was an old-fashioned high-winged twin-engined bomber which had been relegated to the status of a transport. It had a broken tail wheel and rudder but, with the aid of a corporal fitter, they got to work on it.

'Will it hold up?' Dicken asked.

'I reckon so, sir. Just.'

Cotton and his team arrived soon afterwards with his Lockheed and an abandoned Fairey Battle they had found.

He greeted Dicken warmly. 'Just in time,' he said. 'It's all finished here. Just as I'm finished in England. I've heard the Air Ministry's going to sack me. Feller called St Aubyn. How are you off for transport home?'

'We've got an old Bombay and you look pretty full already.'

Cotton grinned. 'Even an English secretary and her dog.'

The service policemen had managed to find a place on another aeroplane by now but there were plenty of

63

ground crew who crowded aboard the Bombay and in the end Dicken found he had a group of twenty-one. Five more turned up just as the corporal fitter started the engines.

There were no maps and Dicken had never flown a Bombay but he put it to his passengers and found they were all willing to take a chance. Taxiing to the end of the field, he swung into wind with the tail wheel rattling and clunking as they rolled over the ruts. The fitter was sitting in the co-pilot's seat, his eyes glued to the dials.

'Shout out if you see anything happening that shouldn't happen,' Dicken said, then swinging into wind he pushed the throttles wide open.

The clunking of the tail wheel grew louder and it began to sound desperately fragile. There was a bang and immediately Dicken thrust the stick forward and they thundered ahead with the tail in the air. Reaching flying speed, he eased back on the controls and felt the rumbling of the wheels cease. As they lifted, they could see the bomb-pitted aerodrome and the crowds of refugees stretching across the countryside, cramming every road. Spirals of smoke seemed to rise from every village and town.

Climbing to a thousand feet, he tried a cautious turn.

'If anything happens I'll put her down near a ship or something,' he said.

They followed the river to St Nazaire. Below them they could see a huge ship lying on her side. All round her there were boats and clusters of black bobbing heads.

After a while, he tried another turn and saw Brittany passing beneath him. The Channel was full of ships, all engaged, he imagined, in rescuing what was left of the BEF. Turning slightly east, he saw the Channel Islands. The engines were making strange noises and one of them was sending out a great deal of blue smoke, so that he expected it to burst into flames at any minute, and it was with some relief that he saw the Isle of Wight passing below. Immediately the naval guns at Portsmouth began to fire at them.

'Get on the Aldis,' he said to the wireless operator. 'Give them "We are friendly."'

The guns stopped but the wireless operator came back grinning. 'They replied, "Bugger off," sir.'

Recalling the losses at Dunkirk and the immortal words of one of the Lords of the Admiralty before the war, engraved on the hearts of all airmen, 'Their Lordships do not consider that any warship competently handled is in danger from aerial attack,' Dicken frowned. 'Give them,' he suggested. '"We'll meet you here tomorrow with bombs and then we'll see who buggers off."'

The airman with the Aldis lamp gave him a startled look and he smiled. 'Perhaps, after all,' he said, 'you'd better not. Co-operation between the services is bad enough already.'

As he swung north-east, he turned to the corporal fitter. 'Where do you come from?' he asked.

'London, sir.'

'Well, since you got the thing going, I reckon we ought to drop you as near home as possible.'

Navigating by railway lines, as they began to descend, their minds still full of the horror that was France, they saw a game of cricket in progress. It seemed unbelievable.

'Pity we haven't got a bomb or two to drop on *them*, sir,' the fitter observed. 'Just to make 'em realise there's a war on.'

Dicken nodded. 'I have a suspicion, corporal,' he said, 'that they won't have long to wait.'

Six

Everybody who could be spared had been brought south to handle the hundreds of bewildered men arriving from France and among the first people Dicken saw was Hatto. He looked tired and had been on his feet without sleep for three days.

'Madly war, what,' he said. 'Dowding's treating it as a run-up to the battle for Britain and Keith Park's holding Eleven Group in readiness for the first attacks.' He sighed. 'At least we no longer have anybody to let us down and we've now got Churchill running the show instead of that old Birmingham umbrella manufacturer, Chamberlain.'

Seen in a clear light, it wasn't a promising prospect nevertheless. Hitler ruled all Western Europe from Tromsø to the Pyrenees, and the threat of invasion was being countered by tearing down all signposts, railway signs and anything else that would indicate to an invading force where it was, while the ringing of church bells was forbidden except as an alarm. Since there were no weapons, there wasn't much else they *could* do.

Somehow, however, there was a strange confidence that came down from the top. Churchill had no doubts about the outcome and said again and again that Hitler would never defeat England or even land an invasion force and, though RAF reconnaissance planes were already bringing back reports of landing barges gathering in the French Channel ports, everybody believed his powerful rhetoric.

The disaster in France had started up a new uproar over the old question of dive bombers and a bitter argument was going on over the RAF's interpretation of the army's close-support requirements. One group was struggling to convince the Air Ministry that its request for such an aircraft was thoroughly justified by recent events and, though the Air Ministry would concede nothing, was urging the design and production in quantity of large numbers of small attack dive bombers to work with the ground forces. The campaign got nowhere.

To his surprise, Dicken found himself appointed with increased rank to command a fighter station at Thornside. Having lost all his kit in France, however, he requested a few days' leave in London to refit himself and, as he headed into the Grosvenor for a drink after a visit to the tailor's, he bumped into a familiar figure. It was older and thicker round the middle than when he had last seen it but it had fought alongside him for months in France and Italy in the last war, and he had last seen it in the United States while searching for his erring wife, Zoë.

'Walt Foote!' he said.

'Dicky Boy!' Foote grabbed him and hugged him. 'Nearly did a gloat dance,' he said. 'Remember how we used to do a ring-a-round-the-roses whenever we shot down a Hun or defeated Percy Diplock.'

'What are you doing here?'

'Just back from China. I got to be a judge and the government sent me out to handle a few things for them.

I've just been to see your Foreign Office and I'm now on my way home to warn ours.'

'About the Japanese?'

'The war in Europe's not going to be the only one. The Japs are going to take advantage of the fact that the British Empire's fully occupied in Europe.'

'Will America let them?'

Foote grinned. 'America doesn't give a damn about them grabbing what belongs to you, but they'll soon start yelling if they lay their hands on anything in our sphere of influence.'

'And will they?'

'Brother, I've been operating China and Japan for years and I sure as hell think they *will*.'

As they talked, a woman in the uniform of an American Ambulance Corps appeared in the hotel and Foote stood up.

'I'd like you to meet my niece, Katie,' he said. 'She's just arrived from France.'

The woman laughed. 'Paris,' she said, pointing at Dicken. 'June 7th.'

Foote was staring at them. 'You've met?'

Dicken grinned. 'You Feete get around.'

–

Foote remained in London only for one more day before going to Southampton to catch a ship for the States. Katie Foote was to remain in England, doing ambulance work, and she and Dicken agreed to take care of each other. As a free agent since his wife had died, it was something that didn't fail to appeal because she was a tall attractive woman just getting over the trauma of a broken marriage.

69

They saw Foote off on the train together and exchanged addresses.

'Let's meet,' she said. 'There should be time.'

Thornside was one of the London fighter stations with a Sector Operations rooms and satellite aerodromes at Beaston and Pewton, and Dicken found himself busy sixteen hours a day seven days a week.

An air fighting development unit was operating there and the aerodrome defences had all been attended to. But the hangars had been camouflaged during the Phoney War with brown and green paint to break up the regularity of the lines and, flying over it, Dicken pointed out that because it was surrounded by houses, it had not been camouflaged at all, simply made more conspicuous.

The experts, who had been trained to believe that camouflage meant trees, not houses, disagreed violently, but after a great deal of argument, the hangars were disguised as more houses with bright red roofs, windows, doors and gardens and the result was so effective that the pilots of the three squadrons stationed there complained they could never find the damn place and the adjutant finally conceded that the idea worked, claiming he'd just seen two swans crash-land as they tried to alight on an artificial stream.

With all three squadrons watching the sea as the Germans stepped up their attacks on Channel shipping, the place was often vulnerable to attack, so a station defence flight was organised, with any pilot – including Dicken – who happened to be available taking off in any aircraft that was handy.

Soon afterwards he was told to report to London to be briefed about a Polish squadron that was due to be attached to Thornside. There were a lot of things to remember – chiefly that the Poles had all reached England through France, Spain and North Africa, and were all a little touchy about their pride. They also had a lot of strange customs and after their defeat considered their honour important, but though they were itching to get at the Germans they were not to be allowed near them until they had learned some English.

The briefing took most of the morning. In the afternoon, Dicken contacted Katie Foote who agreed at once to meet him for a meal. The restaurant was crowded with men in uniform and there was now even a sprinkling of women in them, too. Also, where once all the uniforms would have been those of officers, now there was a mixture of other ranks as the crisis swept everybody into the services. Fathers with red tabs sat alongside sons in plain khaki without a single badge beyond their regimental flash. Like Dicken, Katie Foote was also in uniform and, like all American uniforms, it was perfectly tailored and showed her figure.

She was intelligent with a lively humour and Dicken enjoyed his evening more than he had expected. What had been only a polite gesture to Foote had turned out to be exciting and it was suddenly important to meet her again. As he found her a taxi, she leaned out and kissed him gently.

'Thank you, Dicken,' she said. 'You're a nice guy.'

'I'm an *old* guy.'

'Not that old.'

'Nearly old enough to be your father.'

She smiled, ignoring the comment. 'It was a lovely evening.'

'We'd better repeat it.'

'Please God.'

Two days later the Poles arrived at Thornside. Wearing their own strangely-shaped wings, they were stiff and wary, feeling they knew far more about the war than their British hosts. Though they had all fought against the Germans in Poland, they were new to Hurricanes, however, and knew nothing of retracting undercarriages and flaps. There were several cases of belly landings or overshooting and their understanding of English was not sufficient for them to be controlled from the Operations Room.

'But ve haf come here to kill Germans not to learn Anglish,' their senior officer complained.

Their arrival resulted in another hurried visit to London where the problem of foreign aircrews was being thrashed out. They were arriving now from France, Belgium, Holland, Norway and Denmark, and they all had to be integrated into the RAF. In the evening, Dicken picked up Katie Foote again and they walked together through Hyde Park in the summer evening. In the distance they could hear the mutter of guns and the sky was full of the distant sound of aeroplanes because the raids, though not yet directed at London, were still continuing.

'I've got a flat now, Dicken,' she said. 'And having got it, having decided I was going to enjoy it, they've told me I've got to go home. Some nonsense about London being too dangerous.'

'Don't you want to go home?'

'I've nothing to go home for. My marriage's sunk.'

'This marriage of yours. Don't you think you keep it too much to yourself?'

'Who else is interested?'

'I'll listen.'

'There's nothing to tell. My husband wasn't to blame. We got married too soon. I was too eager. More eager than he was. I guess he'd probably rather have played tennis. He was keen on tennis. I think I talked him into it.'

They were silent for a moment, both of them deep in thought, Dicken faintly depressed. All his contacts with pleasant women seemed to end as soon as they started.

'When?' he asked.

'When what?'

'When do you have to go?'

'I don't know yet, but they say I've got to.'

It was impossible for Dicken to stay long in London because the Poles were itching to get into battle, and they said goodbye at the door of her flat. Standing with his hands on her hips, Dicken kissed her on the lips. As he did so, her arms went impulsively round his neck and she kissed him back urgently.

'Oh, Dicken,' she said. 'Why?' There were tears in her eyes. 'It's this damned war. It makes you feel like a bitch on heat with all the bravery and the dying, yet when you get to the crunch it always gets in the way.'

For a moment they clung to each other before he dragged himself away. 'Perhaps it's best you go home, Katie,' he said.

'No. Never. Why should it be?'

'War's a rotten time to get attached to someone.'

'I don't see why you're so afraid,' she said bluntly.

'There are a variety of reasons,' he pointed out. 'You're an American and no part of the fight over here, and you're also a great deal younger than I am.'

She replied by kissing him again. 'I see no problem at all,' she said. 'Uncle Walt pointed out quietly before you left that you weren't at all bad-looking – which you're not – that your wife was dead, and that he thought you looked lonely. The fact that I'm American also has no point, because although we *are* no part of your fight, I have a suspicion we shall be before long, and age doesn't really matter very much because as you get older it seems to level off and the difference eventually becomes negligible. If I stay here long enough—' she gave him a quick smile '—we'll be the same age. And I would if you wanted me to. I could give up the American Ambulance and join the Red Cross. It wouldn't be difficult.'

His urge was to say, yes, do it, but at the same time he felt he was asking too much. They hardly knew each other and too many people were snatching at the chance of a little love in the middle of the killing.

He left her in tears, his face set and frowning, and returned to find the Poles being difficult. Though they had started to learn English, they didn't agree it was important, and he had to have several sessions with their senior officer, trying to explain that they would never defeat the Germans by isolated attacks. The Germans were obviously trying to destroy the RAF so they could invade and they had to avoid committing their machines and pilots in penny numbers. They could only attack when they had a hope of succeeding and isolated attacks without co-ordination could only result in attrition without achieving much.

Experimenting with a camera gun because too many claims were being put in and the authorities were anxious to have proof, from time to time Dicken watched the Poles as they practised formations and attacked training Wellingtons. Their moves were always made from incredibly close in and he constantly expected to see a collision as their enthusiasm ran away with them.

Flying across London, he saw a formation of twenty-one Dorniers escorted by 109s approaching him unmolested. The sky was empty of anti-aircraft fire and he could see no sign of British fighter formations, and he was just about to turn away when he realised he was in an ideal position for a frontal attack and that he might even carry it out before the 109s, which would have to cross the bomber formation to reach him, could intercept.

The Dorniers were approaching him in three lines of seven machines in line astern and it even began to appear that the German fighters hadn't seen him. As he lined up on the bombers they were so close to each other in such perfect formation he could see the whole of one line of seven aircraft one behind the other in his gunsight, almost as one target. As he opened fire and half-rolled to pass beneath the formation he saw bombs bursting below him and decided that, if nothing else, he had forced some of the bombers to jettison their cargoes. Then, looking up, he saw there were now only eighteen bombers and that the centre of the three lines contained not seven but four. Staring about him, he saw three fires burning on the ground and came to the conclusion that he must have hit three bombers at once. It didn't seem possible and when he landed he was very cautious with his enquiries.

It eventually appeared that three crashed Dorniers had been found within a ten-mile radius of his attack, every one of the pilots killed by .303 bullets from the front. Nobody else claimed them and he could only assume he was responsible.

–

'I saw none of them crash and neither did anyone else, so I made no claim. It would have looked too much like a line-shoot.'

Dicken looked across the table at Katie Foote. Her flat had belonged to a naval officer's wife who had gone to Northern Ireland to be with her husband, and it had a look of studied comfort about it. Katie had cooked the meagre rations, plus a few she'd been able to wheedle out of a neighbouring grocer, and they were sitting back now sipping their coffee.

'The Poles found out, of course,' Dicken went on. 'And promptly made it a good reason for demanding once again that they be allowed into action. "You, sir—"' Dicken sat up stiffly to mimic the Polish commander '"—are destroying Jairmans – even at your age. Why can't we?"'

She laughed then suddenly became serious. 'Are you old, Dicken? I mean for this sort of thing.'

'A bit, I suppose. But so far it doesn't seem to have affected me much. Perhaps I've been lucky.'

'I'm scared.'

'What about?'

'That you'll get hurt. Aren't you afraid?'

'Being afraid's one of the reasons I'm still around. I take no more chances than I have to.'

She was silent for a while, then she lifted her head. 'They've told me again I've got to go home, Dicken.'

His heart sank. He had tried to put off thinking about it but here it was again. She had begun to light up what had been for too long an empty life and he wanted to hold on to her.

'No date?'

'Not yet. I keep fighting them off.' She shifted in her chair and put down her coffee cup. As she stretched towards the table, the line of her body was slim and curving.

She rose and he could see tears glinting in her eyes. 'Now I'm just being sorry for myself,' she said.

He rose to stand alongside her. 'I'm not being sorry for you.'

She turned quickly and, picking up the dishes, turned to head for the kitchen. 'You can stay the night if you wish, Dicken,' she said quietly.

He nodded towards the settee. 'On that?'

'If that's what you want.'

'It wouldn't be what I *want*.'

She slapped the dishes down and turned to him. 'Well, there's only one bedroom and I think you'd be damned uncomfortable on it, anyway.'

He put his arms round her and she swayed a little and took a step towards him that brought her shaking legs against his.

'It took you damned well long enough,' she said.

'I've just told you. Being afraid's one of the reasons I'm still around. There've been plenty of women who've wanted to get into bed with me. I've not been interested because I knew they weren't what I wanted.'

She put her arms around his neck. 'Normally, it wouldn't be what I wanted either. But life's suddenly too short to play kneesy-kneesy, Dicken. You've got to grab things while you can. Tomorrow – tonight even – a goddam great bomb might come down the chimney and that would be the end of Katherine Ironmonger Foote and all her hopes, even her goddam itch to be in bed with Dicken Quinney.'

'Is that what you want?'

She looked him straight in the eye. 'Yes. That's what I want. There are a thousand and one reasons why it's what I want.' She leaned her head against his shoulder and gave a little sigh. 'I can't help it,' she said.

'Why bother?'

She lifted her lips to him. 'Exactly,' she said. 'Why bother? But perhaps you could turn out that light first.'

–

It was clear that the German strategy was to use the bombers to lure the British fighter squadrons up in large numbers and destroy them with the accompanying Messerschmitt fighters, but Dowding and Keith Park, in command of 11 Group, which was doing all the fighting, aware that a battle of the sort the Germans wanted could destroy their defences in one stroke, fed in their squadrons cautiously and played on the 109s' inability to remain long overhead. But, because of the urgency and the losses, by this time pilots were arriving on squadrons barely trained, some barely able to control a bicycle let alone a Spitfire.

With casualties reported in the evening, replacement aircraft always arrived the following day and all-night work by the ground crews had them ready, wearing squadron letters, their guns and sights harmonised and with ammunition in place, ready for action the following morning. One of them turned up piloted by an elderly pilot officer whom Dicken recognised at once as Joshua Rivers, one of his first COs in France. He had been wounded early in the previous war and had a metal plate in his skull which was supposed to be affected by the heat of the sun so that his temper rose accordingly. He had long since retired but was now back in uniform in a junior rank, ferrying aircraft.

'I think, sir,' Dicken said gravely, 'that you could probably do with a sherry.'

'I think, sir,' Rivers agreed with a smile, 'that I could.'

They were just downing their drink when the tannoy went. 'Station Defence Flight, Scramble.'

Almost immediately, the commander of the air fighting development unit lifted off in an old Gladiator. It was hopelessly outclassed by the Messerschmitt fighters but it was sailing into the air bravely, followed shortly afterwards by a Blenheim, flown by the chief flying instructor, a man of forty-three, like Dicken wearing first war medal ribbons. In a fury, Dicken ran for the Hurricane Rivers had brought.

The ground crew helped him in and, setting the compass, he checked the pressures and waved away the chocks. Almost immediately, he was vectored on to a Junkers 88 approaching from the south at 17,000 feet. Followed by the two out-of-date machines, he reached 20,000 feet, but because of the clouds he could see nothing. Then directly below him, through a gap in the white, he saw German crosses.

The crew of the lone Junkers saw him at the same time, however, and immediately turned south and bolted for home. The Gladiator and the Blenheim disappeared, unable to keep up the chase, but the Hurricane, with its emergency boost pulled, was gaining ground. The Junkers sought cloud cover and Dicken fired three long bursts at it in the hope of turning it off course so that he might gain on it. As he dived towards it, it joined a group of five more and almost at once he spotted a flight of Hurricanes below him and to the right. Immediately, he recognised them as his Poles and started yelling at them to keep out of the way. As they ignored his instructions and manoeuvred into position for an attack, he sat back to watch. Two minutes later, the Germans were split up all over the sky, two limping home, one a burning wreck on the ground, and three others spiralling downwards trailing columns of smoke. The air was full of excited cries in a foreign language.

Rivers met him as he landed and took rather a poor view of the aeroplane he'd just delivered being oil-covered and dirty after its long chase.

'That was clean when I brought it,' he said. 'I hope you caught him.'

'*I* didn't,' Dicken said cheerfully. 'But my Poles did.'

As he spoke, the Poles came in over the aerodrome, waggling their wings in triumph. As they landed they could see the pilots leaping up and down and doing jigs in the dispersal areas.

'Gloat dances,' Rivers observed dryly. 'They seem to have picked up that habit of yours and Hatto's and Foote's.'

–

Despite his doubts, Dicken had continued to see Katie Foote. She was intelligent, attractive and efficient and he found himself growing more fond of her than he felt he ought. They no longer dined in restaurants, preferring to eat in her flat. They also no longer made any pretence of what they wanted from each other and, lying alongside her, listening to her quiet breathing, Dicken stared at the ceiling, his mind busy.

Outside in the street somewhere someone was singing. It was raucous and sounded like a sailor on leave heading home from a pub. It was surprising how many people still went to pubs despite the bombing. Particularly servicemen on leave. As if they were determined to enjoy themselves and, finding there was nobody around they knew because they had all joined the forces, they were driven to the bars.

As the singing died, Dicken's thoughts took over again. Katie was warm alongside him, her head on his shoulder. Did he love her? Did she love him? Or was it just the heightened tempo of the war? A lot of people were rushing these days into marriages they would later regret. Yet there were others whose marriages, hasty as they were, would endure and flourish. The time was all out of joint, though. It was hard to identify what was real about the emotions and what was false. The war, the bombing, the dying, made falling in love seem like sitting on a bicycle and back-pedalling. You put in a lot of hard work and got nowhere. Love included having a future and there didn't seem to be one just at that moment.

He felt her stir. 'What are you thinking?' she asked.

'Nothing.'

'Yes, you are. You're thinking you might be killed and I'd be left a widow.'

'Well, something like that.'

'Well, stop it. I wouldn't mind. It's been wonderful. Things are so haywire and you're the only permanent fixture. One of the other girls got engaged to a man flying Wellingtons and he was killed last week.'

'I'm flying, too.'

'You don't have to.'

'I can't refuse to fly when I'm sending young boys up every day. I have twice the experience and skill they have and—'

'And you're twice as old!'

His age seemed to have become an obsession lately and she constantly brought it up.

'It makes little difference,' he said, 'I've heard that an old CO of mine, Cuthbert Orr, has gone to Bomber Command and that he's flying on ops occasionally. He's older than I am.'

She gave a little laugh. 'One day you'll have grown too fat to fly. Perhaps then I'll feel secure. Only—' she sighed '—you're not the type to get fat. You'll always have the figure of a jockey. I'll be the one who gets fat. The Footes always get fat. Look at Uncle Walt.'

She seemed to be talking for the sake of talking, to stop herself thinking.

'When are you coming again?'

'I don't know.'

'Don't back out on me.'

'No. I won't do that.'

'Not even for your goddam Poles.'

When the heavy attacks on London began a note arrived at Thornside from her. 'I'm scared stiff,' she wrote. 'I'm not keen on having bombs dropped on me. But there's a lot to do and a lot of people are getting hurt. When can you come and see me again?'

He decided it was time he took a weekend off. He tried to make sure his pilots and staff took time off but it occurred to him that he hadn't had a complete day off himself in over a month, so he telephoned her and arranged to see her the following day. Somehow, he had a feeling that between them they could make marriage work. Should they get on with it and settle the thing? It didn't really need a proposal because he knew the answer already. Tomorrow, he thought. When I see her tomorrow I'll fix a date.

–

The Poles had been an instant success. Their claims had sounded preposterous but proved quite genuine and, watching from above as they tackled a large formation of German bombers, Dicken saw that, while the rest of their squadron took up a position behind the Germans, two of them climbed ahead and above them then dived vertically into the formation with their guns blazing. Realising that even if they survived the bullets, they were in danger of a collision, the Germans broke and the waiting squadron pounced on the scattered machines individually. In moments the air was full of burning aircraft, fragments of wings and descending parachutes.

Finding himself behind one of the Heinkels, Dicken saw the rear gunner throw up his hands and disappear as he fired, but almost immediately he felt a thump in his back that knocked the wind out of him and, glancing round, saw two 109s on his tail. His instinctive reaction was to half-roll into a dive but he was trapped between the bomber and the attacking fighters. As no further firing came in his direction, however, he realised the Germans were unable to fire for fear of hitting the bomber too, so he moved in as close as he dared and waited there until the fighters turned away.

The thump in his back had knocked all the breath out of him and he could feel blood moving down his spine. There was a gaping hole behind him and he decided that a shell from one of the 109s had knocked his armour plate off its fastenings and crashed it against his seat. But the oil pressure was sound and the temperature correct, though the hydraulics had gone, the radio was dead, and oil was oozing over the wing close to the fuselage. As he entered the circuit at Thornside, to his relief the undercarriage came down safely, but his flaps refused to function and he had to land short to avoid overshooting the runway.

The control tower had seen the hole in his machine and the fire tender and the ambulance had followed him. His knees were already beginning to buckle as he climbed out and they caught him as he collapsed.

'Christ,' he said, 'it's fast these days!'

He was patched up hurriedly at sick quarters before being moved to Uxbridge for an X-ray, and then to Halton where some thirty-odd fragments of shell, radio, armour plate, aluminium seat, armour-piercing bullet and its copper sheath were removed from his back.

'You've been lucky,' the doctor said dryly. 'An inch to the left and your spinal column would have been severed. An inch to the right and the bits would have been in your lungs and heart. I'm afraid you're going to be here for a month or two.'

'That,' Dicken commented, 'is a pity, because I had a date in London tomorrow.'

'And that,' the doctor said shortly, 'is a pity, too, because you're not going to be able to keep it.'

Seven

By the time Dicken emerged from hospital the Battle of Britain was over. They had hung on throughout the summer, though nobody knew quite why, because they were utterly defeated, thrown out of Europe and in danger of starving as the U-boats sank too many ships, and the only thought was 'Shall I survive today, or the week or next week?' Every day you managed it was a bonus, so that nobody worried about the more distant future, while what was to happen after the war was something nobody contemplated because certainly no pilot expected to see it.

The Luftwaffe had suffered such a mauling it had switched to night bombing but it had been a near-run thing, with RAF machines and pilots being lost faster than they could be replaced and, now that it was over, the schemers in the RAF were starting to busy themselves with stories that Dowding had lost the confidence of his pilots.

Unexpectedly promoted to air vice-marshal, Hatto made it clear what was happening. 'There's a move on to shove him out,' he said bluntly, 'Leigh-Mallory of Twelve Group's sore he didn't get into the battle and win himself a little fame, and he's being backed by – guess who – St Aubyn and our old friend, Parasol Percy.'

He had just come from a meeting at the Air Ministry in which the conduct of the recent battle had been investigated. 'All the big shots were there,' he said. 'And it was the sort of inquest you get after a disaster, not a victory. According to a paper Diplock wrote, Dowding's conduct of the battle was overcautious.'

Dicken exploded. 'Coming from Diplock, that's the joke of the year! Why didn't they sack the bastard for running away from France?'

Hatto screwed his monocle into his eye. 'Nothing was in writing,' he said. 'And he'd obviously spent a long time working on his excuse. They put it down to a misunderstanding and St Aubyn was there to back him up.'

–

Soon afterwards they learned that Dowding was being retired and that Park had been removed to Training Command. Leigh-Mallory had taken over his job, while, with the shuffling that went on, St Aubyn had picked up a job in Coastal Command with Diplock, as usual, following as his chief of staff.

'All set for an air marshal's job,' Hatto said grimly.

London was a strange place in the winter of 1940/41. Almost every night the sky was lit with the crimson of burning buildings, and again and again Dicken found himself sheltering in doorways as fragments of shrapnel showered down on nearby pavements.

He was surprised not to have heard from Katie Foote since he'd been wounded. At first he'd expected her at the hospital every day but gradually the eagerness to see her had died and he could only assume she'd finally been sent home. He found it didn't hurt as much as he'd expected and accepted that they'd both been carried away by lone-liness and the need people felt among the dying to belong to someone.

Then an indignant letter arrived from Boston claiming that she'd been told he was dead – she sounded almost as if he *ought* to be dead, and was cheating by being alive – and because of it, numbed by the news, she'd allowed herself to be sent home. When she'd found out he wasn't dead, she'd immediately made plans to return, but it wasn't easy to return from the States in wartime so, since it obviously wasn't going to be long before the United States were in the war, too, she was intending to join the Women's Auxiliary Air Corps so she could be one of the first to come back.

The letter was bursting with energy and determination but, despite the affection in it, it made no mention of marriage or of love and he decided that she had decided, as he had, that they'd been swept along by the feeling of living in a holocaust and had been snatching at a little gentleness while there was still time. Nevertheless, like the letter that came from Foote, it was warm and encouraging and made Dicken feel that, despite the absence of allies, there were good friends across the Atlantic.

He was attached for the time being to the Air Ministry but his duties were vague and he had the feeling they were vague because nobody knew what to do with him. Part of his job concerned the high-speed air/sea rescue launches engaged in picking up from the sea pilots who had been shot down into the Channel, and it seemed a good idea to see exactly what was happening. Journeying to Dover, he took passage in a launch heading out on a mayday call.

There was a strong wind and high waves and the launch seemed to spend more of its time below water than it did on the surface. They picked up the pilot, who was dragged aboard like a drowned rat after floating half-dead in the icy sea in his Mae West, only to find that he had shot down the Messerschmitt which had destroyed his Hurricane. Another hour's search found the German pilot, ensconced happily in a rubber dinghy, far better equipment for survival than anything the RAF possessed, and Dicken found himself savagely aware that the same sort of thinking by types like Diplock had forbidden parachutes in the earlier war in case pilots decided to abandon their machines too soon.

The German pilot proved to be an arrogant specimen who spat at the man who tried to help him to the deck of the launch.

'I don't wish to associate with Britishers,' he said in perfect English. 'I insist that you tow me in my dinghy to the shore.'

Dicken solved the problem. 'Tow him,' he said. 'Just as he says.'

The crew of the launch gave him sidelong glances but a line was passed to the German which he attached to his inflatable dinghy, and the launch swung about and slowly headed north for the coast.

'I said "Tow him",' Dicken pointed out cheerfully. 'But I didn't indicate at what speed. Personally, I would suggest *full* speed.'

The launch skipper gave him a startled look then he grinned and pushed the throttle controls as far forward as they would go. The launch leapt at the sea, dragging the inflatable dinghy behind. At one moment it was ploughing into the crest of a wave, drenching its occupant, the next floating through the air, high above the waves, its occupant hanging on for dear life.

After only a few minutes, panic-stricken cries were heard and, on Dicken's signal, the launch's engines were throttled back.

'I will come aboard,' the German pilot announced as he arrived alongside.

Dicken gestured. 'Get the poisonous little bastard below,' he snapped. 'And if he opens his mouth to complain, hit him with something heavy.'

–

Still without a proper job, Dicken was ordered to take over a bombing and gunnery school at Nortonby. He had sixty aircraft, ranging from out-of-date Whitley bombers to small noisy American Harvard trainers. The pilots' duties were to fly in pairs, the air gunners firing at towed drogue targets, but none of the aircraft was armed and when the Observer Corps telephoned with a complaint that there was a German aircraft over Tenby and why didn't he send something after it, he could only stare in fury through the window, knowing he could hardly use the public telephone system to inform them that he didn't have a single machine suitable for air fighting.

Slamming the instrument down, he decided that perhaps he'd better have a go himself and, calling for his car, he drove out to the dispersed aircraft and climbed into a Henley. While the RAF had still been using Harts as dive bombers, they had searched for a properly-stressed machine to do the job properly and the Henley had been the result. It had been superior to all other types but the RAF had already lost interest in dive bombing and, though the fact that the Henley's steeper dive gave accuracy was admitted, the air staff had come to believe that aircraft with clean lines would reach too high a velocity to be safe. 'Our pilots have not yet developed the Oriental desire to meet Allah,' one stiff-necked senior officer had stated, and as a result, though 200 Henleys had been built, fast, clean-looking and vaguely like the Hurricane in shape, they had been relegated to the humiliating job of target towing.

Climbing into the sun, he found a Junkers 88 taking photographs over the dock area. The sun was to the south so he flew out to sea before turning to approach and, climbing to 15,000, rolled into a dive with the throttle fully open. There was only a Very pistol and a clutch of coloured cartridges in the cockpit but, as the lights floated down in front of him, the German pilot obviously thought he was being attacked by something lethal and, seeing the Henley turning away, assumed it was part of a squadron of Hurricanes. Going into a sharp flick turn, he dived vertically into the clouds.

When Dicken landed he found Hatto waiting for him.

'Where the hell have you been?' he demanded.

'Chasing a German.'

'In a Henley?'

'Not only in a Henley, but with a Very pistol.'

'Don't tell me you shot the bastard down.'

'Not this time.'

'I wouldn't put it past you. Well, you can pack your bags. I've got you a job. You're going to run Hornton.'

'What's Hornton?'

'Fighters. Brand new station. There are three squadrons of Spitfires there and they need shaking up. We're starting Channel sweeps. It's Churchill's idea to make the Germans realise that not only have they not won the war, from now on they're going to start losing it. We're to harass them on *their* side of the Channel for a change.'

'There's a catch, I'll bet.'

'Yes, there is. All our fighter squadrons have had hell knocked out of them. There aren't many of the original bods left and those who are, are either recovering in hospital, taking a well-earned rest or commanding squadrons of their own. What's left are the latecomers who saw just enough of the battle to be frightened to death. They all came into the RAF wanting to be like Errol Flynn in *The Dawn Patrol* and they've suddenly discovered that when it's for real people get killed and that when you're dead, you're dead for ever. They're understandably nervous.'

'So?'

'There's nothing basically wrong with them. They're properly trained and they're not lacking in guts. They're just lacking in leadership and they're sloppy because Dugdale, the chap you're replacing, fell apart at the seams. He was always a bit odd. He used to keep half a dozen bull terriers in a car as a kennel and his wife in another, and he finished himself by doing a shoot-up for the Air Raid Precaution people – unfortunately without remembering to warn them first. The telephone was white-hot.'

Hatto smiled. 'Those chaps of his are walking round showing off in scarves instead of ties and their flying's just as sloppy. You'll also find that you've been lumbered with deadheads from other squadrons, too, because when

Hornton opened, other stations were told to supply drivers, fitters, riggers, service policemen, clerks, Waafs and so on. Most of them responded by taking the opportunity to get rid of their duds. It'll be up to you to sort them out.'

Hatto paused. 'As for flying, it'll be your job to show 'em what to do. It requires somebody with experience and a touch of madness, and as you're about the maddest bugger I know, you should fit the bill. You'll have a full complement of aircraft by tomorrow and we start operations on the first fine day next week.'

Eight

Hornton had been carved out of the fields like so many other airfields that were springing up across the country. Hedges had been levelled and ditches filled and the result was an uninteresting open space fitted with single-storey buildings, a control tower and a water tank. It looked new, impermanent and faintly arrivée, as if someone was trying to impress the neighbours. Instead of the impressive buildings which had been wished on the RAF in the Thirties by men like Diplock and St Aubyn in an effort to make the RAF seem as important as the navy and the army when the money might better have been spent on aircraft, the mess was a long low-roofed structure no different from station headquarters, the sergeants' mess, the Naafi and the airmen's billets.

Dicken found his pilots in the ante-room. They looked a normal enough group of young men but they were dressed in what had come to be thought was the proper dress for a fighter pilot. The top buttons of their tunics were undone, some of them were wearing silk scarves, and one or two wore flying boots. He let them know at once what he thought of them.

'Flying clothing will *not* be worn in the mess,' he said. 'Neither will scarves. When you're flying, you can go up in a suit of combinations as far as I care, but away from the hangars you'll be dressed like airmen. I've noticed that the sergeant pilots have picked up the same bad habits but I can hardly tick them off while you lot are setting a bad example. I shall be seeing them later when they'll discover that leather gloves and suede shoes do not go with a sergeant's uniform. From tomorrow we shall be flying. In formation. Next week it will be against the Germans. You have six days to pull yourselves into shape. See that it's done.'

There was a little muttering but when Dicken entered the mess at lunchtime he noticed that the scarves and flying boots had vanished and tunics were properly buttoned. Almost at once among the wearers he saw a familiar face and, crossing to the young man, a pilot officer who looked as if he had barely started shaving, he asked his name.

'Diplock, sir. George Diplock.'

'Son of Air Commodore Diplock?'

'Yes, sir.'

'I know your father.'

'Indeed, sir?' There was something icy in the reply.

'*And* your mother. In fact, I was married to her sister, which makes you my nephew.'

'I was aware of that, sir.'

'Then I hope you'll have a drink with me when we next meet in the mess.'

The following day Dicken drew young Diplock aside and pushed a half-pint of beer into his hands. The boy had inherited Annys' good looks rather than his father's plump pasty features.

'Why did you join the RAF?' Dicken asked.

The boy shrugged. 'It's the done thing, sir, isn't it? If your father's a general, you become a soldier. If he's an admiral, you become a sailor.'

'And what about *your* views?'

'I'd have preferred the navy. I don't think I'm a very good pilot but, because my father's an Air Commodore, nobody argued when I asked for fighters, which most of my group asked for. We all knew about Mannock and Ball and McCudden and Baron von Richthofen, you see, sir. I expect *you* knew them personally.'

He sounded bitter and Dicken hesitated. 'I could have you transferred, if that's what you wish,' he said. 'To Bomber Command or Coastal Command. Or even Training Command as an instructor.'

Young Diplock shrugged. 'Under the circumstances, sir, I'll stay where I am.'

–

Training started at once, the squadrons flying in the loose formations that the Germans had proved to be far more effective than the tight wedges with which the RAF had entered the Battle of Britain. But there was *too much* looseness and day after day Dicken assembled his pilots in the hangar to tell them what was wrong with their flying.

When they weren't flying he had them aiming at targets on the ground or at towed drogues, practising their radio techniques and making mock attacks in pairs on aircraft from training stations, one man the leader, the other to watch his tail.

'Forget all that nonsense you read in schoolboys' magazines about aces,' he said. 'Air fighting's teamwork. And this war isn't basically different from the other one and height is still important, just as attacking out of the sun is. Your guns have been synchronised for 250 yards so fire at that distance. Short bursts and only when your sights are definitely on. Then think of nothing else. Concentrate.'

The faces in front of him seemed incredibly young and innocent, pale and pinched-looking almost.

'And remember it isn't all attack. You're going to have to defend yourselves. So keep a sharp lookout. Remember to keep your height, always turn to face an attack, never fly straight and level in the combat area, and make your decisions quickly. It's better to act quickly even if what you do isn't always correct.'

As the aircraft disappeared on their training programmes, Dicken turned to checking his ground staffs. As Hatto had warned, squadron commanders had played the age-old service game of getting rid of people they didn't want, and there were several outrageous duds, one or two known service criminals who had come from detention, even one or two men called up from civilian life who had done time inside civilian jails. Among the Waafs, he discovered, there were three who were pregnant.

'Send 'em back,' he told the adjutant. 'I'm more interested in the birth of a decent station than the birth of a new generation.'

The first sweep across the Channel was a ragged affair with Dicken sitting up above to watch how it went. The aircraft hit the French coast at Dieppe and flew in a wide circle, firing at anything that moved. A train was stopped and a convoy of lorries shot up, but the pilots, from being nervous, were now overeager. The formation became ragged and as they turned north Dicken saw he had lost several of his machines.

As they landed in England, he was already down and waiting. All the missing machines turned up later, some of them having landed first at other airfields. This time he didn't criticise their spirit, only their flying discipline.

The second attempt was much better and they shot down a Junkers and a Messerschmitt. It wasn't much but it was a start and everybody in the mess that night celebrated their first successes. The third sweep was even better and they came back this time with a score of three, one of them shot down by young Diplock.

'Next time let's make it four,' Dicken suggested.

In fact, it turned out to be five. Hatto turned up to see them off and Dicken himself led the sweep this time. When he landed he was surrounded by young men with their arms on their shoulders doing what was a fair imitation of the gloat dance he and Hatto and Foote had been in the habit of doing.

'Now where the hell,' Hatto asked, 'did they learn that?'

The adjutant smiled. 'They read, sir,' he said. 'And it seemed appropriate to adopt it themselves.'

The following day they had their first casualty. There were no gloat dances this time but Dicken was pleased to see there was also no sign of depression. It was a period of excitement but also of sadness as the sweeps brought more deaths. Nobody had any doubts that they were harassing the Germans, but it was hard for Dicken to watch them leave, knowing that one or two would never return. Many of them came from the higher echelons of society but a lot of the NCOs had grown up in depressed areas and had not had easy lives, so that it was amazing how prepared they were to give their lives for a system that had never done much for them. They were all so young, too – like the sons he'd have had if he'd had any – and they made him feel ancient even as they tried to treat him as one of themselves. They weren't even very different from the men he'd flown with twenty years before. Only their language had changed. Aeroplanes, known then as 'buses', had become 'kites', and something good was 'wizard' instead of 'hot stuff'. He no longer worried about how they dressed and, for the most part, they gave him no cause to, because they'd realised that to be brave you didn't have to look brave.

The hard flying was beginning to take its toll by this time and the mess alternated with heavy silences or the chatter of overexcited frightened young men. Occasionally he caught one of them staring into the distance, held by unimaginable terrors that he couldn't – and didn't wish to – put into words.

The year advanced, with Dicken leading a sweep whenever he could. Hatto didn't approve.

'That wasn't the idea, old lad,' he said. 'You were supposed to tell them what to do, not do it yourself.'

'I can't ask men to do what I'm not prepared to do myself.'

'These chaps are twenty,' Hatto pointed out. 'We're over forty and too old for it. Well,' he conceded, 'perhaps *I* am, but *you* don't seem to be, I have to admit. Just take care, though, old lad. Things move faster these days than they did.'

The following day, as Dicken prepared to leave on another sweep over Dieppe, he heard that Cuthbert Orr had just been killed flying a Wellington over Essen as an air vice-marshal. The news left him a little depressed but he snapped out of it quickly and, banking the squadron, began to close them into a wing formation in line astern and set course at 170 degrees. A fourth squadron joined them, tagging on behind, and he found he was leading forty-eight fighters streaking south.

Switching on his gunsight, he roared across the Channel, keeping low to avoid radar detection. It was a bright day with white puffballs of cloud and the sea a slatey blue. As they approached the French coast, his earphones became full of noise as he began to pick up the cries of pilots already involved in a fight.

'That's Jimmy going down!' he heard. 'Get out while you can!'

Somebody was having a rough time just ahead of them and he tensed, straining his eyes to search the sky in front. The hairs on the backs of his hands began to prickle under his gloves and he felt the strange unwillingness he had always felt before going into a fight. When the fun started it would vanish quickly enough, but it was always a little like plucking up the courage to plunge into a cold bath.

Suddenly, from nowhere, he saw a fighter approaching him head-on, then another lower down, then several more, all heading homewards. He recognised them as Spitfires and Hurricanes. With Dieppe only ten miles away, he began to climb and the machines knifed their way upwards. He could see the town below him now, a column of smoke rising from the port area. The aeroplanes eased into a looser formation, then just ahead he saw wings glinting in the sun and almost at once he heard the voice in his earphones of young Diplock, who was flying as his wing man.

'Dyton Leader. Large gaggle of Huns eleven o'clock high.'

'Dyton Leader, I see them.'

The enemy machines, thirty to forty FW 190s and ME 109s, were manoeuvering to dive.

'Break port!'

The cry in his earphones made him stamp on the rudder and jam the control column over. The Spitfire stood on one wing as he turned into the attacking enemy, and the formation broke up into desperate manoeuvering. More Germans streaked down and the Spitfires separated into sections and pairs. Still climbing, Dicken pulled into a sharp turn and an FW 190 rose up ahead. As he lined up behind it, he realised that the German wasn't aware of him. The machine was squarely in his sights but farther away than the 250 yards he advocated and he decided to try a long shot. Pulling the stick back to allow for the drop in the trajectory he pressed the button and the Spitfire shook as the 20-millimetre cannons roared. Immediately the Focke-Wulf reared up, trailing a thin stream of smoke and as the range shortened he fired again. The FW's wheels dropped and the smoke grew thicker, then it rolled over and began to drop towards the sea in its final plunge. Pulling the Spitfire round in a tight turn, he saw more Germans diving to the attack and, as he banked to stay out of their path, he caught sight of a big formation to the east. Diplock's voice came, calm and unemotional.

'Dyton Leader. Strong reinforcements coming in. Fifty plus, slightly inland.'

By this time the fighting had scattered all over the sky. Then, as he came out of an S-turn, he saw a lone 109 just ahead. As the enemy grew larger and came within range, he pressed the trigger button. Diplock fired at the same time and the German machine began to lift sharply. At once, Dicken's windscreen went black with oil leaking from the German and as he wrenched the Spitfire aside, the 109 exploded. He felt the Spitfire shake as something hit it and realised it was no longer under control.

Dropping below the fight, he heard Diplock's voice. 'Dyton Leader, are you all right?'

'I'm all right,' Dicken replied. 'Get the hell home. There's nothing you can do.'

The Spitfire was plunging out of the sky now in a twisting spiral. Eventually, he managed to lift the nose but the machine wasn't responding properly and he knew he was too low to bailout so he had no alternative but to put the machine down.

The ground below consisted of small fields and high hedges, but then he saw a road and decided to land on that. Throttling back, fighting the machine's tendency to drop its nose, he swung into his approach as the road straightened out. As he did so, however, a German lorry came round the corner. He managed to hold the machine up and float over it, and the driver gave him a scared look and ran off the road into the ditch. Almost immediately, another lorry appeared. Great Ned, he thought, killed in collision with a lorry! Dog-fighting with German transport! What a bloody epitaph!

Then he saw a cemetery on his right, with, running down the centre, a wide straight road. At least he wouldn't meet any German lorries there. The quick and the dead, he thought. He was quick enough now, but he might soon be very dead. His wheels touched the gravel but it was deep and soft and as they sank into it the machine's nose dipped and the tail kicked up. Snatching the stick back and touching the brakes, he felt the machine give a frightful lurch, then the port wingtip struck a stone angel which dissolved into several pieces and the machine slewed round and thumped into one of the family vaults that filled the cemetery. It looked like a telephone box and had the words *Famille Dunois* carved across it and, as he slammed into it, his face banged against the front of the cockpit and everything dissolved into lights and shooting stars as he felt the tomb collapse on top of the aeroplane.

Recovering his senses, he saw a Frenchman in a smock and beret running towards him through the tombs. Behind him several German soldiers were climbing the wall of the cemetery. Wearily he climbed from the cockpit and leaned against the fuselage, dazedly eyeing the damage he had done to the *Famille Dunois*' last resting place. One eye was closed and his face was sticky with blood from his nose so that he had to breathe through his mouth. He wanted to be sick and was certain the Germans would shoot him.

They were all round him now, waving their weapons and shouting, and he braced himself for the beating he was expecting.

Then he realised they were laughing, and one of them, a corporal, slapped him on the back. '*Ein Klavier aus dem fünfsten Stock,*' he said, and Dicken recalled Udet's expression for an aircraft crash – a piano falling from the fifth floor.

The German fished out a cigarette and offered it. 'You haf landed in a goot place,' he said in a thick accent, his face wreathed in smiles. 'Vat a pity you did not be killed. We could haf buried you here.'

Part Two

One

Half-blind in one eye and still snuffling the blood from his nose, Dicken was led away. As they reached the huts, one of the Germans sat him on a bed and a middle-aged man wearing a Red Cross brassard bathed his face.

At dusk, he was marched under guard to a nearby village where he was handed over to the German Feld-polizei who noted his name, rank and number and searched him to make sure he was unarmed before locking him in a small, dark, bitterly cold room on the top floor of an old stone building which he assumed was the *Mairie*. Flopping on to a low iron bed, he was suddenly caught by an attack of the shakes. His teeth chattered and he couldn't stop himself shuddering. Eventually a German doctor appeared to staunch the bleeding and give him pills to stop the trembling.

Feeling better, he now began to suffer from reaction. Again and again he'd told his pilots that if they were forced to land in enemy territory the first five minutes were the most important, and he had often quoted the case of the pilot who had deliberately fooled the low-flying German fighters which had shot him down by lying back in his seat so that he appeared to be dead, then, as the fighters disappeared, had bolted for the woods and managed to reach England. He could only excuse himself with the knowledge that it had been at least five minutes after his crash before he had collected his senses enough to know what was happening.

During the evening two officers appeared in the doorway. As Dicken rose, the senior of the two started to shout at him. Dicken's German was good enough for him to understand that a salute was being demanded but he thought it wiser to keep his knowledge of the language to himself.

The German continued to shout and eventually the other officer stepped forward. 'The major insists that you salute him,' he said in English.

'Oh, does he?' Dicken said. 'Well, tell the major that I am the equivalent of a full colonel and that in the RAF it's usual for a major to salute first.'

When the officer translated, the German major gave him a glare, but he didn't pursue the matter and proceeded to question him on the type of aircraft he'd been flying. Since the wreckage was in the cemetery only a mile or two away, there seemed to be no point in refusing the information.

'You were shot down. Our airmen are good, are they not?'

'Not as good as ours,' Dicken retorted. 'Because I wasn't shot down. I shot down two of yours and was close enough to the second to have my machine damaged when the stupid bugger blew up.'

The following morning he was awakened by the sound of shouted orders in the street below. Standing on the end of the bed, through the window he saw a column of men, some of them wearing naval uniform, some civilian clothes, one or two even in RAF blue, halted in the street below. As he stared out, the door opened and the elderly man who had bathed his face the night before grinned up at him.

'It's no good trying to get out that way,' he said in his halting English. 'You're joining the column out there in the street. Captured crews of merchant ships, a few naval men from our sinkings, one or two of your own kind. We've been collecting them in Dieppe. You're en route for Germany. You'll have to walk, so I brought this.'

He offered a cup of the ersatz coffee and a portion of a French loaf filled with cheese.

The sergeant in charge of the column signed a receipt held out by the Feldpolizei who had held Dicken prisoner, as if he were receiving a registered parcel, and he was pushed into the column. The sailors were at the front, the officers at the rear, and one of the naval men, stumbling alongside, fell into conversation.

His ship had been torpedoed and the survivors had been brought into Dieppe with a lot of merchant seamen in a German freighter. 'We kept hoping that perhaps the navy would arrive alongside,' he said. 'Like they did with the *Altmark*.' He gave a wry grin. 'But this is France, not Norway, and it's 1941, not 1940.'

They had been kept for several days in a football stadium converted into a temporary prisoner of war cage, a lot of the time in freezing rain, and they were all in a pathetic condition. The German guards were truculent and several of them struck out with their rifle butts. One elderly merchant sailor was having difficulty keeping up and the German corporal kept shoving at him until eventually he fell. As the German wrenched him to his feet, Dicken appeared alongside him.

'Do that again, Corporal,' he said quietly in German, 'and I'll make sure you're reported.'

'So!' The German swung round, his rifle at the ready. 'So we have an Englander here who speaks our language, eh?'

'Well enough to report you where it'll count.'

The German sneered but it was noticeable that he left the sailor alone after that, and eventually Dicken persuaded the sergeant in charge to have him placed in the lorry that was following them.

The rain came again and the march became a shambling stumble over the wet road, all of them drenched to the skin, bedraggled, woebegone and weary. Shuffling into a village called Hine, they were herded into the church to spend the night. Straw was placed on the floor and the church filled with exhausted steaming men, one even asleep on the altar. The old sailor was near Dicken, sucking at a cigarette.

'Kind of you to put in a word for me,' he said. 'Speaking German could be useful if you tried to escape. Going to 'ave a go?'

'You bet.'

The old man sucked at his cigarette again, then he nodded. 'I expect something'll turn up,' he said. 'They'd never miss one, would they?'

During the night, as Dicken dozed off in an uneasy sleep, he was wakened by an elbow jabbing into his ribs. It was the old sailor.

'The place's on fire,' he said cheerfully.

Sitting bolt upright, Dicken saw that the straw alongside him was smouldering and sending up a column of thick smoke.

'Did you do it?'

The old man grinned. 'They'll 'ave to let us out and it's dark outside. Them gravestones would make a good 'iding place.'

'You coming with me?'

'Not likely. Too old. I'd only keep you back. As soon as we're outside, make a run for it.'

'Right.'

'Ready?'

'Yes.'

'Okay.' The old man put his head back and began to yell. 'Fire! Fire! Let us out! We're burning to death!'

By this time the straw was crackling into flame, and smoke was filling the church. For a minute or two Dicken began to wonder if they were going to be burned to death or choke on the smoke but then the door crashed open and the sergeant and two German soldiers stood in the entrance, holding lanterns.

'*Gottverdammte!*' the sergeant yelled in fury. 'Rouse the others, then get the priest and tell him his church's on fire and we'll need help.'

Eventually more German soldiers appeared, some of them only half-dressed, and began to shepherd everybody into the rain. As he went outside, Dicken felt the old sailor give him a shove.

'Dark patch over there,' he pointed out. 'Under them trees. Go on, while you've got the chance. If you make it,' he went on as Dicken squeezed his hand, 'go and see my old lady. Mortenson's the name. Twelve, Waterloo Street, Wapping. It's not 'ard to remember.'

As the prisoners were herded away, Dicken dived behind one of the tombs. Its bulk shielded him from the light and, wriggling on his stomach, he headed for a neighbouring headstone. From there he made it to another tomb and then to the shelter of the trees. Crouching in the long grass, he saw one of the prisoners try to make a run for it but the German sergeant fired at him and the man stopped dead, frozen to immobility until two of the guards grabbed him and swung him round to fling him in among the others.

Lights were being brought now and two lorries had arrived to shine their headlights on the dilapidated group. Then the priest arrived, bareheaded, followed by several of his parishioners with pitchforks who dived inside the church to re-emerge with bundles of smoking straw. Dicken watched until the last bundle had been dumped, then the German sergeant and his men began to push the prisoners back inside.

'This time there'll be no straw,' he roared. 'You can sleep on the floor; and I hope you freeze to death.'

Slamming and locking the door, the Germans stood in a group, lighting cigarettes, then the sergeant posted doubled sentries and the lorries disappeared. As the place went back to darkness and he heard boots crunching on gravel, Dicken turned away and headed into the dark fields.

–

By first light he had walked several kilometres and the only person he saw was a woman milking a cow in a farmyard. At first she didn't move then she beckoned, but as he stepped into the road, he saw her change her mind and hurriedly give him a warning signal. There was nowhere to hide. He could already hear the noise of a motorcycle so he turned his jacket inside out and pulled his trousers outside his flying boots. As the motorcycle combination came in sight, he was bent over the ditch hauling a rotting log aside. As the Germans passed, he lifted the log to his shoulder and walked boldly on to the road. As the motorcycle combination disappeared, he looked towards the woman but she once more signalled care. This time it was a convoy of two lorries but again they took no notice of him and, as they disappeared, he waved his thanks to the woman and headed into a clump of brambles.

He decided to head for Paris and travel after dark. But he continually ran into barbed wire or fell into ditches and the following morning, wet with dew and shivering with cold, he decided he had had enough of night-time travel and, finding a length of cord holding a gate, he made himself a bundle of long sticks and tied them together as if he were a labourer collecting fuel. He was desperately hungry by this time but could see no chance of obtaining food.

After dusk he heard a cow bawling to be milked and decided to try his luck. But he had nothing for a container so he searched around until he found a reasonably clean tin and, washing it in a stream, managed to direct the milk into it.

The following morning he found a deserted farm with a yard containing a battered lorry. There was a loft full of straw which he decided would give him a bed for the night, and in the house he found a bottle of sour wine and a stale loaf and in the hen house several newly-laid eggs. Using the pump, he washed the grime off his hands and face and took stock of his possessions. As he did so he realised he was still wearing his RAF watch, so he shoved it hurriedly into his pocket. Deciding to abandon his uniform jacket, he scraped the grime off an old coat he found and, building a fire, dried it sufficiently for it to be wearable. Then he boiled the eggs in a tin and began at once to feel more capable. Examining the lorry, he discovered that the key was missing but using his penknife, he managed to turn the ignition on and start it. Knowing he could now move faster, he removed the rotor arm and, climbing to the loft, buried himself in the hay and fell asleep almost at once.

Searching the house the following morning, he found a pantry with a mouldy quiche in it but there were more eggs in the hen house and, catching two of the chickens, he killed them for use as barter. He couldn't imagine why everything about the place had been abandoned and could only put it down to some sudden raid by the Germans on someone suspected of helping the British.

Tossing the chickens into the lorry's cabin, he replaced the rotor arm and started the engine. The petrol gauge didn't work but, by poking into the tank with a stick, he came to the conclusion that there was enough fuel to take him further south. Loading the lorry with straw to give him an excuse for being on the road, he hadn't gone more than a few dozen kilometres, when it ran out of petrol. As he was checking the tank a man dressed like a farmer came along on a bicycle.

'In trouble?' he asked.

'Out of petrol,' Dicken told him.

'What happened to your eye?'

'The starting handle caught me.'

The Frenchman studied him for a moment. 'Where were you heading?' he asked.

'Paris,' Dicken said. 'Want to buy a lorry?'

The farmer gave him a sidelong look. 'Are you English?'

Dicken admitted the fact and the farmer smiled. 'Wait here,' he said. 'I can raise enough to help you.'

As he cycled off, Dicken stared after him, wondering if he'd made a mistake and the Frenchman had gone to fetch the Germans. For safety, he hid in a nearby wood, but an hour later the farmer came back with a can tied to his handlebars. Stopping by the lorry, he looked round him, puzzled, then began to pour the petrol into the tank. When Dicken stepped from the trees he waved.

'Three hundred francs,' he said. 'It's all I can raise but it ought to help.' He fished into the pannier on the back of his bicycle and produced a haversack containing a loaf, a tin of meat and a bottle of wine. 'I've brought you some food, a hat and a coat that's a bit better than the one you're wearing.'

As the lorry rattled away, Dicken set off southwards again, more confident in a passable coat and hat. He reached Paris four days later and headed for the American Consulate. The woman who interviewed him looked a little like Katie Foote. She studied the scar over his eye. 'That's a nasty injury you've got there,' she said. 'It needs attention. Have you anywhere to spend the night?'

'No. But I have money if you can recommend a quiet hotel.'

'You'd better come to my apartment,' she said softly. 'Wait outside until you see me leave then follow me. Don't speak to me.'

To kill time, he made his way to the Champs Elysées. The Germans were just marching from the Etoile to the

Place de la Concorde. The Parisians were boycotting the parade, their eyes averted as the Germans passed, kettle-drums beating the step in a triumphant note, file on file of soldiers, their bayonets fixed, a polished, unhurried symbol of France's humiliation.

The woman from the consulate said she had offered her help because she was convinced that America would eventually enter the war on Britain's side. She bathed his eye, gave him a meal and for the first time in days he had a bath and slept in a proper bed. The following morning she provided him with a pair of trousers to replace his RAF ones, a pair of shoes in place of his flying boots, and a battered bicycle. By that evening, he had covered 220 kilometres and had almost reached Tours, where he spent the night in a shabby hotel before passing through the checkpoint between Occupied and Unoccupied France. The Germans were demanding papers but there was such a crowd of gesticulating people that, by waiting his opportunity, he was able to slip by as if he were a member of a party moving south seeking employment.

With a French loaf tied to his handlebars, he looked like a French labourer and he found nobody looked twice at him. With the money he had obtained for the lorry, he was able to sleep in small hotels and, though a few people eyed him curiously, none of them asked questions.

He remained on the south coast close to the Spanish border for over a fortnight, trying to make contact with the British Consul in Barcelona. The area seemed to be full of disguised British soldiers trying to reach neutral territory but, though everybody seemed to know who they were, none of them was prepared to admit their identity because the German secret police were busy in the area. Several times Dicken had to bolt down a side street, and once he saw several of his companions being marched off to jail. The local gendarmerie seemed willing enough to help, however, and eventually a sous-brigadier who was crossing the frontier smuggled Dicken over in the boot of his car.

After that it wasn't difficult to reach Madrid, from where he was flown to England. Put on the train to London, he was met by Hatto.

'You look like an onion seller, old lad,' he said cheerfully. 'You smell a bit like one, too. Fancy a meal at the Ritz?'

They were halfway through the meal, with Dicken tackling it as if he hadn't seen food for months, when Hatto dropped his bombshell.

'The king's heard about you,' he said. 'He wants to meet you. After that there's a job for you. You're growing too old to get yourself shot down. How fit are you? When Basil Embry got back he found he'd contracted a form of scurvy and needed two months leave.'

'A week or two'll do me.' Dicken looked up from his plate. 'I've got someone to see – a Mrs Mortensen in Wapping – and then I'm yours. Where am I going? If you say to a wireless school, I'll resign and join the Home Guard.'

Hatto grinned. 'No need for that, old son. It'll be Greece.'

'What the hell's happening in Greece?'

'You'll remember Mussolini had a go at the place and got a kick in the pants for his trouble. We sent a few RAF types from North Africa to help the Greeks and, like

116

Topsy, British Air Force, Greece, has grown and they're now in need of senior officers to help carry the load.'

Dicken was silent for a moment. 'What makes you think the Germans won't go to Mussolini's aid? They'll never allow us to get a foothold on the mainland of Europe.'

Hatto smiled. 'My view exactly,' he said. 'But Churchill wants us not to break faith – or something else equally high-sounding and political. Personally I think it would be a much better idea to kick the Eyeties out of North Africa first. However—' he shrugged '—I don't make the plans. So, if you don't want to be kicked out of the bum end of the Balkans before you've even gone in, it would seem to me a good idea not to delay.'

Two

'Someone,' Babington said, 'boobed badly. We'll end up losing both Greece *and* North Africa. We're short of pilots, aeroplanes, weapons, radios, mechanics, vehicles and petrol, and because of that the Italians, whom we'd fought to a standstill, are beginning to recover their spirits.'

Arriving in Athens via the Middle East as senior administrative officer to the air vice-marshal in command of the RAF in Greece, the first person Dicken had met was his senior signals officer who turned out to be Babington, by now a flight lieutenant. His warrant officer was Handiside.

'It's like an old comrades' club,' he said.

The first thing he had seen as he landed was a shuffling procession of Wolves of Tuscany, Indomitable Centaurs, or other bombastically labelled members of Mussolini's vaunted Army of Victory, but there were also dozens of legless Greek soldiers, evidence of frostbite during the fighting of the severe winter. After eighteen months facing the Germans across the Channel, it was also strange to be passing the German Legation – lying arrogantly side by side with the American Legation – every time he left the Hotel Grand Bretagne to go to headquarters, and stranger still to meet German officers at Greek tea parties.

But the war in Greece was officially against the Italians and didn't concern the Germans, and every British serviceman arriving at the Piraeus by sea from North Africa was greeted by the swastika flying over the German consulate, while it took only twenty-four hours to discover that the Germans were deliberately flaunting themselves in the bars that were popular with the RAF. Despite the fact that Britain was supposed to have gone to the aid of the Greeks, there were many influential Greeks who were clearly unfriendly and Babington pointed out that their attitude varied according to the news, and warned of Fascists who waylaid British airmen who strayed away from the main streets.

'It's because they know damn well the Germans will be joining in before long,' he explained.

Drawn from the Desert Air Force, the RAF consisted of Blenheims and Gladiators, together with one squadron of Hurricanes. Other aircraft were constantly arriving but it was very clear there would never be enough when the Germans attacked. There were eight headquarters and maintenance units and a total strength of over 4000, but because a headquarters in Greece had never been contemplated, what existed consisted of officers drawn from a variety of other headquarters who had never before worked together. Operations were being conducted by a wing in the north-east and a wing in the north-west, and the overburdened senior administrative officer was trying not only to run his own organisation but also to co-ordinate the activities of other administrative departments. With a routine of early-morning conferences where instructions were given and difficulties were ironed out, there was little time for pleasure flying, because the shortcomings arising from the hasty entry into the campaign were becoming daily more obvious and Babington's complaint had clearly not been a frivolous one. There were not enough airfields and landing grounds and there was a complete lack of aerodrome defences because there were no spare weapons and no personnel to man them. There were also no blast pens and nobody to construct them, fitters were in short supply and there were not enough vehicles, aircraft or spare parts.

Babington was working overtime as impassioned signals flashed to Air Headquarters, Middle East, begging for supplies. The replies were always disappointing because there was fighting in Eritrea and Abyssinia and in the Western Desert where recent victories had suddenly gone into reverse, and, because of the need to show an aggressive face to the Continent of Europe, none whatsoever available from Britain itself. In Cairo there was even a tendency to regard Greece as a sideshow.

They still had the whip hand over the Italians, however, and had destroyed ten times as many aircraft as they had lost, but it was obvious it wasn't going to last, if only from the influx of war correspondents and the arrival in civilian clothes of a large portly gentleman with a sharp sense of humour who spoke down his nose as if he had permanent catarrh – the general who was to be in command if and when British troops arrived.

'Goddab silly,' he claimed. 'I bet the Gerbads dow I'b here eved if dobody else does.'

A Blenheim was available for Dicken's use but when he had to visit tricky landing grounds near the Albanian or Yugoslav borders, he landed at a neighbouring aerodrome and had himself flown in by someone familiar with the terrain because the unpredictable Greek flying conditions were among the worst in the world.

He found Larissa in ruins, not from bombing, but from an earthquake which had occurred the week before. The whole town looked like a house of cards which had collapsed on itself and police and soldiery were still digging out the bodies. Heading for Paramythea and Yannina on the Albanian front, he had to fly along the Gulf of Corinth and up the coast to Corfu before swinging in to land. As he descended he found himself over a lush green valley flanked by snow-capped mountains. The airfield looked like an English meadow carpeted with spring flowers, the grass kept short by a flock of grazing sheep. There were no runways and no hangars, and aeroplanes were hidden among the bushes and undergrowth. A mud-spattered bus took the pilots to their billets in the town.

Enormous numbers of Greek soldiers were moving northwards through the cobbled streets, all bearded and all dirty, with thousands of mules carrying heavy packs. The RAF men had had a terrible time during the winter, the pouring rain making the town's main street a river and the temperature dropping several degrees below zero. Fresh crews and aircraft parts were being flown in by ancient Junkers of the Pan-Hellenic Airlines but they were still having to fill tanks from drums when the bowser was out of action and only the fact that the Greeks were in worse condition had kept their spirits up. The Greek wounded were housed in appalling conditions and all the doctors could do was try to prevent the spread of infection and disease. The town had been badly hit by Italian bombing and there were still the rusty remains of cars and lorries in the streets and buildings scorched by blast.

The aerodrome lacked facilities but the field was covered with thousands of alpine flowers with a tremendous range of mountains in stark silhouette to the east. The airmen were living among the olive groves, alongside a fast-moving stream which had been blocked so they could bathe. There was no restaurant in the town and for a mess the officers sat on wooden boxes, eating rations cooked inside a tent. As Dicken arrived a pair of Greek PZLs, obsolete high-wing monoplanes, came in to land, one of them from the wrong direction so that they met in an abrupt halt in the middle of the field. Neither pilot was hurt but both were shouting and gesticulating in rage.

The RAF men were experimenting with whistles. They had attached them to their bombs to create panic among the Italians as the Junkers 87s had in France, and were even wondering if they could attach them to their aircraft for ground-strafing.

'If you drop a bottle it sounds like a bomb,' one of them said.

'So why not drop a latrine bucket?' another suggested. 'That ought to make 'em jump.'

Flying back to Athens, Dicken was enchanted by the beauty of the country under the cloudless sky. He could see all the way from snow-covered peaks to indented rocky coasts with a sprinkling of white dolls' houses and the green of olive groves running down to blue waters which seemed to be clear for a hundred feet down. As he appeared in his office, he was greeted by Babington with a long face.

'It's starting, sir,' he announced. 'We've just received information that the Germans are massing on the Greek frontier. A British Expeditionary Force's on its way.'

The first convoy of troops arrived at the Piraeus two days later and it was clear that nobody was deluded about what they were facing. As the soldiers marched from the transports, the sailors shouted their farewells. 'See you again,' they yelled. 'On the way out.'

Babington was as cynical as everybody else as he thrust a signal flimsy into Dicken's hand. 'They're planning to build us up to twenty-three squadrons,' he pointed out.

Dicken's eyebrows rose. So far they had nine, of which only two flew machines modern enough to handle the German fighters. 'I hope they're not Blenheims and Glad-iators,' he said.

There was little to give much cheer as the British troops moved to their positions and nobody was kidding themselves that the crisis was far away. For the life of him Dicken couldn't see the thinking that had enabled anyone to believe that a campaign in Greece could be anything but a disaster. Everything for its support would have to come across hundreds of miles of sea, while the Germans would have no difficulty in advancing by road all the way down the Balkan peninsula.

His flights to the outlying aerodromes intensified. The strain on the faces of the pilots was obvious as they begged for more vehicles, more materials, more men, more machines, which Dicken was well aware he couldn't provide. When he returned to Athens early in April he was tired enough to drink a large whisky and to flop into his bed exhausted. He seemed to have been asleep no more than a few minutes when he was wakened by his batman with a cup of tea.

'A fine morning, sir,' he announced. 'We've just heard that the balloon's gone up. German troops have crossed the border.'

Swallowing the tea as he dressed, Dicken headed for Babington's office. Babington arrived at the same time and Handiside gave them the news together.

'They've also gone into Yugoslavia,' he said. 'And the Luftwaffe's bombing Belgrade. It's Rotterdam all over again.'

The news was grim. The Germans had thirty-three divisions, six of them armoured, and the Yugoslavs were trying to oppose them with men on horseback. The Luftwaffe seemed to be having it all its own way, while along the Greek border the dispositions of the Greek and British forces were thrown off balance by the collapse of the Yugoslavs. The main body of the Greek army was facing the Italians in Albania, with the British army and three Greek divisions deployed on a line between the Aegean Sea and Yugoslav frontier. Three more Greek divisions watched the Rupel Pass.

'It's a bloody long front,' Dicken growled.

They had learned that reinforcements of Hurricanes were aboard a ship in the Piraeus, and the AOC was understandably worried. Apart from Kalamata in Morea, Pireaus, eight miles to the south, was the only port of any consequence and its importance was paramount. Inevitably the Germans would try to bomb it and during the morning Dicken drove down to find out what had happened to the aeroplanes.

The harbour was congested to the point of chaos. Nobody had thought to appoint a British naval officer in charge and the port captain was struggling on his own to clear the congestion. Certain the Germans would bomb the place, he had already ordered all ships to clear the harbour but an ammunition ship, *Clan Fraser*, was still lying alongside. The decks had been emptied of the motor vehicles and stores she had carried but her cargo of explosives had been only partially cleared into lighters which still lay alongside, and there were still 250 tons of TNT aboard.

Another ammunition ship, *Goalpara*, lay alongside the Sea Transport Office and *City of Roubaix*, also carrying ammunition, lay with *Clan Cumming* near the Custom House. Outside the harbour, in the calm of a fine evening, lay the cruisers, *Perth, Calcutta* and *Coventry*, and several destroyers.

'We all know what'll happen,' the captain of *Clan Fraser* said. 'As soon as the air raid alarm goes the stevedores'll bolt.'

Before the morning was out it was clear the Germans were trying to cut the Allies in half by isolating the troops in Albania. At the same time they were attacking Salonika and trying to cut off the Greeks in Eastern Macedonia. The Greeks were withdrawing from Thrace and the Germans were breaking through the Rupel Pass and the Monastir Gap, while the British troops, barely settled into their positions, were already moving into reverse under fierce air attacks. Intelligence showed that the Germans had around 800 aircraft against which the British Air Force, Greece, could put up only eighty machines out of the total of 150, the rest unserviceable for lack of spares.

Air raid warnings kept sounding but no German aircraft appeared. Early reports indicated that Blenheims had made successful attacks on German armoured columns and motorised units heading south while Wellingtons were bombing strategic targets. They all knew the success was only temporary, however, because, as soon as the Germans seized the Salonika Plain, they would establish landing grounds south of the mountains and fly in fighters.

The operations room in Athens had been dug out of the rock near the crest of Mount Lycabettus in the centre of the city, and when the air raid sirens went for the fifth time that night, instead of heading for the shelter everyone moved on to the terrace to see what was happening. The night was pitch dark but they could see one or two search-lights probing the sky and could hear aircraft droning above.

Almost immediately, there was a series of explosions to the south and it became obvious at once that the Germans were trying to neutralise Piraeus harbour. In silence they saw anti-aircraft tracers stabbing upwards and the flickering lights of their shells bursting. Then, as they watched, there was a tremendous explosion from the south-west. The whole sky went red and in the glare they could see a mounting cloud of black smoke lifting in the form of a mushroom as it reached the upper air and began to spread. More explosions followed so that the windows shook and the blast seemed to stagger them, even though they knew it came from eight miles away. Then, as the glare changed to a variety of colours, the telephone behind them jangled. Babington snatched it up.

'Jerry's hit *Clan Fraser*,' he said. 'When she went up she set off other explosions. She's now a wreck and adrift with the lighters still alongside.'

When they arrived at the harbour, it was a scene of devastation and confusion. One bomb had crashed on to *Clan Fraser's* foredeck, a second into the engine room, and a third had struck aft. The bridge and upperworks had vanished, showering debris over the ship and injuring the master. Nearby, *City of Roubaix* and *Goalpara* were also ablaze, their cargos in imminent danger of exploding. *Clan Cumming*, so far undamaged but berthed near *City of Roubaix*, was clearly also doomed.

A naval officer trying to organise tugs was in a fury of frustration. 'The only bloody way we can avoid the complete destruction of the harbour and the installations,' he stormed, 'is to tow the damn ships out!'

Soon afterwards they saw a tug threading its way through the glare of flames, the naval officer and two of his men in the bows, half obscured by the smoke, the drifting dust and the glittering fragments of burning material drawn up by the fierceness of the blaze. They had just reached *Clan Fraser* when there was another colossal explosion. Diving behind the stone-built building, Dicken saw the car he and Babington had used flung end-over-end and the next moment they were surrounded by falling fragments of stone, iron, steel and wood. His lungs emptied as the blast drew air from them and his ears filled with sound. When he looked up all that remained of *Clan Fraser* were two shattered ends. The lighters alongside had erupted and the tug, empty of life, lay wrecked and drifting alongside. All round them buildings and small craft had been ignited by blazing debris. Warehouses had been reduced to rubble and red hot corrugated iron sheets were skating down through the flames and smoke like huge razor blades.

Almost immediately, another violent explosion convulsed the harbour as *Goalpara* blew up, and a few minutes later a third giant explosion tore *City of Roubaix* apart. As she settled by the quayside, flames erupting from her decks, alongside her, her bridge and upperworks damaged by the blast, *Clan Cumming* began to blaze.

They found themselves trying to organise ambulances and dragging away charred and bleeding dock-workers, their clothes blown from their bodies. Everywhere among the smoking debris were the mutilated remains of men, women and children. Bloodstained people were being carried away on blown-off doors, and others, shocked by the destruction, were screaming and tearing at their hair. Cars, twisted out of shape, had been flung against buildings that were nothing more than piles of rubble, their white walls splashed with blood.

–

Eleven ships totalling more than 40,000 tons had been lost and the damage was enormous. Not a building had any glass in its windows and dozens of the small houses surrounding the area had been flattened. The Pireaus had ceased to function. Communications had vanished, seven of the twelve berths were useless, the port's administration had collapsed and the twenty merchantmen still waiting outside the harbour were unable to take on water and fuel. The Greek harbour pilots, like the stevedores and dockyard workers, had fled inland for safety.

When they returned to headquarters, it was to find that the Germans had pushed through the Rupel Pass, that fighters were beginning to operate from the Salonika Plain, and that British troops in the north were already under fierce and unrelenting air attacks. Blenheims were still trying to get at the German columns but now they were facing Me109s and they were being shot out of the sky by the faster German machines from airfields supplied by transport aircraft. Greek morale had plunged.

'We're pulling out of the Vardar front to Mount Olympus and the Aliakman River,' the AOC said.

Only the Hurricanes had the slightest chance against the German fighters and there were too few of them, while every one of six Blenheims sent to bomb Monastir failed to return. It seemed to Dicken that with the resources at their disposal they were not going to be able to hold on and if retreat were left too late they could lose everything, and he began to organise the withdrawal of the squadrons further south before they were overwhelmed.

Preparing an administrative instruction for a redistribution of units, he was about to issue it to unit commanders when it occurred to him he had better show it to the Air Officer Commanding. To his surprise the AOC was not alone. In the corridor outside his room were several parachute bags and inside a group of officers. Their uniforms were neat and, unlike most of the men struggling to keep things going in Greece, they did not look tired or harassed.

'Dick,' the AOC said. 'We've been sent help. You know Air Commodore Diplock, I think. I believe you're related, in fact, aren't you?'

'We've come to organise the situation,' Diplock said coldly. 'We were sent out from England to try to see things clearly. We arrived yesterday by flying boat.'

Dicken pushed forward the plan he'd written. 'Doubtless you'll wish to see this then,' he said. 'It's an instruction for the redistribution of RAF units. In case of withdrawal.'

Diplock gave him a contemptuous look. 'We're not here to retreat,' he said. He took the sheets of paper, glanced at them, then let them skate from his hand to the desk. 'We'll start worrying about retreating when we have to. At the moment we need to maintain a measure of secrecy, and plans to stay where we are are better than panic plans for a withdrawal.'

As Dicken silently filed the report, Babington looked up. 'Aren't we issuing it, sir?'

'Not now.'

'But, sir—'

'Dry up, Bab!'

Babington frowned and said nothing. A moment later Dicken looked up. 'Sorry I was rude, Bab,' he said. 'It isn't your fault. It's just that there seems to be an unnecessary obsession here with secrecy that doesn't seem to have much point.'

By this time the retreat was increasing in momentum, and it was clear that even when they were established on their new line it was going to be almost impossible to hold it because whole battalions and brigades of Greeks were already surrendering and another retreat had started from the Olympus Line to the Thermopylae Line.

'Isn't that where Leonidas and the Spartans held the Persians in 480 BC?' Babington asked. 'I seem to remember reading about it at school.'

Dicken frowned. 'They all died,' he said. 'Let's hope our people aren't all going to die.'

Three

'I'm praying the Germans don't think of dropping parachutists there.'

Bending over the map, Dicken had his finger on the narrow isthmus that joined the Peloponnese to Hellas and the rest of the country. It was cut by a canal which was crossed by a single bridge, the loss of which would mean that the whole of the British force of 60,000 men would be trapped, because the Piraeus was now barely useable and there was little hope of embarking them in the northern half of the country.

The Greek authorities had finally agreed to leave the handling of all shipping to the Royal Navy, a general headquarters had been set up in Athens and, though no one else appeared to have thought yet of evacuation, the navy, with its experience of Dunkirk, was already reconnoitring suitable beaches to the south, and scouring coastal villages to charter caïques, motor boats and other small craft.

As a systematic blitz of airfields and aircraft began, news came in of increasing numbers of enemy machines and the loss of more and more British machines.

'We have nine aircraft left in the three bomber squadrons in Thessaly,' Babington reported. 'The three fighter squadrons have twenty. After that, nothing.'

Diplock's committee, known by this time as the Clear-sight Committee because of its avowed intention of looking at things clearly before issuing its plan, was busy in a set of offices it had taken over. So far little had emerged and Babington produced the information that they had decided it would be unwise to remain in Greece – 'I can believe that of Diplock,' Dicken growled – but that they hadn't yet come up with any ideas.

Then, without waiting for Diplock's decision, the AOC decided he'd had enough and, ordering his squadrons south, signalled Middle East Headquarters urging immediate withdrawal. Another flurry of orders brought the instruction from the Clearsight Committee to Dicken to send off the Redistribution Plan.

'It's too bloody late now,' he snapped. 'The roads are already packed with traffic!'

By means of despatch riders, he was able to get instructions to three of the squadrons which immediately started to move, but the delay had gone on too long and the other squadrons had made their own decisions and were already making for the Athens area. The situation was beginning to fall apart. As the western of the two RAF wings was forced south, the Greek Epirus divisions folded up and the Greek army started to disintegrate, so that it began to seem highly improbable that any substantial part of the British force could hope to escape.

This is going to be worse than Dunkirk,' Babington said. 'We've farther to go and we haven't got fighter cover.'

–

That afternoon, Babington came in with a report of large formations of German bombers approaching, escorted by

Meııos. There were only fifteen Hurricanes to send up against them and, as they watched from the roof, they could see the fighting swaying over Athens, the Piraeus and Eleusis. There were huge cumulus clouds in the sky and the aircraft kept disappearing to reappear moments later at the other side. There were bursts of firing, then a machine slid out of the sky, trailing its sacrificial column of smoke, before the fight finally broke up and the aeroplanes vanished, as aeroplanes always did, as suddenly as they had appeared. The tally soon arrived. There were now only five serviceable Hurricanes left.

That evening, as Dicken and Babington ate at a small restaurant near headquarters, the shadow of catastrophe lay over the whole city. The army was still clinging to the last ditches of Thermopylae but there was the constant drone of German bombers above and the echo of explosions at the Piraeus and anywhere else where there might be a hope of embarkation.

Deciding not to wait for Diplock's decisions, which seemed to have atrophied behind the closed door of his committee room, Dicken arranged for the remaining bombers in Greece to be flown to Crete, where the navy had established a base, and what was left of the Hurricanes to an improvised airfield at Argos in the Peleponnese. By this time conditions were changing like a kaleidoscope as the German advance proceeded almost unchecked. Orders became outdated before they could be implemented and confusion was spreading like ripples in a pond, the situation became more chaotic by the hour as the air attacks continued with an intensity that stunned the senses.

Returning to headquarters, Dicken found the Clear-sight Committee still in session. 'What about the evacuation?' he demanded.

'They've decided nothing yet,' Babington said.

Heading for Eleusis, he found the RAF men packing furiously.

'When are we to be evacuated, sir?' the squadron leader in command demanded.

'I don't know,' Dicken admitted.

'Well, where to, sir?'

'I don't know that either.'

Diplock's committee had been working in monastic seclusion for four days now but not a word of a plan had appeared. The army, which was now in control of all movements except by air, were still clinging to the hope that they could hang on and were issuing no instructions, so that it was a period of orders, counter-orders and lack of orders, of men waiting patiently to be told what to do and where to go, of troops passing through the city with no notion of where they were heading.

'Sir—' Babington arrived with unexpected news '—one or two ships have started evacuations of their own, and merchantmen and ferries are loading refugees in the Piraeus and at Salamis!'

That afternoon the Germans came over again and that evening they learned that a yacht taken over as a hospital ship and packed with Greek and British wounded, Australian nursing staff, and British, Maltese and Cypriot women and children had been hit and almost everybody on board had perished in a vast funeral pyre. Even the jetty had caught fire and the few survivors who had escaped had done so only by jumping overboard.

After a frantic day of issuing orders, withdrawing them, reissuing them, of trying by car and telephone to make sure they reached their destination, Dicken sank into an armchair to drink a cup of coffee, only to awake with a start to find he had fallen asleep and spilled the coffee on his chest. Babington was standing alongside him, his face haggard with weariness. 'You're wanted at army HQ, sir,' he said. 'They've decided on a withdrawal and they're having a conference on implementing their order for the evacuation. It had nearly ended when somebody noticed they hadn't informed us.'

There were profuse apologies from the brigadier in charge but nothing from Diplock.

'Why were the bombers flown to Crete?' he demanded.

'Because they were no use here,' Dicken snapped back. 'We'd only have lost them.'

'Who issued the orders?'

'I did.'

'You didn't ask me.'

'You were never available.'

Diplock's pale features reddened and, as he stared defiantly back at him, Dicken realised just how much he disliked him for his physical and moral cowardice. He had obviously been sitting on his plans because he hadn't the courage to issue them.

'There's a great need for secrecy,' Diplock snapped.

'Why?' Dicken snapped back. 'The Germans obviously know our evacuation ports because they're already bombing them.'

The meeting ended in confusion, ill temper and hostility, with the brigadier trying to cool hot words, and they spent the rest of the night drawing up instructions for the assembly of RAF men at railway stations the following morning.

The German attacks didn't cease for a single day, and even as they issued their orders and repeated them by telephone in case they didn't arrive, the Piraeus and the airfields were bombed again. But key personnel were by this time being flown to Crete and they started to burn confidential documents and destroy unserviceable aircraft and transport. It was less than a year since they had been doing the same thing in France.

Driving to the station the following morning to make sure the men were safely on the way, Dicken and Babington found the train they were expecting was two hours late and, after frantic telephoning from the station-master's office, discovered there was a good chance it wouldn't come at all.

'Bab,' Dicken said. 'We're wasting our time. I'm sending everybody to Argos by motor transport. And we'll go with them.'

The next day he heard he was to be evacuated that evening in a Sunderland with the AOC, Diplock's committee, other members of the staff, the King of Greece and the British Minister. But, during the afternoon, he learned unexpected difficulties had arisen at Argos where, because of the bombing, ships were having to arrive after dark and leave before 3 a.m., so that it needed considerable organisation to make the best use of the few hours available.

'We need a senior officer down there to organise things,' the AOC said. 'Accounts will let you have funds to hire caïques. The place's too small for anything else.'

As they left Athens, the Greeks were lining the streets and, as the car stopped for the traffic, an old man climbed on the running board and kissed Dicken on the cheek. 'You'll be back,' he said. 'We'll be waiting for you.'

The drive developed into a nightmare. The little towns were full of burning houses, bewildered Greek troops and confused columns of mules and bullock carts. Babington drove, while Dicken sat watching the sky, yelling to him to stop as the German bombers appeared, so they could dive for the ditches. A lorry just ahead went up in flames and a Greek transport column of mules was caught, so that they had to struggle past screaming animals and lopsided carts.

The road was narrow and twisting and the traffic jammed nose to tail for miles. Buses and private cars, Greeks riding horses or trudging along on foot, were all crowded among army transport and an occasional gun. The halts were interminable and every time they stopped the weary drivers had to be roused from sleep by cursing officers and NCOs hammering on their helmets with the butts of revolvers. The road was littered with discarded clothing, ammunition, harness, dead mules and horses, the inevitable sodden papers and office files which had been thrown away, and dozens of abandoned vehicles and requisitioned lorries from every province of Greece, side by side with British three-tonners, Italian tractors and mobile workshops captured in Albania and now left to be returned to their original owners. Some were bogged down in ditches. Others were tipped at crazy angles into bomb craters. Others were burned or shattered by gunfire.

As dawn drew near they were unable to disperse off the narrow road and the port of Nauplia was almost impassable, so they decided to halt in the town. It was beginning to look as though Nauplia was becoming unusable, and eventually an officer, exhausted and depressed at the poor chances of getting any more men away, arrived to confirm the view. A Greek ammunition ship had blown up and the Stukas were using the flames to drop more bombs.

'We're hiding ships in small coves along the coast,' the officer explained, 'and taking the troops out by small boat from Nauplia Pier. I don't think we're going to be able to keep it up much longer because no ship's captain will come near the coast in daylight.'

They continued to wait in a small bar where messages could be sent and finally a message arrived that Kalamata on the south coast might be used. When they arrived to check, however, they found hundreds of bewildered men bivouacking on a nearby airfield, around them the smoking ruins of all that remained of the British Hurricanes in Greece.

Four

Returning to Nauplia and sending 300 men and an officer to Kalamata to prepare for the arrival of the others, Dicken formed the rest of the men in a hollow square round him. There were almost 2000 of them.

As he explained what he proposed to do, he saw they were pleased to have a senior officer in charge. Their own senior officers had already left by air, followed by aircrew and specialists, and what were left were men from Stores, Accounts, Cyphers, Works and other non-combatant branches. Their officers were unused to command in a situation such as now faced them and the men knew it.

'I'm going to try to get you to Crete,' Dicken announced. 'Whether I succeed or not will depend on you plus a bit of luck. I've already got men at the coast trying to find caïques and I promise you I shan't go myself until the end.'

Keeping behind sufficient transport to get the whole party to the coast, he gave orders for the rest to be damaged beyond repair. Immediately the air was filled with the clang of hammers as engines were smashed, tyres gashed and chassis members cracked.

As he walked among the struggling men, one small airman looked up. 'I never thought I'd enjoy anything so much, sir,' he grinned.

Dicken turned to Babington. 'Look, Bab, I want you to go down the Kalamata road with two hundred and fifty men and head for Gythion.' He opened a torn map. 'It's here, south-east of Kalamata, and should increase the number of caïques we can find to take us across to Crete. We'll follow you as soon as we can.'

As the lorries began to roll away, a telephone call came from Kalamata. The men he had sent there had arrived and the officer in charge, not very long ago a mere stores officer, had managed to get them billeted in an empty brewery. 'I've asked the port controller for ships,' he said, 'and he promises them in the morning.'

It was beginning to grow dark as Dicken organised the remaining men into groups, as far as possible under the NCOs and officers they knew and were used to. The bombing of Nauplia went on throughout the night in spasmodic attacks, and as first light came, a Greek officer arrived to say he had commandeered everything he could.

'I also have a coaster and a fast caïque arriving by evening,' he said.

As they talked, the air raid alarm sounded and they heard a crackle of firing. Going outside, they saw a Sunderland circling above the red-tiled roofs of the town as it lined up for a landing in the bay.

'Well, that can take away sixty bodies for a start,' Dicken said. 'Let's have them down at the harbour. I'm going to find a boat to row me out.'

As he bumped alongside the towering grey sides of the flying boat, the pilot appeared in the doorway. 'We got your Gythion party away, some with us, some with boats. We can take sixty men. We might even make it seventy.

We'll be back tonight. But at Kalamata, not here. It's no longer going to be safe at Nauplia.'

As the flying boat started its engines and swung into wind in the first light of the next morning, it had eighty-seven men aboard, six of them in the lavatory. There was a slight lop on the surface of the sea that made the take-off easier and she headed south-east into the rising sun. Returning to Argos, Dicken found Babington hadn't gone with the Gythion party and was waiting for him.

'Thought you could do with some help, sir,' he said. 'The army's on its way. Now that Nauplia's out of action, they're arriving in groups and wondering what the hell's happening. Chap in charge is a Brigadier Beddington.'

Beddington was a tall unflappable man with a bony nose who had established his camp among the olive groves. He seemed unperturbed to find there were large numbers of RAF men in the vicinity.

'We're expecting the navy to send vessels in tonight or tomorrow,' he said.

The news seemed too good to be true but Dicken continued with his own arrangements just in case. By dark he had three parties waiting by the jetty, one large one for the freighter the Greek officer had promised, a smaller one for the caïque, and one for the Sunderland. As the freighter came alongside the men began to file up the gangplank but the caïque didn't turn up, nor did the naval ships Beddington had been promised.

The freighter had just disappeared into the darkness when they heard the drone of Bristol engines and they listened in the dark as the flying boat circled above him. They had arranged for a line of dinghies to lie out in the harbour carrying hurricane lanterns in a crude flare path and the Sunderland circled for what seemed hours. Then they saw a red Very light descend in a slow arc and, as it reached the water, the pilot throttled his engines back and they waited expectantly for the splash of the great machine sliding into the water. Instead there was a tremendous crash, then silence.

Villagers began to appear and fishing vessels and rowing boats set off across the water to where they could hear the men in the dinghies shouting for help. Out of the whole crew only four were found alive, among them the pilot, a young Rhodesian flying officer called Cotter, who had a broken leg, a broken arm, broken ribs and a broken nose. As they were taken to the little hospital behind the town, he was profusely apologetic.

'Sorry about that, sir,' he said painfully. 'It wasn't as easy as we thought it would be.'

'Never mind,' Dicken said, bitterly aware that his resources were dwindling rapidly. 'There'll be others.'

'That's just it, sir,' Cotter said. 'There won't. The navy's growing worried and the Sunderlands have been taken off the evacuation for reconnaissance.'

–

The search for vessels started again with daylight. By this time there were thousands of soldiers in Kalamata and their morale had reached rock-bottom. Many of them no longer carried weapons and they were exhausted and half-starved after their long march south. A pall of defeat hung over them like a leaden mantle and their only hope lay with the navy. Many of their senior officers seemed to have given up hope and one brigadier even told Dicken he hadn't bothered to organise his men because they were too tired.

It was a dispiriting interview but Dicken still had his men ready, properly organised in groups so that if the navy did arrive they could go aboard at once. By this time the hordes of soldiers had been joined by Greek, Cretan, Yugoslav and even Bulgarian civilians fleeing ahead of the Germans. They all seemed to have a great deal of money and a lot of them seemed unsavoury characters who appeared to be profiteers and crooks getting out of the country while the going was good.

Babington had managed to obtain two caïques and they placed Handiside in charge with armed guards and orders to shoot anybody who tried to take them over. As they returned to their headquarters in the harbourmaster's office, the naval officer who was organising the evacuation turned up from the north. He looked exhausted but for the first time he had full information on what was to happen.

'Jerry's collared the Corinth Canal bridge,' he said. 'And the swastika's flying from the Parthenon. They'll be here before long.'

They sent for Handiside's group and everybody was waiting by the water's edge when the navy arrived. There was no indication of their approach but suddenly the piercing shaft of a searchlight came out of the darkness and lit up the mole. The waiting men immediately erupted into cheering, and Morse signals flashed between ship and shore. Within half an hour two destroyers were berthing alongside, and the spirits of the waiting men picked up at once. There were three troopships in the bay which couldn't get alongside, and the destroyers began ferrying at once.

Going aboard one of them, Dicken got off a signal to Crete informing them of the situation. As he waited for the reply he downed at a gulp the gin the ship's captain offered him.

'Better get below,' the naval man said. 'You can use my cabin.'

For a moment Dicken was tempted. His job was finished and he had no wish to be a prisoner again. But he shook his head.

'Thanks,' he said. 'But I think I'll stay. I've heard there are stragglers around Kalamata. I'll need to get them away.'

The naval officer gave him a sidelong glance. 'Sooner you than me,' he said.

Standing on the jetty watching the destroyers pull away into the darkness, Dicken had never felt so much alone.

–

Next morning the bombing attacks started again. The olive groves began to burn and houses cascaded into the water, and Dicken and Babington spent most of their time dodging bombs or crouching in ditches as the Germans machine-gunned the place.

Beginning by this time to despair, they sent the rear party along the coast to Kandimili and, still sheltering in ditches and doorways as the bombs came down, arranged with the hospital for the injured to be collected. As they were doing so, to their surprise, they learned that another Sunderland was coming in that night and decided to get away those injured who could stand the transfer.

The flying boat arrived after dark without problems but with only one pilot because of the short trip across the sea and the need in Egypt for every spare aircrew. Leaving a boat guard of the engineer and a gunner, he arrived in the office Dicken had set up to see which of the men at the hospital could be transferred, and it was decided that they could all go but Cotter, who'd been too badly injured. They were helped into the back of a lorry and, returning inside the hospital to thank the staff, Dicken had no sooner turned his back when they heard the scream of a bomb. The blast blew him through the door and when he lifted his head the lorry containing the wounded was only a smoking crater fringed by bleeding bodies and fragments of flesh. Sickened, he lay his head on the side of the ditch and felt the tears starting in his eyes. There were no survivors and now they had a perfectly good flying boat and nobody to fly it.

As he clambered from the ditch, he heard firing and a soldier on a bicycle came tearing into the town to say the Germans had swept in and captured Beddington and the naval officer. Counter-attacks had cleared the lower part of the town but fighting was still going on in the northern outskirts and with no naval officer to issue orders, the evacuation was starting to go awry. The destroyer captains had refused to enter the harbour because they had heard the Italian fleet was out and were afraid of being caught at a disadvantage, so loading was being done by rowing boat and it was painfully slow. Remembering the caïques on which he had placed guards, Dicken persuaded an officer in command of a company of soldiers to follow him to Kandimili. The soldiers were none too keen. As at Dunkirk, they assumed they had been let down by the

RAF and grumbled and sneered at what they called the Bluejobs, the Riff Raff and the Rafwaffe. A few even began to sing a ribald ditty Dicken had already heard too often –

'Roll out the Nelson, the Rodney, the Hood,
The whole bloody Air Force is no bloody good.'

One man blew up a rubber lifebelt. 'This is all the bloody air support I expect to get,' he said.

But the caïques were still there, still guarded by Hand-iside, and when they saw them the soldiers' attitude changed at once.

Bottles appeared and cigarettes were handed round, and as they began to line up on the quayside, a small wrinkled soldier held out his dixie to Dicken. It contained pieces of cooked chicken.

'Food!' Dicken said. 'Where did you get it?'

The soldier grinned. 'It attacked us, sir, and we had to kill it in self-defence.'

There was no compass and nobody in charge of the caïques, but a wounded Cretan said he knew the way and, with a padre as helmsman for one of the ships, offered to lead them south. There was only a small group of them left now and, back at the hospital, Cotter listened as Dicken explained what had happened.

'I reckon,' he said, stirring in his bed, 'that the rest of us had better use the Sunderland.'

'You can't fly a Sunderland like that.'

Cotter managed a grin. 'No, sir,' he said. 'But *you* can. It'll have to be after dark because of Jerry fighters and we'll have to make it a conversion course and first solo in one.'

They pushed the wincing Cotter into a car and drove him to the beach. Babington had organised a small motor boat and, standing up to their thighs in the water, they managed to lift the injured pilot aboard.

The engineer and gunner of the Sunderland had heard what had happened to the rest of the crew and were nervously watching the sky. Manoeuvring the boat alongside in the darkness, they made fast and began to edge Cotter aboard. It was difficult with his bandages and plasters and several times he yelled out in pain. But they managed it and finally got him established, panting and exhausted, in the co-pilot's seat, and the machine was filled up with all who were left, all of them understandably anxious, because they were well aware of the situation. Dicken strapped himself into the pilot's seat.

'Right, Bab?' he asked.

Babington looked up from the navigator's table and held up his hand with his fingers crossed. 'Right, sir.'

Cotter, who had recovered a little by this time, dragged himself upright. 'It's not too difficult,' he said. 'The procedure's much the same as with a Wellington, except that you've got four engines and four throttles instead of two.'

'I've got big hands,' Dicken said grimly.

'Right.' Cotter studied his surroundings. 'Well, first of all, you have to bear in mind that a flying boat's like an ordinary boat. You haven't got brakes. But it's *unlike* an ordinary boat in that it can't go astern, so you've got to think ahead and not get into a jam. You've got to be on the lookout for anything that might be in the way and—' he paused significantly '—there seem to be a hell of a lot of craft in this bloody bay. Right?'

'Right.'

'When we start up,' Cotter went on painfully, 'we rev up on one engine so the chap in the bow can get the anchor in. Once she's up you'll be all right. You can almost but not quite loop these things and they're super to handle, especially at the end of the trip, when they're lightly loaded.'

He seemed to be talking for the sake of talking and Dicken suspected that, like himself, he was scared stiff. 'Let's concentrate on the beginning of the trip first,' he said.

'Right, sir.' Cotter lifted his free hand and made circles above his head. 'Start up. Inners first, sir, to get clear.'

As the huge engines roared to life, the machine began to edge forward and the gunner, standing in the bow, began to haul in the anchor. The wind was light and the machine swung easily. As he shouted that they were free, the outers were started and Cotter gestured.

'Keep one at full revs,' he said. 'And the other throttled back to keep her straight. You'll soon work it out. There aren't any rules. It's usually a case of suck it and see because water makes everything different.'

As the huge machine began to edge through the swell, Dicken found he was drifting sideways as the breeze caught the slab-like sides and Cotter's head turned painfully as he watched what was happening. They had edged out into the bay now and were facing into wind, Dicken mentally praying that there were no small craft ahead of them in the darkness.

'Sometimes it's not easy, sir,' Cotter warned. 'If there isn't a lop on the water the buggers won't come unstuck and then you have to plough up and down for bloody hours and even ask somebody to create a wash with a launch so you can take off across it. You ready?'

'Ready as I'll ever be.'

Shoving the throttles wide open, Dicken felt the surge of power as the huge machine began to gather speed, and in the darkness it was like flying into a mine shaft. The great square fuselage began to cut the water, throwing out a flat spray on either side and trailing a deep white wash behind. The few dim lights they could see ashore became a blur, then, as the enormous wing began to take the weight and the machine moved on to the step, Cotter nodded. 'Gently back on the stick and you've got her.'

The rumbling of the water beneath the hull grew less and finally stopped.

'Airborne,' Cotter said. 'Just keep her going. We set the two inner engines by ear, synchronise the outers with the Aldis from the window and cruise at a hundred and twenty knots. Coming in's the same. You fly her all the way down and I'll tell you when to let go of everything. Now, if you don't mind, sir, I think I'm going to have a nap.'

Five

Apart from total defeat, things couldn't possibly become worse. Britain was beleaguered everywhere, and in addition to the losses off Greece, they heard that *Hood*, the pride of the navy, had been blown up with her whole ship's company in battle with the German *Bismarck*.

They had passed over Suda Bay in the first light of dawn. There had been one or two nightmarish moments as they saw flights of Junkers 87s and 88s in the distance, but none of them had taken any notice of the Sunderland, and in the growing daylight, they could see vessels of all kinds gathering in the outer islands, caïques, motor boats and small local craft from harbours and coastal villages on the mainland.

As they landed in Egypt, ships packed with soldiers were moving in and destroyers from Greece were disembarking troops as fast as they could. By this time the evacuation had become a matter of pure invention. Men with initiative and courage were still trying to get away and the destroyer crews were splicing slings for stretchers and lashing drums together to make rafts, because it soon became clear that the only men who would get away would be finding their way out from the beaches on anything that would float.

The RAF in the Middle East was at its wits' end to find aircraft either for strikes against the enemy or merely to provide air support for the navy. Suspecting that Crete would be the next battleground, Diplock and his committee had not stayed long there and by the time Dicken arrived in Egypt, he was already on his way back to England. Cairo was in a turmoil and the naval and air force commanders-in-chief, each certain the other was demanding too much, were at each other's throats as the struggle began to fortify Crete before the German attack, which everybody knew was about to start. By the time it ended, another 13,000 British prisoners had been added to the 11,000 captured in Greece.

It made gloomy reading. The enormous naval losses were almost more than could be borne while the army and the RAF were both looking over their shoulders, wondering where their reinforcements were coming from. The only satisfaction was that the Germans had found that, though they had once again convinced the world of their power, this time it had cost them dearly. Seventeen thousand of their finest soldiers and 170 troop-carrying aircraft had been lost in Crete and one of Hitler's most effective weapons had been blunted, while the British were beginning to find the answer to the dive bombers and they had been lost in dozens.

But with the British in disarray, the whole of the Middle East was in a turmoil. The Iraqis had risen in revolt and, fully occupied with a new offensive towards Tobruk which was already in difficulties, the British had been obliged to go into French-held Syria, while Malta appeared to be on its last legs, bombed, battered and desperately hungry.

Just when things were at their blackest, however, they heard that Hitler had attacked Russia. Nobody knew much about Russia. It had been a blank space on the map since the Revolution in 1917 and the only thing in everybody's mind was the memory of what had happened to Napoleon in 1812, the fact that they at last had an ally and that Hitler had committed himself to that bogey of all strategists, a fight on two fronts.

–

Despite the hopes that had lain behind Hitler's attack on Russia, by October the Germans were at the gates of Moscow. The desert army, now known as the 8th Army, had been pushed back once more, the aircraft carrier, *Ark Royal*, had been lost, followed soon afterwards by *Sydney* and *Barham*, and finally the appearance of the Japanese.

The news that they had attacked the Americans brought shouts of joy because they knew that at last they had an ally of tremendous potential, but the shouts soon died when they learned that the American Pacific Fleet had been annihilated at Pearl Harbour. Three days later they learned that the Japanese had landed in Malaya and that the battleships, *Repulse* and *Prince of Wales*, had been sunk by bombing.

'So much,' Dicken said dryly to Babington, 'for the navy's claim that no ship properly handled need fear anything from bombs.'

It was a gloomy Christmas with the Japanese in the Philippines, and Hong Kong and Singapore in danger. What they all felt must surely be the last disaster was the escape of *Scharnhorst*, *Gneisenau* and *Prinz Eugen* up the

Channel from Brest right under the noses of the Royal Navy and the Royal Air Force.

Dicken's duties took him all over the Middle East and there was hardly a day when there was not some air action to initiate or sustain because, even with the army temporarily lying low, the RAF still had to maintain a programme of bombing, fighter defence, ground attacks and intruder trips. Flying a Hurricane, he visited Syria, Palestine, Cyprus, Malta, and the desert.

The recent string of defeats in North Africa had started up angry demands for success, however, and twice in a year the general in command had been sacked, while at home the repercussions from the loss of *Repulse* and *Prince of Wales* and the escape of the German battleships up the Channel were shaking people out of comfortable jobs by the dozen. Even in the lethargic atmosphere of Cairo, senior officers were being shed by all three services and newer men with more energy and more initiative were taking over almost overnight.

The backbiting was clamorous and, ordered with Babington to England, Dicken found he wasn't sorry to go. They arrived just in time for the inquest on the escape of the battleships up the Channel. There had been a whole series of misunderstandings, and a great lack of initiative and, calling at the Air Ministry to see Hatto, Dicken found that their old enemy, Air Marshal St Aubyn at Coastal Command, was finally about to get the sack.

'He helped shove Dowding into limbo,' Hatto said. 'Now it's his turn. Guess who fixed it?'

'Surely not Diplock?'

'His old chum.' Hatto frowned. 'It makes you think, doesn't it. You'll remember Sidney Carlin, a retread like us, who lost a leg in the trenches and managed, wooden leg and all, to fly SE5s. He succeeded in becoming an air gunner and was killed by a sneak raider, hobbling to his aircraft. When you see gadgets like Diplock flourishing it makes you wonder where all this God's mercy we read about has got to.'

'What happened?'

'Having shown his usual aggression in Greece, he'd just settled into his job back here when *Salmon* and *Gluckstein* bolted up the Channel.' Hatto's face was grave. 'It was a bloody poor show, y'know. A whole squadron of Sword-fish was sacrificed for no end at all, and a lot of good young men were lost through somebody's bloody sloppiness.'

'However—' Hatto gestured '—Bert Harris, who's just taken over Bomber Command, wasn't really sorry to see them go. He'd had his machines constantly tied up trying to hit them in Brest but now they've disappeared back to their own little rathole, both damaged by mines laid by us, and, in the end, apart from the poor young devils who didn't live to see it and a bit of propaganda value to the Germans, we're probably better off.'

Hatto even managed to sound optimistic. 'Why not?' he said. 'In addition to the Russians who seem at last to have brought the Germans to a full stop – we now have America in and the days of fighting a war with two men, a boy and a flying hearse are over. Things will tick from now on. And, if nothing else, all those defeats have finally shaken loose all the useless bods at the top who've been proved too old and too slow.' Hatto shrugged. 'As usual in the case of a national disaster, however, the final stage's the apportioning of the blame, and Diplock, of course, was in there at once protecting his own arse-end. He put in a paper, full of protestations of loyalty to St Aubyn but also full of claims that nevertheless he felt he had to speak out. Parasol Percy at his best. St Aubyn's still wondering what hit him.'

'Is he hoping to get St Aubyn's job?'

'He got it. Like God, bad leaders only reveal themselves when it's too late. However, he didn't win what he expected. He'd hoped for a bomber group but Harris has old memories of him in Iraq and won't have him within a mile of him.'

Hatto pushed a packet of cigarettes across. 'You know Harris. He always thought all the leaflet dropping we were doing was just giving the Germans enough toilet paper to last them through the war and when he had Five Group he found his Hampdens were inadequately armed so he had gun mounts made to increase their fire power. Privately. Because he knew it would take months for his request to work its way through the red tape. And he ordered a lot, because he knew if he ordered only a few he'd have to pay for them himself.' He paused. 'How are you on multi-engined jobs?'

'I've just flown a Sunderland.'

Hatto nodded approvingly. 'I always did think you could have flown a three-ton lorry if somebody had fitted wings to it. What else?'

'Everything. Bombays. Hyderabads. Vernons. Wellingtons.'

'That's good. Because we got splendid reports of what you did in Greece and Bert Harris has asked for you.'

'Is he getting me?'

'Temporarily.'

'Willie, I'm sick of temporary jobs. I'm always getting temporary jobs!'

Hatto smiled. 'That's because you're good at flying.'

'What do you mean by that?'

'I'm an office type these days, old lad.' Hatto slapped the desk top. 'I fly these. Mahogany bombers. But I'm a wizard at clearing away the bumph.' He indicated a waste-paper basket full of files. 'My predecessor's,' he pointed out. 'But *you're* not and never have been and when they need some fat pulling out of the fire they send for you. You're going to Twenty-one Group. You'll be based at Rumbold Manor. Once belonged to an uncle of mine. Pity you're not married. You could have had your wife with you. You'll have the rank of Air Commodore and Tom Howarth's running Harwick, one of your stations.'

Hatto beamed and started to polish his eyeglass. 'We're beginning to think that the idea of putting all our money on heavy bombers might at last begin to pay off,' he said. 'They're going to knock hell out of Germany, and the Germans, who put their money on dive bombers and two-engined jobs, are going to find they don't pack enough punch. All that's needed is to build up the bomber force and Harris has a few ideas about that. Go and see him. He's here and he wants to talk to you. He says he'll give you a lift back to High Wycombe where there'll be a car waiting to take you to your headquarters.'

As Dicken opened the door, Hatto called him back. 'Oh, by the way,' he said. 'There's an item of news you might be interested in. Erni Udet shot himself. We've just been informed. It seems his face didn't fit in with the Nazis any longer.'

Dicken was silent for a moment. A straightforward man who was never a political animal, Udet had always been completely at sea among the ambitious and perverted minds of the Nazis and Dicken remembered something he'd said when he'd last seen him just before the outbreak of war. 'I put a noose round my neck when I put on uniform again.'

'Thanks, Willie,' he said. 'But I don't think old Knägges was ever really part of the set-up.'

–

Harris hadn't changed much. The red hair was sprinkled with grey now and the hot temper had mellowed a little, but not much. He signed to Dicken to get into his canvas-topped Bentley and started talking as soon as they left London.

'All this damned involvement in the army's campaigns has reduced Bomber Command to the level of everybody else's skivvy,' he growled. 'There's a lot of talk now of invasion but it's a waste of breath before we've smashed German industry. Besides, it's time the Germans had a taste of their own medicine. Agreed?'

'Agreed, sir.'

'The good old British sporting public is beginning to ask when we're going to start hitting them back and Winston doesn't disagree. But when I took over Bomber Command I found we had only about seventy-five more machines than we had in 1939, yet nearly twenty squadrons were added last year. They've all been lost to Coastal Command and North Africa. The only bright spot is that we've got forty or fifty heavies, Stirlings and Halifaxes, and there'll be two squadrons of the new Lancasters very shortly. However, they're all due for Coastal Command, too, and most of the mediums and lights are due for the Middle East, while what can be spared will go to Russia. What it amounts to is that the Admiralty and the War Office are trying to divert practically the entire bomber force to tasks for which it's not designed and not trained. I've started to get 'em back, and this time I'm going to keep 'em. But to do that I've got to do something that'll make the bloody politicians realise that they've got a potential war-winner in their hands. It's got to be something that will fill the newspapers and make those fat-heads in Parliament understand that you can't whittle away a good weapon just to help out the army and the navy. I'll expect ideas from you.'

Harris concentrated on his driving for a while. 'It's going to mean that a lot of young men are going to die,' he went on. 'But from now on I'll want to know why. You know me, Dicken. Most people go in healthy fear of me. But it's best that way. It makes people work harder. If a chap makes a genuine mistake I'll do all I can for him. But God help the buggers who dissemble. You and I know one or two like that, don't we?'

They were heading along the Great West Road now and approaching ninety miles an hour.

'There's a police car behind me,' Harris said. 'I expect he wants to tick me off but if he goes on the way he is, all he'll do is kill himself.'

With a sigh he drew the Bentley to the side of the road. The police car swerved in front. The policeman who appeared saluted gravely.

'Do you realise, sir,' he said, 'that you were doing almost ninety?'

Harris gestured. 'Have a look at the front of the car. There's a plate on the front bumper clearing me of all speed limits. Sometimes I'm called on to deal with emergencies.'

'That's all very well, sir, but you're liable to kill people.'

Harris gave a grim smile. 'I'm paid to kill people,' he growled.

As he drove off, he was frowning. 'I hope I wasn't too rude,' he said. 'But it'll get back and everybody'll think I'm a ruthless commander and that's what we want just now. They call me "Butcher", did you know?'

'I'd heard.'

'It worried me a bit at first but then I learned it had started simply as "Butch" among the Commonwealth crews and doesn't mean anything.' Harris swerved round a milk float pulled by an elderly horse. 'I hear I haven't got you for long.'

'I heard that, too.'

'Well, no matter. We've got around four months and that's enough for what I want you to do. Your group's a bit lost. We've expanded too fast and we're losing far too many crews. I want to know why.'

'Can I pick my own staff?'

'No. I want them there when you've moved on.' Harris paused. 'But I see no reason why you shouldn't have one or two who've worked with you. Got any ideas?'

'Chap called Babington, sir. He's Signals but he's worth much more as an organiser.'

'He's yours. Ask for him. Do you mind giving up your leave?'

'No, sir. I have no family wanting to see me.'

Harris grunted. 'I heard about your wife. She was a good flier.'

'Not quite as good as she thought, unfortunately.'

Harris was silent for a moment. 'That's probably the trouble with a lot of the crews. They've been trained too quickly and all the good ones from before the war have gone because of the bloody stupidity in the Houses of Parliament that failed to give them the machines they deserved. As it is—' he shrugged '—well, as usual they all see themselves as Richthofen or Albert Ball, which is the one thing they're not, and I've come to the conclusion that the much-advertised destruction of precision targets is quite mythical. Most of our crews can't hit a target 250 yards long in broad daylight on their own doorstep. I want to change that and I'm taking steps to make sure I do. I want *you* to make sure that 21 Group fits into the picture.'

Six

Rumbold Manor was a mid-Victorian manor house, with panelled walls, ivy poking in at latticed windows, a magnificent entrance hall and a splendid if over-decorated oak staircase. It was full of specialist officers of all ages, some of them men who never flew, some wearing RFC wings and ribbons of the last war, one or two of them younger men with new ribbons who had been through the mill of the present conflict and managed to survive. One of them Dicken recognised at once as Fisher, the trainee who had shot him a line on flare path duty. He was wearing a DFC and a DFM and was now a flying officer. He walked with a heavy limp and was working in Signals.

'You've come a long way in two years, Fisher.'

Fisher smiled. 'I might add also, sir, that I've never shot any more lines.'

Dicken smiled back. 'I should say that it doesn't matter much now. How many tours did you do?'

'One complete one, sir, and twenty of the second. We were hit over Essen and crash-landed at Bassingbourn. We all survived, but none of us walked away. Fortunately, she didn't burn.'

'You're probably the man to supply me with the information I want. The C-in-C wants to know why the losses among the crews are so high.'

Fisher shrugged. 'Lack of experience, sir. Once they get a few missions under their belts, they seem to survive. I suspect some of them just get lost. I did the first time we went very far. Fortunately, I had an intelligent observer and, instead of panicking, he went through his calculations again and found his mistake.'

'Would you be prepared to fly again?'

'They said I couldn't.'

'Suppose I say you can?'

'Then, yes, sir, of course.'

'Not across the Channel, though you might have to, but with one or two of these new crews to see what they're doing wrong.'

'I'd be glad to, sir.'

'Anybody else around here with experience who's growing bored?'

'One or two, sir.'

'Get me a list. Pilots, navigators, wireless operators, engineers, bomb aimers, gunners. A few of each. I think we're going to be busy.'

--

With Tom Howarth in command of RAF Harwick nearby, Dicken arranged to receive a thorough grounding in the new four-engined Lancaster there and, moving into the mess, he spent several days getting his cockpit drill correct, learning where every single switch and tap lay, so that he could put his finger on them without having to look. Every movement had to be made automatically,

163

because a glance away from the instruments at the wrong moment could well mean the difference between life and death.

When he arranged to be checked out, Howarth took him on one side.

'I've asked one of my chaps to go through everything with you,' he said. 'He's a flight lieutenant and he's good, intelligent and brave. You've met him before and I'd like you to meet him again. His name's Diplock.'

Dicken gave him a look of alarm. 'Does he know he's going to be checking *me* out?'

'He does. He knew you were here. He's spotted you about the place.'

'Does he mind?'

'He's pretty level-headed.'

When young Diplock appeared, he looked ten years older than when Dicken had first met him. His face seemed bonier and the boyishness had gone. Only over his cheekbones was there any colour; the rest of his face was pallid and he seemed to be in a different world from Dicken. Under his wings was the ribbon of a DFC.

'I had a bad crash in a Spit,' he explained, 'and I decided my reactions had slowed down so I asked for a conversion course. Somebody in the family has to do some flying.' The way he spoke told Dicken that he had managed to find out about his father's record and had felt he had to do something to redeem it.

Diplock passed him out without difficulty, demonstrating the characteristics of the Lancaster then handing it over to him to fly. After two or three landings he told him he was competent to fly solo, so he carried out another three and a half hours flying that day and a further two the following day, mostly doing circuits and bumps. Returning to the mess, he suggested Diplock might like a drink to celebrate a good job well done.

Diplock smiled. But it was an empty smile as though he wasn't a young man who saw a lot of cheer in his life. 'Even my father said you were the most natural flier he'd ever seen, sir,' he said. 'And I've heard older officers say you flew like a sparrow with a cat after it.'

It seemed only polite to ask after the boy's parents. 'How is your father?'

Diplock shrugged. 'Safe in London as usual, sir. Especially now the bombing's stopped.'

'Do you see much of him?'

'I prefer not to, sir.'

It was obvious the boy had a chip on his shoulder and Dicken didn't push the questions but unexpectedly Diplock spoke again.

'I go to see my mother instead, sir. She's taken over the house at Deane.'

It sounded unlike Annys, who enjoyed the social round, to retire to Deane when she could have shared the more sophisticated life Diplock must be enjoying in London. It had come alive with the arrival of the first Americans, who never permitted the war to interrupt their enjoyment of life, and parties were constantly being organised to allow the two sides to get to know each other.

There was another long silence, then Diplock spoke again. 'She doesn't often see my father these days,' he said. 'You'll have heard of the Waaf, of course.'

Dicken guessed what he was getting at but he answered warily. 'As a matter of fact I haven't, so perhaps you'd better not tell me.'

'I thought everybody had heard of her. And I'd prefer to tell someone. And, since we're related, I suppose you've got to be it, sir. I'm sorry. Perhaps I've been talking too much.'

'Perhaps we'd better just have another beer instead.'

Diplock smiled. 'My turn, I think, sir. I've just got engaged.'

'Someone from Deane?'

'No, sir. She's on this station. Section Officer Paget. She works in Ops. She's the one who looks after the blackboard. Puts down the time as the crews land. I try to make sure she always has mine.'

–

When Babington arrived he promptly insisted on his name being added to Fisher's list.

'Later,' Dicken said. 'I'm upping you to squadron leader. I want you to keep an eye on this place while I'm away.'

It didn't take him long to find out how hard it was to find targets at night, even in good weather and without the distraction of enemy fire. At the conferences that were held, he made it clear that targets needed to be marked.

Harris had already thought of that one. 'Targets *will* be marked,' he said. 'I've asked for marker bombs. In Iraq we improvised our own by fastening Very lights to twenty-pound practice bombs and I've been badgering the Air Staff for something similar.'

There were other innovations. Pilots had had nothing more to guide them in instrument flying than a bubble and an airspeed indicator and at night, with poor visibility and no horizon, it wasn't enough, except for the most experienced crews, so that Harris was already having stabilised instrument panels with artificial horizons fitted and car headlamps mounted as landing lights. Listening to Dicken's description of the Americans' electrically-lit flare paths, he demanded the same for his aerodromes to replace the out-of-date gooseneck flares.

'Well,' he said as the conference broke up. 'We're making progress. But it's only just starting and it looks as though we're going to be fighting a major battle every night and making major decisions every twenty-four hours, on weather, conditions and where to go. I just hope to God we can measure up to it.'

–

Within a fortnight, Dicken found himself flying on a raid on Stuttgart. He had three times taken new crews on short operations. Their attitude to him and the rows of medal ribbons he wore was less one of awe than of sheer terror, but he briefed them carefully, explaining that he was there merely to show them how it was done. By this stage in the war, the standards of education, lowered when the war had started, had been lowered still further and there were all kinds of men in command of the huge machines. They were a mixed bunch and they ranged from eighteen – some Dicken suspected were even less – to the middle thirties, all enthusiastic but all slightly nervous of their responsibilities.

As each new crew arrived, he took them flying on a course round England, watching everything the pilot did, with Fisher somewhere behind him watching the wireless operator and an experienced navigator watching the navigation. Some of them had their skills at their fingertips but some had been trained far too rapidly, pushed through to keep up the numbers, and as he watched them bombing the targets in the sea off North Wales, he found he had to send several back for extra training. A few who were over-confident were cautioned, though he tried to be gentle with high spirits, knowing they were born all too often of nerves.

Making a point of visiting the squadrons as often as possible, he found he was beginning to receive grins of greeting and was startled to discover that for the first time in his life he had a nickname.

'They call me "Daddy,"' he said to Hatto.

Hatto grinned. 'You're lucky,' he said. 'They call me "Old Bum and Eyeglass".'

The group contained a nucleus of experienced crews but the new men had a lot to learn. In addition to a sea crossing of around 100 miles, they had to cover another 120 miles of German-occupied air space before entering Germany itself, and an unbroken line of radar zones stretched from north to south right across their route. In these zones night fighters were waiting to pounce and behind them were the searchlights and the flak – so thick, one youngster claimed, he had to fly through it on instruments. Their job done, they then had to do the whole thing in reverse and do it thirty times before they were entitled to a rest. Like all aircrews they were deeply attached to each other but they managed to remain unemotional, and when one of them died it was under-stood that his friends should help themselves from his kit before waiting with only mild curiosity for the new arrival who was to take his place.

By April, the group was taking its full share of the raids. Occasionally Dicken accompanied them but most nights he waited in the Ops Room of one of the stations – usually half-dozing in a chair until the aeroplanes returned. He had learned to live a completely different kind of life because no commander who needed his sleep was much use in Bomber Command. As the hours passed, he found himself staring at the attractive Waaf behind the telephone and the large blackboard on the wall on which were written the names of the captains taking part in that night's operations, their bomb load, the time off, and the names of their crew. The most important space was left unfilled until they returned – 'Time landed'. As they appeared one by one the girl, Diplock's fiancée, Section Officer Paget, rose, mounted the ladder and filled in the final space – *X-X-Ray, 0520. S-Sugar 0522, M-Mother 0525* – while Dicken and Howarth sat smoking cigarette after cigarette until it grew daylight and an orderly came in to draw the blackout curtains.

Harris was still seeking his 'something big' to shock the authorities into giving his command the support it needed, but time seemed to be growing short because, with the war still going against the Allies, the cry from the other services was always for bombers and more bombers, and there was always the danger of squadrons being taken for other theatres.

There was still fierce criticism of the control and direction of the RAF. Both the army and the navy were convinced that it was the province of the Chiefs of Staff to advise on the allocation of aircraft and that it was quite unacceptable for the RAF to decide these allocations itself. The argument even reached Parliament where it was being debated whether the continued devotion of a considerable part of the war effort to the building up of the bomber force was the best use of resources. The chances of Bomber Command surviving in its present form were beginning to look very slight.

Then in May Dicken was called to a conference at Harris' headquarters. That it was important was obvious from the fact that all station commanders and group commanders were present, together with Harris' Radar Officer, his chief research scientist, his meteorological and intelligence officers and the Group Captain, Operations. Flanked by his Chief Staff Officer, Harris arrived with his peaked cap pulled down over his ginger-grey hair. Unlike the others, who all wore battledress, he was dressed in his best blue, his shoulders in their characteristic hunch. Taking off his cap, he handed it to an aide. Around them, as he sat silently in his chair, with his Chief Staff Officer on his right, were the wallboards of station, squadron and aircraft figures.

'We have our "something big",' he announced at once. 'I've got you here to explain what it is and to ask what you can contribute.' He paused for a moment, took a packet of American Camels from his side pocket, tapped it and drew out a cigarette, then, lighting it with a lighter from his other side pocket, pressed it into a stubby cigarette holder. Flattening a chart that lay before him, he looked up.

'We're going to put a thousand bombers in the air over Germany,' he said. 'In one raid. On one city. We're going to obliterate it.'

There was a murmur as the message sank in, then Harris continued. 'I must be the first commander in history to commit the whole of his first-line strength, his reserves and training back-up in one battle. Failure will mean the end of Bomber Command but, since they're talking of taking it apart, anyway, we don't seem to have much to lose. I propose to make use of conversion and training machines, instructors and if necessary pupils. That way we can double our front-line strength to seven hundred plus. The Prime Minister has been informed and, with his support, we shall have transferred back to us all bomber aircraft and crews which have been transferred in the past twelve months to Coastal Command. That adds another 250 machines and brings us within reach of a thousand. The remaining fifty we can raise by using the machines which every squadron already maintains as replacements and by demanding more replacements for machines which have not yet been lost. Any questions?'

There was a moment's silence as they all absorbed the incredible news. They all knew what it meant and to a man they supported Harris' action.

'One, sir.' It was Howarth. 'What's the target?'

Harris looked up over his spectacles. 'At the moment it rests between Hamburg and Cologne, both of which are easily recognisable. The final decision will be made when we see what the weather does.'

'When's it to be, sir.'

'It'll take three or four days to get the force together, carry out the plan – hopefully, with a back-up raid to follow – and disperse the machines back to their aerodromes. A full moon's desirable – perhaps even essential – which makes it between May 26th and 30th. That would be just about right. We can't afford too long a delay because of security.'

Nobody spoke and Harris continued. The problems of using so large a force would be greatly simplified by the use of Gee, the radar guide to the target, and Gee-equipped aircraft would drop markers.

'We expect to have four hundred aircraft so equipped,' Harris said. 'Including Lancasters, Halifaxes and Stirlings of the conversion units.'

He took off his half-spectacles and began polishing them. Howarth spoke again.

'One thousand aircraft are lot of aircraft, sir. The collision risk will be considerable.'

Harris had the answer to that. 'We propose to have more than one aiming point, and will route the groups on parallel tracks. Heights will also be staggered. By this means we can get the whole force over the target in a matter of ninety minutes with a collision risk over the target of one per hour, which I think we can accept. If we're successful, and I think we shall be, we shall overwhelm the defences and the lessons we can learn will be of enormous value. A successful operation will not only raise morale throughout the whole force but will finish for ever the demands for our aircraft.' He paused. 'Doubtless the target can be patched up afterwards but the impact of a raid of this magnitude and the inherent threat of further raids is bound to have a profound effect on Germany's entire strategic thought. They'll have to retain fighters for the defence of their homeland and that will have the effect of reducing the dangers in other theatres – which is what the advocates of dispersing the force are trying to do, anyway. I want to know now what you can raise in the way of machines and crews. Go back. Think about it and let me know the absolute limit to which you can go.'

As he headed for his car with Dicken, Howarth's face was grim. 'You know what the world's going to say of us, don't you, Dick?' he said. 'We'll be accused of mass murder. There are plenty of people who'll say that all Germans aren't bad and that under Hitler they had no say in the bombing of Warsaw and Rotterdam and London.'

Dicken shrugged. 'Doubtless there *are* such Germans,' he agreed. 'And there'll be a lot more after this raid. But, you know, Tom, I've never heard of any of them while Hitler's been winning everywhere. If Germany starts getting hurt, they'll come out from under the stones as they always do in such circumstances, and say we're a lot of dirty dogs. But whatever's said about this war being a crusade against an evil regime, it's more than just that. It's first and foremost a battle for survival and, because we've got to win it, anything goes.'

Seven

The task of assembling the bombers was expected to take all of forty-eight hours. In addition to the operational bomber groups, approximately 200 aircraft from Flying Training, Army Co-operation, Coastal Command and Bomber Training Groups were involved and it was essential for security that nobody should notice what was happening. Meanwhile plans had been laid for diversionary attacks on German fighter airfields along the route and in the target area, while air/sea rescue patrols were to be set up from daylight onwards.

The final operation order was issued on May 26th. The raid was to take place the following night or any night afterwards when the moon was on the wane. The order was simple. It was estimated that a force of 1081 bombers would be employed, led by Gee-equipped Wellingtons and Stirlings which were to set the centre of the target alight, to be followed in the next hour by the entire force except the new four-engined Lancasters and Halifaxes, which were to drop their bombs in the last fifteen minutes. Zero hour was fifty-five minutes after midnight, all aircraft turning for home by 0225 whether they had bombed or not. There were to be no bomber operations for a full forty-eight hours beforehand to enable ground crews and aircrews to prepare.

From his own group, Dicken had raised over a hundred machines when at the last moment he heard that Diplock, leaned on by the Admiralty, had withdrawn Coastal Command's 250 Wellingtons, Whitleys and Hampdens. Called to the Admiralty at the last moment when it was too late to make changes, he had given way.

Harris was furious. 'We'll plan without them,' he snapped.

The problem was not so much aircraft as crews, and the order went out that pupils, men on rest, and scratch crews from station, squadron and group staffs were to be asked to volunteer. By May 26th, the number of machines available had been pushed up again to 940 but several untried crews, hampered by the need for wireless silence, had come to grief even as they flew to their advanced bases. Reading the figures, Dicken frowned. If they couldn't fly across England, it would be God help them when they came to fly across Germany.

Doubts that he hadn't had before came to him. Harris had made his view of the Admiralty and Coastal Command – and of Diplock in particular – forcefully clear, and it was known that he was determined to have Diplock's scalp. But now, though he was behind Harris on the need for the raid, Dicken found himself wondering how much sense there was in using untried crews. It seemed to be pushing the case almost into the realms of political necessity. It had already been made clear that personnel under training were to be used only at the discretion of their senior officers, the idea behind it that insufficiently trained men would not be thrown into the raid. Once they had heard what was happening, however,

it was going to be hard to remove them from the order of battle.

On the morning of the 27th, the weather was dull and information came in that thundery conditions and heavy cloud existed over Germany. Watching the window with Babington behind him reading the weather reports, Dicken's face was bleak. The same thing happened the next day and again on the 29th.

'Harris' hope of a back-up raid won't wash any more,' he said.

'If this weather continues, sir,' Babington commented, 'we'll be lucky to get off the ground at all. Something's got to give soon. We can't disrupt operational and training programmes for more than another day or so.'

On Saturday, May 30th, they heard that there was a fifty-fifty chance that the cloud over Germany would disperse by midnight and that the target would be Cologne.

'What about the bases?' Dicken asked. 'We can't have nearly a thousand aircraft trying to get in on their return with the airfields covered.'

'They expect them to be clear, sir.'

'I hope to God it's clear over the target because if it isn't we'll have to abort and that'll finish it for good. The fillip it's given the command will disappear and just leave bitterness.'

'I have my fingers crossed, sir.'

Dicken was silent for a moment. 'I'm flying on this one, Bab,' he said quietly, and Babington looked up, startled. 'I can't ask my chaps to go into a thing like this unless I'm prepared to go as well.'

Babington threw down his pen. 'Then I'm coming with you, sir.'

'No, Bab, you're not. I want you to stay here and hold the fort. Carry the can if you like, because if I don't come back there'll be a hell of a row.'

Babington was silent for a moment. 'Very well, sir,' he said. 'I'll contact the squadron commanders and find out if you can fly with one of them.'

'No, Bab, that won't do. Which are our most doubtful starters?'

'Sir?'

'Which crew's the most likely to make a cock of it. Get lost. Bomb London by mistake. You have your ear to the ground, Bab. You must know.'

'Wing Commander Gregg at Harwick has a Lancaster from one of the training units. He doesn't think much of the crew.'

'Isn't Gregg's squadron the one young Diplock flies with?'

'That's correct, sir.' Babington turned over a sheet of paper, checking. .

'Very well, what's the name of this chap he's doubtful about?'

'Pilot Officer Scrivens, sir. His crew are all sergeants. Gregg's considering returning the whole crew for further training.'

–

During the afternoon, Dicken drove over to Harwick to meet Scrivens. He was a tall young man who looked about eighteen, thin, peak-faced and dark-haired, with large brown eyes like a spaniel. His machine, Y-Yoke, had been giving trouble and, having to flight test it, he seemed more than willing to have Dicken along as a passenger.

'Have you flown on ops before?' Dicken asked.

'No, sir.'

'Any of your crew?'

'No, sir.'

Sitting in the co-pilot's seat was a youngster called Hopper, who was flight engineer and, at Dicken's suggestion, the rest of the crew had come along, too, for experience and familiarisation. Scrivens introduced them: Norman, the navigator, a fair-haired boy with a dreamy expression; Ortton, the bomb aimer; Davis, the wireless operator; and the gunners, Barr-Lewis and Baker. They all looked terribly young, all uncertain of their future and all nervous of having a senior officer with them.

'I'm not here to tell you what to do,' Dicken pointed out. 'Just to find out what happens over the target. Please carry on.'

Scrivens looked at him for a moment then he swallowed with difficulty. 'Switches off,' he said into his microphone.

'Switches off,' the flight engineer said.

'Inner tanks on.'

'Inner tanks on.'

They went through the list of checks carefully and Dicken was pleased to see that Scrivens knew his drill.

One by one the questions were answered until the list was finished. There was a pause and Scrivens seemed to be deep in thought as he spoke to the flight engineer. 'Prepare to start up.'

'Contact. Starboard outer.'

One by one the four great engines roared to life with the harsh crackling noise peculiar to Merlins.

'Chocks away.'

Glancing through the window, Dicken saw a man twenty feet below him dart from beside the huge wheels, dragging away a chock. Someone stuck a thumb in the air and Scrivens released the brakes. There was a hiss of air and they began to sway and rumble along the tarmacadam. At the entrance to the runway Scrivens stopped and ran his engines to full power, checking everything as he did so.

When they returned the mess was noisy. Squadron life played on the nerves of its members like a violinist, plunging them from the treble of gaiety to the bass depths of despair. There was a lot of laughter but not much drinking, though there was a lot of talk about going for a burton or getting the chop – pithy phrases that hid the horror of one of the most unpleasant forms of death there was.

Young Diplock was among them but he was quiet and keeping well to one side. With him was Section Officer Paget, and they were talking quietly together. They stood up as Dicken approached but he signed to them to sit down again. 'How do you feel?' he asked.

'All right, sir. I've heard you're coming with us.'

'That's right. With Pilot Officer Scrivens.'

'Scrivens?' Diplock's jaw dropped. 'But he's—'

Dicken nodded '—in need of a little help perhaps.'

The briefing was noisy because everybody was a little on edge and, until Howarth arrived, there were a lot of ribald shouts between the crews. Taking a seat with the senior squadron officers at the front, Dicken waited quietly until the briefing officer, a tall man with a bony nose who looked like a solicitor in civilian life, got going.

'Cologne,' he said, 'is one of the most heavily defended cities in Germany and one of the most important. In and around the city are more than five hundred heavy and light anti-aircraft guns, and about a hundred and fifty searchlights. But this will be a large force and the belief is that the ground defences will be overwhelmed.'

There was a mutter of 'Tell us another' from the back of the room.

The briefing officer was used to the nervous comments of strung-up young men and went on to explain the fighter intruder operations which had been designed to kill the night fighter stations but warned that inevitably there would be some about.

'Tall gunners,' he said. 'There'll be a large number of friendly aircraft over the city so don't mistake our two-engined jobs for Junkers 88s.'

He explained that the key to success lay in saturation and that depended on getting a thousand aircraft over the target in the shortest possible time. They were to make sure of accurate timing, not only to swamp the defences but also to avoid collisions. Exact heights were impor-tant, but the boffins had decided that the collision risk was negligible. 'We have assessed the chances at one in a thousand,' he said and there was a yell of laughter and someone bawled out from the back. 'Have you worked out which two aircraft it will be?'

There was another gust of laughter but the briefing officer didn't bat an eyelid. 'I have it,' he said, 'on the highest authority that it will be a Tiger Moth and an Anson.'

The sun was sinking over the Fens as the crews began to pull their flying kit from their lockers. As the dusk faded, the flare path lights began to twinkle. Tractors were towing aircraft into position and petrol bowsers were topping up fuel tanks. Lorries carrying aircrews were dumping their noisy cargoes round the field, and as the figures, lumpish in their flying clothing, were swallowed up by the aircraft the bombers stood silent and sinister, heavy with their loads. Then the pistol crack of ignition started, and the pounding roars as engine after engine roared and rumbled into life. The crew of Y-Yoke stood back to allow Dicken to board first and, as he pushed his parachute into its place, he heard Scrivens talking to Norman, the navigator.

'Get it right this time,' he said fiercely. 'Okay?'

'Right, Skipper.' Norman sounded nervous. 'I've got it right. I've checked and rechecked.'

The sky was clearing and the weather had improved steadily during the afternoon. As far as they knew, Cologne still lay under a blanket of cloud and would remain so until midnight. Would it disperse in time? Were the Met boys correct? So much hung on the success of the operation, failure didn't bear thinking about.

By this time the aerodrome was reverberating with the roar of engines as machines strained against brakes and chocks, then gradually it subsided to a steady throbbing, before finally breaking into a series of aggressive crescendos as signal lamps flashed green, and one by one the great machines, pregnant with menace, began to move heavily forward.

'Control. Y-Yoke calling. May we take off?'

'Okay. Take off. Listen out.'

A string of orders from Scrivens followed.

'Flaps thirty.'

'Radiators closed.'

'Lock throttles.'

'Prepare to take off.'

'Okay behind, Rear Gunner?'

As the engines roared, the brakes were released. The acceleration was enough to make Dicken grab the back of the seat.

'Full power.'

The air speed indicator was registering 110 miles per hour and the aircraft shaking had stopped. They were airborne. 'Climbing power. Wheels up. Flaps up.'

As the huge machines, their navigation lights still burning, dragged themselves into the air, tucking up their wheels and circling for height, the sound of their engines came from half a dozen directions at once, from the dispersal areas, the perimeter tracks, the runway, over-head, combining half a dozen different notes into one great orchestrated iron clamour.

The sky was still glowing from the sunset and the clouds were still tinged with crimson on their undersides as the din began to fade. The air still shuddering under the racket of the mass take-off, the aerodrome lapsed into an empty silence as the sound of engines died and the aircraft began to turn east on to their course.

Scrivens' voice came. 'Course, please, Navigator.'

'One-three-oh, Skipper, to Goedereede on the Dutch coast.'

They were on their way. Harris' plan had come to fruition. The great raid was on.

Eight

Despite his reputation, Dicken was impressed by Scrivens. He seemed to know *his* job, even if the rest of the crew didn't.

He wondered what they were thinking. The force heading across the North Sea was made up of every kind of available aircraft from Lancasters down to Whitleys and Hampdens and beyond, from fifty-three airfields and carrying 4000-, 100-, 500- and 250-pound bombs and canister after canister of incendiaries.

It wasn't the force propaganda would make it if they were successful. But if they *were* successful it wouldn't matter. People wouldn't bother to ask questions. Only if they failed would the questions rain down on them. Harris would be removed and doubtless many of his subordinate commanders who had agreed with him would be removed too as the search for scapegoats started. If Harris succeeded, Diplock was out – and about time, too – but if he failed Diplock would be the first to defend himself with a cry of 'I told you so.'

'Bomb Aimer to Navigator.' The voice broke in on Dicken's thoughts. 'Coast ahead.'

They drove out above the sea, heading over a blanket of thundery cloud with very few breaks in it, the wind pushing them slightly north of their course. They had been promised a dispersal of the cloud but as midnight approached there was no sign of it. To starboard lay a towering mountain of vapour, ugly with protruding anvil-heads so that Dicken was reminded of the Himalayas. Behind them and to port and starboard stretched an unbroken carpet of more cloud. But over it, making it a sea of silvery light, was the glow of a full moon, just as they had been briefed.

As they approached the Dutch coast the cloud began to break up with gaps in it to show the land below.

'I'll have the new course, Navigator,' Scrivens said, and Dicken noticed that his voice sounded particularly brisk. 'Have you got it ready?'

'Yes, Skipper. One-two-five.'

'One-two-five?' There was more than merely a question of figures and Dicken guessed that Scrivens was leaning a little on his navigator.

There was hesitation in the reply. 'Yes, Skip. One-two-five.'

Scrivens said nothing. He seemed calm but there was a lot of unnecessary chattering among the other members of the crew that seemed to indicate they were nervous and uncertain of themselves.

'Pilot to Navigator. Course one-two-five. Okay?'

'Navigator to Pilot. Spot on.'

The navigator had his own compass and it was useful to check that it matched the pilot's, particularly on a long trek over the empty sea.

'Pilot to Gunners. Watch out for other aircraft.'

'Navigator to Pilot. Alter course to one-two-three.'

Dicken saw Scrivens' hand move to his microphone to reply, probably to question the course, but as he did so the rear gunner's voice came, harsh and urgent. 'Rear Gunner to Pilot. There was a kite immediately behind us just now. He was bloody close.'

'Roger. Keep watching. There are lots of aircraft around.'

'Bomb Aimer to Navigator. Enemy coast ahead.'

Suddenly the aircraft's wing dropped and it slumped to port as if it had lost its footing in the air.

'Christ—' the rear gunner's voice came in a nervous shout '—that silly bastard nearly hit us!'

'I know that, Rear Gunner.' Scrivens sounded annoyed through the formality of his reply, and his voice was tart.

'I didn't see him coming.'

'Perhaps you should have done. Keep a better lookout.'

'Skip, I *am* keeping a good lookout.'

'Dry up,' Scrivens snapped. 'Where is he now – that's more important.'

'I think he's gone underneath us.'

'Right. Let's all keep our eyes open then, shall we?' Scrivens glanced quickly at Dicken but Dicken said nothing. If he could control his nervous crew on his own so much the better. So far he was managing very well.

They seemed to have lost the other machine. Indeed, they seemed to have lost *all* the other machines and Dicken suspected they had wandered out of the bomber stream and he quietly opened on his knee the map he had brought with him. He had marked off a course himself as a check but the wind was still edging them north and, with the cloud blanketing the ground and blotting out landmarks, he wondered if Norman was allowing enough drift in his calculations.

In the distance as the occupied Dutch coast grew nearer he could see flickering pinpricks of flak, like small sparklers in the sky where the defenses opened up against the leading aircraft, then a searchlight flung its beam upwards and another nearby plane came into action. The beams crossed then, for no apparent reason, the first light went out. The flak came nearer, like fireworks on Guy Fawkes' Night, then abruptly there was a thud and for a moment the bitter smell of explosive in the nostrils. The aeroplane jolted as if struck by a giant fist, rattled, and rode smoothly on.

'Rear Gunner to Pilot. We have a hole aft. Not a big one, but a hole.'

The bomb aimer's voice came in a nervous attempt at humour. 'Indian country.'

Little damage seemed to have been done and every member of the crew reported that everything in his department was functioning correctly. But the chattering had died down now, because they were all aware that Cologne knew all about protecting itself and what they had just experienced was nothing compared with what they would have to face over the target. Cologne was used to aerial bombardment and having, like all cities, grown tougher under the experience, could be expected to hit back hard.

For a long time, beneath the thunder of the engines, there was silence, then Scrivens spoke. 'We should be approaching Germany by now, Navigator, shouldn't we?'

There was hesitation in the reply. 'Yes, Skip.'

'Well, are we or aren't we?'

'I – yes, we are.'

'Aren't you sure?'

'Well, look, I—'

'This has happened before,' Scrivens snapped. 'Are we or aren't we?'

There was a long silence and Scrivens began to stare through the window.

'Pilot to Passenger. Do you see any other aircraft about, sir?'

'No,' Dicken said quietly. 'We seem to have lost them.'

'Pilot to Navigator. Where are we, please?'

There was another thud nearby and the machine shook. 'That was a German gun,' the rear gunner said. 'It sounded more spiteful than the ones in Holland. We're over Germany all right.'

They were still waiting for Norman's reply when they found themselves surrounded by shell bursts. Then there was a tremendous crash that sent the Lancaster skating sideways out of control. The sound was shocking in its suddenness and intensity and immediately Dicken became aware of a cold draught on him that told him they'd been hit again, this time harder than before. But the machine recovered again and seemed to be flying safely.

There was a long silence, then the members of the crew began to report. The last one to speak was Norman, the navigator. The voice was faint and hesitant.

'Navigator? You all right?'

'There's a big hole here. But, yes, I'm all right.'

'Well, will you give me that position, please.'

'I—'

Scrivens' voice became crisp and hard. 'Do you know where we are?'

There was a long silence. 'I think—'

'I don't want any "thinks", Navigator. I want to know for sure. *Do* you know?'

'I think we're over Eindhoven.'

'I don't think we are.'

Dicken, who had been following the course with his map, stared down at the ground and spoke quietly. 'I think we're further north and east, between the Waal and the Maas at Nijmegen. We're still over Holland.'

He heard Scrivens give a sigh of relief. 'Thank you, sir. Did you hear that, Navigator?'

'Yes, Skip. I'll work out a new course.'

'If the Navigator will come forward,' Dicken said, still keeping his voice quiet, 'I can probably help.'

When Norman appeared he seemed almost in tears and terrified of a monumental ticking off. But Dicken gently pointed out the rivers, which they could just see between the broken cloud in the moonlight.

'The wind's been setting us north all the time,' he said.

He pointed out the new course and handed back the map. 'After that,' he suggested, 'I doubt if we'll need a course, because we ought to be able to see the fires the pathfinders have started.'

Norman had just disappeared back to his position when there was a yell from the rear gunner.

'There's a fighter—!'

A tremendous crash drowned the shout and Dickens heard Scrivens, who had just yanked the machine to port, cry out. As they lurched in the air, holes appeared in the side of the cockpit. Scrivens' instinctive move had undoubtedly saved them but he was sitting twisted in his seat now, his head down.

'You all right, Pilot?'

Scrivens' voice came faintly. 'No. I – I've been hit.'

'Right.' Dicken reached for the controls. 'I've got her.' He looked about him. The machine was flying steadily and there was no interruption in the beat of the engines. 'Where's that fighter, Rear Gunner? Can you see him?'

'No, sir. He went over to starboard. He's disappeared.'

'Keep a sharp lookout, everybody. Engineer and Bomb Aimer, come here and help me change seats.'

Blood was pulsing from Scrivens' left leg. The bomb aimer yanked him roughly from his position while the flight engineer held the machine steady for Dicken to change seats. He had just settled down when the rear gunner's voice came once more in a high-pitched yell.

'I see him! He's coming round again!'

'Let me know when he comes in.'

'He's coming in – *now*!'

'Flaps!'

As the flaps opened, the Lancaster wallowed, her speed cut abruptly, and they saw the night fighter shoot ahead of them. As the bomber fell over to starboard in a dive and its speed built up, it began to rattle and shudder.

Hopper, the flight engineer, was sitting in the co-pilot's seat now. 'You all right, sir,' he said. 'Do you need any help?'

The controls seemed solid against the weight of the airstream but gradually they began to move as the flight engineer also applied pressure. The Lancaster's nose came up, the whole machine shuddering and rattling as it did so. The damage turned out to be less than they had expected but, though the engines were still roaring satisfactorily and the flight engineer reported that he could find no malfunctioning anywhere, the aeroplane persisted in flying one wing low.

As they began to regain height, Dicken saw a glow in the sky and other aeroplanes in silhouette against it. Cologne was drawing them towards it like moths towards a candle, but they were on a converging course as Y-Yoke came in from slightly to the north.

'Keep your eyes open, everybody,' Dicken said. 'We don't want a collision.'

'There's an aircraft to starboard, sir,' the mid-upper gunner reported at once. 'I can see him quite plainly. Converging.'

'I see him, too, thank you.'

There was no need for navigation now, and Dicken merely pointed the Lancaster at the glow. The cloud, exactly as they had been told, had fallen away to leave them a clear view of the target and they could see the ground in amazing clarity under the moon. A lake picked up the glow momentarily then turned pitch black, darker than the rest of the countryside. They were approaching the city from the north-west, making their run at 15,000 feet. Hundreds of searchlight were quartering the sky and hundreds of guns were throwing up an incredibly heavy barrage. But the defences had been hard hit by the earlier arrivals and were already beginning to show signs of confusion and panic. Much of the firing seemed to be haphazard, a barrage merely because there had to be a barrage, while the searchlights seemed unable to pick out individual aircraft. When they did, however, the flak was co-operating well, hurling a tremendous fire into the apex of the cone of light.

The shell bursts grew nearer then just ahead of them, there was a bright glow in the sky and a ball of incandescent light fell slowly and gently earthwards. Immediately, all the other machines in the vicinity, whose crews had seen the aircraft explode, began to weave and corkscrew, determined not to be caught, too. Under the circumstances, the safest thing seemed to be to fly straight and level.

Still the mass of bombers forged on and now they could see that, as if caught by some internal explosion, the old city had caught fire.

So far the losses had been minimal but the defences were by no means saturated yet and, with the fear of fighters, there was also the fear of collision. An enormous number of machines were converging over Cologne, and, with the varied angles of the searchlights, there was also an effect of a false horizon that made it all too easy to fall into an uncontrolled spiral.

Rocking in the slipstream of other aircraft, everybody was straining their eyes not only for fighters but also for friendly aircraft weaving nearby. Then, no more than 400 yards ahead and slightly to port, clear in the glow from the fires below, they saw two aircraft settling down into a dangerous position one above the other. Unless someone in the lower machine was looking directly upwards, neither crew would see the other. The top aircraft was a Stirling, the one below a Wellington, both of them easily recognised by their silhouettes against the glow. Then, as the Stirling sagged and levelled out, the Wellington lifted slightly, soaring just too far, and its propellers carved into the Stirling's tail. The two aircraft drew apart at once, as if startled, then they both began to fall. As their noses dropped, the Wellington blew up in a flare of flame and they saw the Stirling hurtle through the blaze and disappear. A few seconds later there was an explosion on the ground where it had struck.

'Jesus!' The voice was the mid-upper gunner's.

For a few minutes the chatter died and Dicken could only hear the roar of the engines and the shout of the wind through the holes the flak had made in the machine. It was less a shocked silence than an awed silence, as though for the first time the crew, with all their idealistic beliefs about the war in the air, had suddenly realised what the reality was.

Because they were approaching from the wrong angle, Dicken knew they would have to cross the target and go round again. Below them the fires were spreading like a plague and major conflagrations were going now like blast furnaces in three enormous columns of flame. Then, as they turned into the main stream, they were hit again. The explosion was just below and to starboard and there was a crash in the cockpit that left a gaping hole in the nose. The outer starboard engine began to run raggedly, the aeroplane developed a shake, and somewhere beneath them Dicken could hear a loud rattle, as if something had been torn loose and was flapping in the slipstream. But nobody was hurt and the flight engineer's voice came quietly.

'The compass's smashed, sir.' He sounded quite calm.

'Thank you,' Dicken said. 'At the moment, I doubt if we need it. How are we, Flight Engineer?'

'Losing pressure on the starboard outer, sir. It's overheating. We look like having to shut it down.'

'Well, that ought to enable us to turn south for the homeward run without much difficulty.'

Beneath them now Dicken could see the outline of the city clearly, the Rhine running almost north and south. A vast S-bend just to the south gave them a steering point as they began their run towards the centre of the city. Ahead they could see the twin central bridges, the Hindenburg-brücke and the Hohenzollernbrücke, and the cathedral floodlit by the surrounding fires.

The defences were growing ragged now and the entire target area was thrown into relief by the moonlight so that individual streets could be seen for their entire length, broken by buildings and by the railways that curved wide tracks round the city. Ortton, the bomb aimer, was already in position. There seemed to be dozens of aircraft around and they were all, Y-Yoke included, clearly visible to fighters against the glow.

'Steady!'

There could be no evasive action during the run up as the bomb aimer lined up his target, and everybody steeled themselves to ignore the shuddering and the rattle and the flak.

'That's it, sir. Hold it there. Drifting a bit to the right. Left a bit. Good. That's fine. Hold it there.'

The flak blasts kept nudging the aircraft.

'Bit more left, sir. Hold her there. Steady. Steady.'

God, Dicken thought, he was growing too old for this lark! He could still remember the terror he'd felt when they'd bombed the Lugagnano power station in Italy in 1918. Curiously, though, the fear now didn't seem so intense. Perhaps as you grew older dying didn't matter so much, while at twenty you felt you still had too much life to live. In addition, these days he had no woman to care whether he lived or not. At Lugagnano, he'd been thinking of Nicola Aubrey.

Concentrating on keeping the aircraft steady, his thoughts drifted to her sister, Marie-Gabrielle, who had said at the age of nine that she wanted to marry him and had said it again when they'd met on the North-West Frontier of India when she was nineteen. She'd be all of thirty now and sometimes as he thought of her he longed for another chance.

'Bombs gone!'

The words jerked him back to the present and, relieved of her load, Y-Yoke lifted, adjusting herself to her new freedom. His mind on the job in hand again, Dicken's hands moved as he retrimmed her. All they had to do now was get home.

–

Limping badly by this time, with one engine dead, Y-Yoke dropped down to Harwick well behind the rest. The runway had been cleared for them and, with Scrivens faint by this time from loss of blood, an ambulance was waiting. As the tyres screeched on touchdown, Dicken saw it move out and start to follow them.

Taxiing to their place on the perimeter, as he switched off engines, there were shouts from the ground crew as they stared up at the holes in the machine. Then as the ambulance arrived and Scrivens was lifted out Dicken climbed with the others into the crew lorry. They didn't speak much but kept giving him sidelong, almost shy glances, as if they knew that, in their inexperience, they probably wouldn't have survived but for his presence in the aircraft.

Hatto was waiting at the debriefing. 'Nice to see you back, old lad,' he said quietly. Holding out a cigarette case, he handed over a mug of tea. 'Harris's livid, of course. Next time, he says, there'll be an order saying that no AOCs are to take part.'

Dicken shrugged. 'That crew wouldn't have made it if I hadn't,' he pointed out. 'As it is, we have one more aircraft and one more crew for tomorrow than we would have had, and there are seven young men out there who are still alive. What's the state?'

'They're still coming in. We've got off lightly, judging by the reports, we've lost around thirty-seven aircraft. Which is what was expected. We can cope with that.'

The returning crews were excited and thankful to be alive, especially the crew of Y-Yoke. Even the return had not been without incident because Norman, once more on the point of tears, had been obliged to confess he was lost once more. With the compass destroyed, a freezing gale passing through the cockpit and the aircraft shedding pieces all the way across Europe, Dicken had flown them home with his map on his knee. He had recommended to Gregg that Norman be sent back for further training.

As the crews began to disperse for breakfast and sleep, he headed for the Ops Room. Howarth was there with Hatto.

'Still one or two to come,' Howarth said.

His hair flattened by his flying helmet, Dicken found a chair, lit a cigarette and sat in silence. Everybody was watching the board, waiting to see that last ominous space filled in with the time the aircraft landed.

Section Officer Paget was sitting behind the table, answering the telephone, getting up every time they heard the roar of engines overhead and climbing the ladder to the board to fill in yet another space. X-X-Ray. S-Sugar. M-Mother. They were all there. One after the other the spaces were filled, until only one remained empty. Section Officer Paget sat silently at her desk. Someone brought her a cup of tea which she drank without speaking, while Dicken sat watching her, still smoking. Above her head the empty space remained, blank and frightening. As Dicken's eye travelled along the line of information – the bomb load, the time of take-off, the crew – he stopped at the name of the pilot: *Flight-Lieutenant Diplock*.

Eventually an orderly came in and drew the curtains and he was surprised to see it was almost daylight. He wasn't sure what to say as he looked at the small pretty face, bleak in its misery behind the desk. He would have preferred to be in the crew room talking to Scrivens' crew or at the hospital checking how Scrivens himself was, but somehow he didn't wish to leave her.

She continued to sit there, staring into space, the look on her face one of incredulity and disbelief. Someone brought her another cup of tea but this time she didn't even notice. Then the telephone rang. This time, Dicken reached it before her.

It was the Observer Corps to say that a Lancaster had just crossed the coast heading in their direction. When he told her, her face lit up, and when soon afterwards they heard the roar of engines her expression became warm and alive. But the aeroplane continued overhead without stopping and her face fell again. When the telephone went once more it was the watch tower to say the machine had belonged to 83 Squadron.

They continued to sit there until the sun came up. Dicken had already quietly persuaded Hatto to ring round the aerodromes to find out if Diplock had landed anywhere else. He hadn't, and Air/Sea Rescue reported that they had checked all ditchings, so he wasn't in the sea. Eventually, he could stand it no longer and, rising, he took the girl's arm and led her to his car.

Nine

The interview with Harris turned out to be less difficult than Dicken had expected. The raid had been a success. Out of 1046 bombers and eighty-eight intruders a total of forty-four had failed to return, a percentage loss of 3.9, which was acceptable and seemed to indicate that the policy of saturation had reduced the casualties. Despite the German propaganda ministry's claim that the raid had been a failure, it was clear that the damage had been on a far greater scale than anything yet seen.

It seemed to Dicken, as he left High Wycombe, that it was time to go and see young Diplock's mother. A signal had gone off to his father in London but it had brought no sort of response and he decided to drive over to Deane.

It was a strange feeling entering the house. It had belonged to his wife after her father's death, but she had rarely lived in it, preferring America to England and hotels and a nomad life to thrusting down roots in the village where she'd been born. It was in this house that he'd first wooed her sister, Annys, Diplock's mother. It was here when, on being turned down because he was late to take her to a dance after he'd been flying, he'd turned to Zoë. The place hadn't changed much. Indeed, he even recognised some of the pictures, and the summer house where he and Zoë had first clutched each other in the dark still stood, though it looked a little decrepit now and sadly in need of a coat of paint.

He was shown in by an ancient maid who, to his surprise, recognised him from the past. When Annys appeared, she was calm and expressionless, though her eyes seemed to indicate that she'd been doing a lot of crying.

'It was kind of you to call, Dicken,' she said. 'Did you see what happened?'

'No,' he admitted. 'I didn't. But I was there and it must have been instantaneous.' He was lying, because he had no idea what had happened. No one knew. Young Diplock had been reported missing, presumed killed and, while his death could have been in one of the instantaneous explosions he'd seen in the air, it could just as easily have been in a Lancaster he had seen spinning away with part of its starboard wing missing, its crew pinned down by the effects of gravity, knowing for every second of that terrible dive to earth that they were doomed.

'Did you know him well, Dicken?'

'I got to know him. I had a high regard for him.'

'He had for you, too,' Annys said, her eyes on his face. 'He told me more than once. He compared you to his father. Did you know that?'

'He talked to me once. Not much, but I learned a little about the situation.'

Annys took a deep breath, as though she were steeling herself to face an unpleasant fact. 'He thought there was little to admire in his father.' She seemed to be scourging herself and he tried to interrupt, but she continued remorselessly. 'He'd made a study of his record.'

'Surely, Annys—!'

'Come, Dicken! We both know my husband., After a time, I didn't find much to admire either.'

Dicken was silent and embarrassed.

'He never comes home now,' Annys went on quietly. Her head was up and she looked surprisingly beautiful. 'He must have been informed of George's death—'

'I made sure he was.'

'—but he hasn't been in touch with me.'

'I expect he's busy.'

'Yes, I expect he is.' Annys' mouth twisted. 'You've heard of the Waaf, I suppose. I left London and came back here. He didn't follow me. He never will now.'

'I'm sorry, Annys.'

She sighed. 'Perhaps it's better this way. At least I know now where I am. If only George—' she hesitated and he thought she was about to burst into tears, but she recovered quickly. 'He was engaged, did you know?'

'I met the girl. I took her back to her quarters when we learned—'He stopped dead and extricated himself with some difficulty, hating himself and wishing he'd never come.

The temporary job with 21 Group Dicken had been given showed no signs of ending and by the time they had reached another year of the war it even began to seem permanent.

The war itself was changing. The Germans were stuck in Russia and their U-boat campaign, after a final murderous flourish, was coming to a dead stop, too. For the first time it began to be possible to see the light at the end of a long dark tunnel. The policy of relying on heavy bombers seemed at last to be paying off while the Germans, who had relied on light bombers, were in trouble. But the cost was high. Bomber Command's losses crept up and men Dicken had known disappeared into the darkness over Germany – men with years of experience just as easily as the young men who arrived, fresh-faced and unblooded and still, even now, with ideals about what they were doing. Mostly they didn't appear to care but he often saw them sitting alone, their eyes faraway, knowing perfectly well that their chances of enjoying the success of what they were striving for were slim indeed, and that when they went their deaths could be agonising and even horrific.

Several times, returning to see his mother, who still lived near Deane, he saw Annys. Once she offered him a meal and when he arrived it dawned on him she had made a special effort, not only with the meal but with her own appearance. He decided to let the matter lie fallow for a while.

To his surprise, when Hatto next appeared in his office, he grinned and said 'I've got a visitor for you.'

It was Walt Foote and Dicken leapt to his feet with a yell of delight. Solemnly the three of them joined hands and circled in the centre of the office, watched with bewildered amazement by Babington.

Foote was wearing the uniform of a colonel in the American Army Air Force. Rimless glasses gave him a paternal look and he was beginning to show the heaviness of increasing age. His grey hair was parted in the middle and showed little signs of thinning.

'They made me a county judge, you remember,' he said, 'and, because I'd always been a reservist, when we got into this war they offered me a colonel's commission and told me they needed me urgently. But when I reported to the Chief of Air Staff in Washington, they didn't know what the hell to do with me and I spent the first month or two in the Army and Navy Club. Colonels were a dime a dozen so they transferred me to the Army Services Forces, only for them to yell they wanted me back a couple of months later.'

Foote grinned at them. 'A lot of people think we should fight the Pacific war first,' he went on, 'but Eisenhower, who was running Operations and Plans, said we couldn't because we hadn't enough shipping and that the first priority was an air offensive against Europe. Roosevelt's noticed that, though the Germans have made Europe into a fortress, they forgot to put a lid on it. I'm at General Eaker's headquarters. He was here during the Battle of Britain as a US observer and he knows Harris, so he set up his HQ at High Wycombe nearby. Used to be a girls' school.' Foote grinned again. 'There were notices in the bedrooms, "Should you desire the services of a mistress, push the bell." There was a lot of bell ringing until Eaker showed he wasn't amused.'

'What are you doing?'

'Administration. Helping to get our bombers into the air over Germany. It's a slow business. So far we haven't gone much beyond France and Churchill's wanting to know why. We'll make it, though, eventually. We still have a lot to learn about bombing.'

Hatto frowned. 'So have we,' he admitted. 'And *we've* been at it for three years.'

–

Foote stayed at Dicken's headquarters studying the war as it continued through its disasters and occasional triumphs.

With the Germans flung out of Africa at last, they were all beginning to think more optimistically of the future.

There had been only two more 1000 bomber raids. The one on Essen was carried out in cloud, and bombs were scattered all over the Ruhr Valley – 'At least,' Hatto said, 'those Nazis with country homes well away from the danger zones must have got a nasty shock' – and the one on Bremen failed because of bad weather. But they were abandoned chiefly because of the great disruption they caused in Operational Training and Conversion Units, and from then on major raids had been carried out by forces varying between 400 and 600 machines.

Foote had news about his niece. She had married and was now safely tucked away in a small Virginian town and was expecting a baby.

'Fortunes of war,' he said. 'He's navy.'

From time to time, he flew with one of Dicken's crews and came back looking worn-out and aged.

'It's a goddam sight more dangerous than it was in our day,' he admitted. 'There's just a lot more of everything, and when it happens, it's twice as big and twice as fast.'

Suddenly, however, in the Pacific the Americans were beginning to make headway against the Japanese who, the year before, had seemed invincible, and there was a lot of talk of help for the Chinese who had been fighting them on and off ever since 1931. The first person to get in on the act was Diplock, whose removal from his job with Coastal Command had been deftly engineered by the unforgiving Harris. Never without influence for long, however, he had promptly had himself put in charge of a military mission to China and had already left for India.

He was shortly expected to fly to Assam, from where they would fly over the Himalayas.

'He's been upped to air vice-marshal,' Hatto said. 'To give him a rank equal to the occasion, and they've promoted Tom Howarth to go as his running mate.' Hatto smiled. 'Actually, he was hoping for the purchasing committee in Washington – a cushy billet in a war-free zone would have been just up his street – and had even arranged for his Waaf to go with him. Instead he's got China, which won't be anything like as pleasant, though Chungking's a long way from the fighting.'

By this time the Americans were coming into the country in large numbers and the American 8th Air Force was beginning to join in the assault on the German home-land, pledged to precision daylight bombing. On their first raids, the 109s and Focke Wulfs had exacted a terrible toll so that they were obliged to think again, but they were committed to daylight bombing and it was one of Foote's jobs to convince Harris of the practicality of it. He almost seemed to be succeeding when he was called to London, and two days later he appeared in Dicken's office again.

'I'm off,' he said.

'Where to?'

'China. They consider that, being a judge and having spent several years there, I know all there is to know about the goddam place. I'm a liaison officer. At least, that's what they say. With Chiang Kai-shek. But I reckon there's more to it than that and they aren't telling me the rest. But I'll be in Chungking. I might even find myself working with Parasol Percy.'

Hatto's wife put on a dinner party and they saw Foote off to India. Two days later, Hatto telephoned. 'Parasol Percy,' he said.

'What about him?'

'They were crossing the Hump in a Liberator. It never arrived. They're looking round for a replacement.'

For a long time Dicken was silent. He remembered all the hurts Diplock had done to him, all the mean tricks that had damaged his career. But now, somehow, he couldn't hold them against him. Diplock was just another casualty in what was proving a very impersonal war.

'Poor sod,' was all he said, and Hatto returned with 'Amen to that.'

It seemed important to see Annys again. She'd suffered two blows in a very short time and, whatever Diplock had done, Annys had never done Dicken any harm.

It was difficult getting down to Sussex from East Anglia because, in retaliation for the heavy raids on Germany, the Luftwaffe had started sneak raids on Southern England and the night before one on Canterbury had blocked the roads.

Annys showed no emotion when he appeared and even seemed to prefer to talk about her dead sister, Dicken's wife. 'I think we both picked the wrong partners, Dick,' she said. 'Zoë was never easy to keep up with.'

Dicken shrugged. 'It wasn't that I couldn't keep up with her,' he said. 'I just never knew where she was going.'

Annys' voice shook. 'Neither did *she*,' she said. 'She was always confused. She wanted to be your wife but she also wanted to be a famous airwoman.' Her face twisted. 'I don't feel much for Arthur, but I can't dismiss him completely because after all we lived with each other from

1917 until last year and you can't forget that. But he was a very selfish man.'

He was also a bloody coward, Dicken thought, as well as spiteful as a ferret.

'I just feel—' suddenly he sensed she wasn't so much in control of herself as she had appeared '—I just feel the load is suddenly too heavy. First my son. Now my daughter.'

'Has something happened to her?'

'She's married to a solicitor in Canterbury. The raid last night destroyed their home. She's in hospital. She was such a pretty girl, but she's been burned.' Tears were streaming down Annys' face and, as she put out her hands blindly and clutched at him, his arms went round her.

For a long time he held her in silence before he could trust himself to speak. 'Are you going to see her?'

'I must.'

'It'll be a hell of a journey from here. Let me take you.'

–

Canterbury was still smoking but Dicken's official car got them through all the barriers that had been thrown up. It appeared that Annys' daughter was not badly hurt and her husband and his parents were taking care of the children. Annys was more cheerful on the return journey, and even managed to smile.

'They never came to see us,' she admitted. 'Arthur didn't like children much.' She paused and gave a little laugh. 'Still, I don't think they liked Arthur much.'

It was late when they reached Sussex. They ate at a small hotel where the food, like all wartime food, was adequate but hardly exciting, but they had a couple of drinks beforehand and split a bottle of wine. On the last stretch of the journey, Annys fell asleep against Dicken's shoulder as he drove and it seemed strange to have a woman alongside him again, warm-feeling, perfumed, and dependent on him.

She stood in front of him in the blacked-out hall of the house as he left. It was there that Dicken had kissed her more than once years before, when they'd both been young and Europe still hadn't been torn apart by the German wars. She stood for a long time staring at him then, without a change of expression, she stepped forward and, putting her hands on his arms, kissed him on the mouth.

'Thank you, Dicken.'

She saw him to the door. 'Come again, Dicken,' she said quietly.

He nodded, not speaking, and drove away deep in thought. It was obvious she was throwing out hints and he wasn't objecting to them. Was he mad? Surely, after living twenty years with Diplock, some of his character must have rubbed off on her. But it was far from unpleasant to hold an attractive woman in his arms again, and his life had been lonely for a long time. In the end, he decided just to let things slide and see what happened. It was a coward's way out but he could think of no other.

It seemed a very easy way to deal with it but when he returned to his headquarters he found that the matter had been taken out of his hands. Hatto had telephoned and left a message that he was to turn over his command to his deputy and report to the Air Ministry in London.

It didn't take much imagination to guess that he was due for another spell overseas.

Part Three

One

He found Hatto occupied with a huge file marked 'China'. As he saw Dicken he stood up and reached for his hat. 'I think this needs a stiff drink,' he said.

As they knocked back pink gins, Hatto explained. 'Diplock,' he said. 'They found them. The whole lot. Crew. Diplock. Tom Howarth and a few others. They've got to be replaced.'

There was a long suspicious silence, then Hatto went on. 'I'd better put you in the picture. The frock-coats believe that if Chiang Kai-shek were defeated in China, Japan would be free to exploit the place without harassment, and that – if and when we've finally assaulted the Japanese home islands – they could continue the war from the centre of China. It doesn't bear thinking about.'

'So?'

'So we're putting tremendous resources into Burma. By the end of the year we expect to go over to the offensive there. There's a new command set-up and a big propaganda campaign to indicate that the Japanese aren't the supermen we thought they were. The aim's to re-establish land communications with China. You'll remember they cut the Burma Road in 1942. We're hoping to reopen it. The Yanks have a general out there called Stilwell, and a fighter group called the Flying Tigers

209

run by a chap called Claire Chennault gave us a lot of support. There was even a Chinese division helping. We're now going to try to pay them back.'

Dicken studied Hatto, puzzled. 'What's your interest in all this, Willie? Are they sending out a British Mission or something?'

Hatto smiled. 'In fact, the Americans are running the show, but you know Winston. He's not going to be nudged out of what were British spheres of influence and he's insisted that we're represented with the Chinese government, even if all we do is hold the Americans' coat-tails.'

'So?'

Hatto smiled. 'So it's become a major preoccupation to keep China in the war. To do so, the Americans have organised their airlift over the Himalayas and, with a little assistance from us, have provided a loan of over five hundred million dollars. Unfortunately, Chiang Kai-shek, for whom I imagine, after your stay in China in 1927, you have no great love, seems to have cast a spell over Washington. Roosevelt seems to show a strange partiality for him – it's almost become a cult in Washington, it seems – but Winston's a bit more sceptical. Chiang keeps sticking his nose into our affairs in India and Winnie thinks Washington's a bit like Titania captivated by Bottom. He feels that, considering the amount of money and aid that's been sent to them, the Chinese are being remarkably unwarlike and he wants somebody to find out just what's going on. So he's sending a little mission of his own.'

Hatto swallowed his drink and ordered another. 'Some of the Americans,' he went on, 'have also started to grow a bit suspicious of Chiang and begun to think he's just leading us all on, so, unknown to Roosevelt, there's a new American mission going too. Walt Foote's running it. After three years' legal experience in the East he's considered as much of an expert on China as you can get. They've upped him to brigadier.'

Dicken frowned. 'Who's leading our lot?' he asked. 'You?'

Hatto grinned at him. 'No,' he said. 'You! They've decided that a man who managed to get himself captured by a warlord called Lee Tse-liu probably knows more about the place than anyone else they can find. They've also heard that you speak some Chinese.'

'*Some's* the operative word. Do they realise how many dialects there are?'

Hatto smiled. 'I don't suppose it's occurred to 'em,' he admitted. 'It usually doesn't to the clever types who think up these things. You'll be flying in from Assam.'

'It sounds hard work just getting there.'

Hatto smiled again. 'You pick your own staff.'

'I'll have Babington,' Dicken said at once.

'What's he got that's so special?'

'He picks me up when I'm drunk.'

'Right. He's yours and he'll carry the right rank. You've also been nudged up another notch, same as Diplock. To give you some elbow.'

Dicken was silent and Hatto looked puzzled. 'Aren't you pleased?' he asked.

Dicken smiled. 'Oh, yes,' he said. 'I'm pleased. I was just thinking that, after twenty-five years of sitting across my career, for the first time Diplock's finally done me a favour. And the only way he could manage to do it was by dying.'

Hatto nodded. 'Anyway, congratulations. It's not before time. If we weren't now elderly gentlemen we could do a gloat dance.'

Dicken smiled back. 'Perhaps we should save it until I come back. Will you be seeing me off?'

Hatto pulled a face. 'Not this time, old son,' he said. 'They need somebody in India to watch things from there. I'm coming too.'

Two

China hadn't changed much. It was still the land of the empty gut.

When they left Assam the rain was falling in solid depressing sheets and the atmosphere was that of a steam bath. Foote's mission still hadn't moved on and he explained the joys of flying unsuitable aircraft in an area of storms, unmapped mountain peaks, icing, overloading, accidents and unpredictable high altitude winds. It was always a toss-up whether a machine would arrive or not and their deputies were not to accompany them just in case.

The weather was kind as they flew into Yunnan, from where they headed by road and river to Chungking, Chiang Kai-shek's new capital in Szechwan. They were met by a cynical young American Army Air Force major called Johnson, who had once been part of Chennault's Flying Tigers and was now part of Foote's mission. He wore a battered cap and a leather flying jacket with a Chinese flag and a message in Chinese characters painted on the back so that if he were shot down the Chinese peasants who found him would know who he was and what to do with him.

'You'll find things a bit crazy here,' he advised. 'Our guys are paid in American dollars, which makes them almost millionaires, but there are also a lot of other guys, European, American and Chinese, who're making a lot of money out of profiteering. And this place has grown so fast nobody knows where anything is. New buildings have spread like fungus. There was no steel to spare so they used bamboo corner poles, no nails so they lashed it together with bamboo strips, and no wood so they split bamboo and made wattles. And we've got every dialect in China here so that if you ask the way in Mandarin like I do, you get answered by a Cantonese who speaks it even worse. Everything's written down, because messengers can't understand what's said to them, and the government's given the streets high-sounding names like the Road of the People's Heritage and the Road of the National Republic, but the rickshaw boys still call them by their old names.'

'Leads to confusion,' Foote said dryly.

'Some,' Johnson agreed.

Despite the war, the city seemed to have lapsed into a state of indifference. It stood on a tongue of land at the junction of the Yangtze and Chialing Rivers, its boundary wall almost intact after five centuries of wear and tear. Once it had been remote and self-sufficient because Szechwan had always been considered backward by the rest of China and for six months of the year a curtain of fog and rain overhung it and coated its alleys with slime. When the Sino-Japanese War had started in 1937, refugees had poured in and government offices had migrated en masse. Pedlars, shopkeepers and politicians had followed and the population had doubled in a few months to 400,000. After the fall of Hankow it had neared a million and it was still rising.

It had first been bombed in 1938 and, with the Chinese anti-aircraft guns ineffectual, incendiaries had started fires which had gnawed out the ancient slums, and in the back alleys men, women and children had roasted to death. But since then a lot had been rebuilt, though the scars still showed in smashed shop fronts, blackened acres of devastation and the bamboo-and-mud squalor of new housing.

Accommodation had been provided for the two missions on the top floor of a block of offices, the bottom floors of which were filled with Chinese government departments. The entrance was swarming with children and outside women were hanging out their washing.

'Wives of the Chinese junior officials,' Johnson explained. 'Everything's kinda overcrowded and mostly they live in dormitories. A family that has a room's very lucky. Most of the clerks sleep in their offices and their families live in the basement. In some ways it's a good idea because it's cold in winter and they keep each other warm.'

Part of the accommodation had been made into a mess but food was difficult to obtain and the British were dependent on the Americans for rations, all of which had to be flown over the Hump. To flush them, the lavatories were provided with a tub of muddy water, which was carried by coolies from the river, and a bath in a few inches of water was a luxury.

Johnson let them know the position. 'The one thing you'll notice is the sound of dynamos,' he said. 'They're always going. They never stop working. One shift takes over as the other leaves. Twenty-four hours a day.'

There were no restrictions and no blackout and you could buy anything – fur coats, champagne, electric razors, silk stockings, army boots, guns, high octane petrol, diamonds, ever permanent waves. Provided you had the money, because stockings were 300 dollars a pair, matches 20 dollars a box. You could buy *Life* magazine for 500 but *Esquire* cost you 2000. When it wasn't raining, the goddam place was always covered with a grey-blue mist, and when there was neither the sun came out hot enough to shrivel you. There was typhus about, too, because of the rats. An enormous number of them lay dead in the streets, so that the dark alleys were noisome with the smell of them, but nobody bothered to collect them.

'It's okay, though,' Johnson said cynically. 'When you get used to it.'

General Clinton R. Loomis, the American officer running things in Chungking, seemed bewildered and indignant that he was wasting his time. 'Those guys in Washington have gone off their nuts,' he said firmly.

He was a large man who was built like a brewery dray, with a deep chest and square shoulders. He liked the British, always called Foote by his civilian title, 'Judge', and most of the time had a cigar like a telegraph pole sticking out of the corner of his mouth. 'Here we are,' he said. 'Sending all this aid, all this goddam money, and that slimy bastard, Chiang, the Generalissimo, is just using it to make sure of his hold on the country.'

He tried to explain. 'Before Pearl Harbour,' he said, 'he decided that if he just held on, Japan would be bound to collide with the US eventually and when she did China could just retire from the fight and leave it to fresher forces – us. The bastard isn't doing a thing! It's just one lousy snafu. Tell 'em, Johnny. You know it as well as I do.'

Johnson added his mite. 'The performance of the Chinese troops,' he said dryly, 'so far has been unmemorable.'

'That goddam Chiang's always threatening that China's on the point of collapse,' Loomis snorted. 'He says his position's calamitous. And the more he makes of it the more effort those guys in Washington make for him. They fancy America taking the place in China of the old imperial powers.' He looked at Dicken and grinned. '*Your* outfit. But the bastard's using all the material and money we send him to blockade the Communists, who *are* fighting the Japanese.'

'Aren't they *both* fighting the Japanese?' Foote asked.

'They're supposed to be, Judge, but only the Communists are achieving anything. They're penning the Japanese into the towns in the north but they don't trust Chiang and won't work with him. Can't say I blame them. It's a bit like a civil war, with the Communists trying to spread their influence and Chiang trying to stop them. Each side's got its own territory and if one moves into the other's they're driven out by force. In 1941 the communist Fourth Route Army was ambushed. It was sheer treachery and there was a lot of fighting and the Commies lost seven generals. Chou En-lai was here in Chungking at the time, too, trying to keep things on an even keel. Now Chiang's using 200,000 of his best just troops to keep the Communists out of his territory because he knows they're dangerous to his goddam regime.'

The general lit a fresh cigar, blew out smoke, waved his hand and sighed. It seemed to diminish him from a military man to a worried executive. 'General Stilwell, who's running the show out here,' he pointed out, 'hates old Dogleg Chiang, but he likes China and keeps trying to get the Chinese to fight, when any goddam halfwit can see they don't have to, because even by not doing anything they're tying down whole Japanese armies. And the reports he's sending on the Communists, because they *do* fight, are so goddam glowing, those guys in Washington are now beginning to think they've got roses growing all over 'em.'

'Does Chiang want to make peace?'

Loomis' cigar circled in the air. 'He daren't. The country wouldn't let him. He couldn't, anyway, and you guys have got to produce proof that his men aren't a romantic army fighting against odds but a military rabble that in some parts of the country have even started trading with the Japs.'

'Stilwell's all right,' he went on. 'But he's got some lousy subordinates and he and Chennault hate each other, while some of the guys they send us might just as well have stayed at home. They think this place's Minnesota or Nevada or Missouri, they call the Chinese "Slopeheads" or "Slopeys", and the US Government "Uncle Chump from over the Hump". Chiang Kai-shek's "Chancre Jack" and Sun Yat-sen's "Sunset Sam". Those people back home have no idea what it's like out here.'

'Do we know anything about a man called General Lee Tse-liu?' Dicken asked.

The general's head whipped round. 'I sure hope you're not goin' to ask any favours for *him*.'

Dicken laughed. 'Not on your life. I'd like to meet him with a Lancaster with a full load of bombs.'

Loomis smiled. 'There are some bastards in Chiang's outfit,' he said. 'But I'd say Lee was the biggest of the lot. He sits on his ass and uses his soldiers to collect rice to sell to the Japanese. He's made a fortune out of the Chinese peasants and he's now making another. But he's Chiang's favourite general and he's here in Chungking at the moment. He's always ass-licking in Chungking. He leaves his troops to his chief of staff, a guy called Colonel Kok, while he organises his loot for the time when he can bolt for somewhere safe. I'll fix you an interview with old Dogleg. You might meet him there. What do you intend to do? Spit in his eye?'

–

The meeting was organised for the following day. The Generalissimo was fixedly calm, his pate clean-shaven – 'So there'll be no tell-tale grey fuzz,' Johnson whispered – and he wore a spotless tunic bare of decorations tightly buttoned to his throat. He greeted them in a clear high voice.

'They say,' Johnson murmured, 'that he lives pretty frugally and that he's incorruptible, but that's because by Chinese standards he's got everything he needs. They say he's slipping, though, and that some of his supporters are beginning to turn against him. Twenty-seven of his generals went over to the Japs, thinking they'd get a better deal.'

Madame Chiang was very different. She was small and beautifully dressed, speaking English with an American accent acquired during her schooling at an American college. Johnson was as unimpressed with her as with her husband. 'They say she's as ruthless as hell,' he murmured. 'They say she signs death warrants with her own hand.'

The meeting produced nothing. Chiang remained poker-faced throughout, saying little and offering nothing, while his wife, chattering gaily, produced only charm.

General Lee Tse-liu, who had grown plump and well-fed and had not lost his strange affected English manner of speaking, clearly failed to recognise Dicken as the man he'd once held prisoner with the American priest, Father O'Buhilly.

'I was studying in England in 1914,' he said as they were introduced. 'I tried to join the British army, don't you know? But, by Jove, they felt they shouldn't enlist Chinese in a British squabble.'

It was a different version from the one he'd told Dicken in 1927 when he'd bitterly described how his enthusiasm for the British Empire had been turned to hatred by a fool in red tabs who'd told him they 'didn't want wogs in the British army'.

'Those were jolly difficult days,' he went on. 'Everybody was jolly well against China then. Now they're friendly because they know we're holding the fort against the Japanese.'

'That the guy?' Foote asked as he moved away.

'That's him,' Dicken agreed. 'It's a pity Diplock didn't make it. They were two of a kind.' He turned to Johnson. 'So far,' he said, 'we've learned a lot about Chiang Kai-shek. How about telling us something about the Chinese army?'

Johnson grinned. 'You know what Ludendorff said about the Austrians in the last war – "We're allied to a corpse." It's the same with Chiang's army. It's tired, discouraged and not even wanted by its own people. The guys are brave enough but they've been neglected, they've got no transport and no leadership, and only the poorest and the stupidest get drafted. The relations between the top officers and the men are goddam terrible and most of the soldiers don't see their families for years. They have nothing to fight for, and for most of them being in the army's just like being dead because the guys at the front live entirely on rice and vegetables – supposed to be twenty-four ounces a day but usually less – with a few beans or mouldy turnips. Meat comes occasionally. At first our guys couldn't understand why Chinese regiments always seemed to be carrying dead dogs. They soon learned when they lost their own pets. Dogs were food to the Chinese and the mutts our guys keep eat as much as a Chinese soldier.'

Foote was listening quietly, clearly a little shaken. 'And what the hell can we do about all this?' he asked.

'Nothing, sir,' Johnson said. 'It's a waste of time. Senior officers are incompetent or corrupt and the campaigns are nothing but foraging expeditions; and when the Japanese aren't lashing out, the result's stalemate, in a belt of No Man's Land fifty to a hundred miles deep right up the middle of the country, because the Chinese have destroyed every road, bridge, railway and ferry and burned the villages and towns. And the blockade's useless anyway, because the Chinese get cloth, rubber, tyres, medicines and petrol from the Japanese in the same way the Japs get Chinese tungsten, tin and other things.' Johnson shrugged. 'It is,' he said, 'a hell of a way to fight a war.'

–

Though the air raids on Chungking had long since died down, in their place had come hunger and discomfort and thousands of people were living in a nightmare of inflation. But the profiteers were being very discreet and there was no bright plumage visible, though they heard of officials' wives having new dresses flown over the Hump from India and of offers being made to Western Transport officers to use their vehicles to make a fortune. Meanwhile, it was startling to find the Chinese press attacking the United States and painting a picture of the riotous life being lived by American soldiers.

The city was notorious for its climate, which produced fog and rain for months, and as the year progressed epidemics began to breed in the alleyways that ran down the slopes, twisting and tumbling over steps polished smooth by centuries of straw-sandalled feet. Sewage and rubbish lay in the same stream from which drinking water was taken and when people became ill they went to herb doctors who organised cures from musk and children's urine. Even when the summer came and the heat poured down, moisture remained in the air, and everybody started rashes of prickly heat, and there were swarms of insects swimming on the drinking water or clinging to the walls. Then the mosquitoes came.

'The bastards work in threes,' Foote claimed. 'Two lift the mosquito net and the third zooms in for the kill.'

Meat spoiled and there was still never enough water for washing. Dysentery spread and the city was full of drifting odours.

It was known now that the Americans, pressing in the Pacific, were beginning to cause the Japanese to look over their shoulders, while in Burma the British were preparing for an offensive to reopen the Burma road. In addition, an excellent airfield had been constructed at Kweilin where the remains of the American Volunteer Group under Chennault had regrouped. Ever since 1941 this grab-bag bunch of young volunteers had been tearing at the Japanese bombers, and when the Burma retreat had ended and the RAF had retired to India, the Americans had retreated to China. They had searched Calcutta, Cairo and the States for new machines, spare parts, fuel and ammunition, and with a few ancient Russian Tupolev bombers, which the Chinese were using, had even talked of bombing Tokyo until Jimmy Doolittle had got there first.

But there was little sign of gratitude from the Chinese government, even to a large extent obstruction, as if the wish were to stop them finding out what happened to the goods that were lifted over the Hump with such heavy losses in men and machines.

'Makes you wonder what the hell we're doin' here,' Foote complained.

Because the electricity was off, the lift wasn't working, so they trudged slowly up the stairs to their rooms, puffing a little by the time they got to the top.

'Shows our age,' Foote grinned.

As Dicken opened his door, he noticed the light was on and wondered if some government spy had been searching his room. Then, sitting bolt upright in a straight-backed chair, he saw a great bear of a figure in the shadows. As he entered it rose quickly.

'Dicken, me boy, do you not recognise me?'

'Sure I do,' Dicken said. 'The only thing as big as you on two legs is King Kong. Father O'Buhilly, by all that's holy! What are you doing here?'

'Still hoping to make you a believer, my son.'

Dicken laughed. 'Father, in all my flying time I've never encountered a single angel.'

'Ah, the pity of it! Doubtless they were lurking behind a cloud!'

For a moment they hugged each other delightedly. As they drew apart, Dicken grinned.

'It's wonderful to see you, Father,' he said. 'What are you doing here?'

'The same as always, me boy. Spreadin' the word of the Lord and the Holy Catholic Church. There are always too many Presbyterians and Baptists pushin' *their* version.'

Remembering the old priest's tastes, Dicken gestured. 'There's no Irish whiskey here, Father. But there *is* a little American rye.'

'A barbarian drink to be sure. But for once I won't turn me nose up at it.'

Sloshing a good helping into a glass, Dicken handed it over. The priest smacked his lips.

'I have cigarettes, too, Father. Do you still smoke?'

Father O'Buhilly fished out a blackened old pipe, its stem bound with twine. 'A pipe these days, me boy. Mind,' he added, 'I smoke cigarettes when I can get 'em. Especially other people's.'

As Dicken offered his case, the priest drew the smoke down with a dreamy look on his face. 'Do you remember, boy, how we shared them in prison, you and I? A puff each alternately to make 'em last.'

They were silent for a moment, remembering the shabby little cell in the village where they'd been held prisoner.

''Twas only the absence of somethin' to smoke that drove me to escape,' O'Buhilly went on. 'But for that you'd never have got me into that contraption you called an aeroplane.' He paused again. 'He's still around, y'know.'

'I've met him.'

'When the Japanese came he contemplated going over to them, but in the end he changed his mind and he's now one of Chiang's most trusted men. Which goes to show how bad Chiang is at pickin' his subordinates. He's Methodist like Chiang, o' course – if he'd been a Catholic I might have made something of him. His army's north of Changjao, where I've come from, but, sure, 'tis a skeleton army padded with the names of dead men whose wages and rations he continues to draw. It's dyin' on its feet, boy, sufferin' from dysentery, malaria and starvation. The Americans offered quinine tablets – I distributed 'em meself – but he sells 'em to the Japanese. Half of 'em have scabies and the rest have the itch. On their hands, legs, bodies, everywhere. They wear the same uniforms day and night all year round, and there's no bathin' because there's no soap. There's beriberi – you can push your thumb into the leg of a Chinese soldier and the mark's there ten minutes later – leg ulcers, tuberculosis, typhus, influenza and worms. The only thing that's missing is venereal disease and that's because their morals are good and they can't afford a prostitute, anyway. Sure, this place's nothing but a cess pool. I pray, of course, but in China you have to shout to be heard. But that's no reason why we should give up. There are still souls who need help, and

225

the strength of me religion isn't in the way it's preached or the way it's offered in books. It lies in the way we apply it.'

The priest seemed low in spirits and Dicken guessed he hadn't arrived merely to renew an old acquaintance. 'Why are you here, Father?' he asked.

The old man shed his gloom with an effort. 'The Japanese are comin',' he said. 'Everybody in Changjao knows they're comin'. Lee knows they're comin'. Chiang knows they're comin'. But nothin's bein' done except by the people themselves. There are textile factories up there, which came up here from the coast, and now they've got to move them again. You should come and see 'em, me boy. 'Twill teach you a lot about China.'

'How did you know I was here—'

'The miracle of modern invention, me boy. You'll remember that meetin' you had with Chiang. They took photographs. Not for the Chinese papers. Most Chinese can't afford a paper anyway. No, my boy, it was for Western consumption. *New York Times. Washington Post. London Times.* Aid to China. Look you at the Generalissimo, surrounded by American and British aides. When I called on one of his ministers, he had them on his desk and I saw your face. Y'haven't changed, boy. Have you been pittin' yourself against those monsters in Germany?'

'Once or twice, Father.'

'God be praised for brave men. The things they've done to their fellow human bein's. I carry no special torch for the Jews. Nor, for that matter, for Anglicans, Presbyterians or Baptists or anyone else who doesn't belong to the true faith. But human beings are human beings. Have you shot many, boy?'

Dicken laughed. 'One or two,' he said. 'But mostly we leave it to the twenty-year-olds. When the Germans shoot back, they're better at dodging. What about you?'

'I wait for an end to the killin'. That's all. 'Twill come eventually and then China will be different. The Communists have ideas for after the war because most of the intellectuals left Chiang long since and joined them. There'll be a great sweepin' away of privilege.'

'Can they do it?'

O'Buhilly shrugged. 'They *will*, boy. Believe me, they'll throw out old Dogleg and his corrupt hangers-on so fast they won't know what hit 'em.'

'Are you a Communist, Father?'

'And believe in God?' The priest looked indignant. 'But I believe in human dignity, boy, as did Jesus Christ in His infinite mercy, and I don't believe in one law for the rich and another for the poor. We know about that in Changjao, y'see. The Japanese are close and there are air raids and the only people who can leave are Lee's people. When you get up you look at the sky. If it's clear you have everything handy for a quick dash to the shelter. If it's cloudy, the Japs probably won't come so you do the longer journeys.'

The priest paused, his eyes filled with sadness. 'Sure, 'tis like withstanding a whirlwind, because the buildings are tinder-dry, the fire fightin' equipment's ancient and the water pressure's never enough. The only thing we have in our favour is the will of the people and that's wearin' thin. When will you be comin', boy? There's someone there I think you'll be wantin' to see.'

Dicken frowned. 'In Changjao? I don't know anybody in Changjao, Father.'

'You know this one, my son. 'Tis Marie-Gabrielle Aubrey, and when I left she was talkin' of leavin' for Yuking. The harvest's goin' to fail and there'll be a famine, and that's where everybody will go.'

Three

They travelled north by railway, on a wide loop that ran westwards away from the front.

The train was a vast amorphous mass of sleeping soldiers and civilians in and on a mixture of flat cars, box cars and old coaches. The carriages were stuffed with people propped on hard wooden benches and the roofs were black with more of them, bracing themselves against the vibration and the curves. Every now and then they saw smashed bodies lying in the roadbed, but nobody looked twice at them because dead human beings were nothing new in China. At every station more tried to climb on while those already there tried to beat them off.

As the train stopped at a small shabby station, peasants appeared, offering scraggy boiled chickens, sausage-shaped waffles of bean flour, vermicelli, sugar cane and hard-boiled eggs. One had a cart pulled by a bright green horse which he explained was really white but had been painted green as camouflage for when the Japanese bombers came over. As they waited, an armoured train used by Chiang came through, its carriages filled with officials.

The station forecourt was filled with soldiers wearing scraps of Japanese uniform, still complete with Japanese insignia. They seemed to be mere boys and they were performing curious exercises which seemed to consist of balancing on one leg staring at each other, with the other stretched out behind like ballet dancers.

'New recruits,' Johnson pointed out. 'They'll never be any good because after the last war old Dogleg hired Prussian officers and rootless Russians to train them. They only know how to goose-step and the tactics of the old Russian Imperial army, and they have to unlearn everything when they get to the front.'

His mind busy with memories, Dicken turned to Father O'Buhilly. 'What's she like, Father?'

''Tis the third time you've asked me, boy. She's the same as she was in Rezhanistan. A beautiful woman still. After Rezhanistan, she studied nursing in South Africa then came out to China because her brother was here.' Father O'Buhilly crossed himself. 'But he died of typhoid, God rest his soul, while she was on her way, so she came to me and we started a hospital. Just a wee one, y'understand, but it's there when people need it.'

The priest looked sideways at Dicken. 'But she's in the wrong place, boy,' he went on. 'She needs to be the mother of children.'

'She won't find a husband in some out-of-the-way province in China, Father.'

'She's doing God's work, boy. Where it's most needed.'

The guard was moving along the platform pushing people back into the train now. As he climbed after the priest to their compartment, Dicken tried a final question.

'Did she ever talk of me, Father?' he asked.

'Sure, that she did. Often. You did her no favour, boy, when you lost her after Rezhanistan.'

'I tried to find her, Father.'

'Pity you didn't succeed, boy. Mebbe now it's too late.'

–

They detrained at a place called Yu-Tsien, a grubby noisy dusty little town where the hotel was like a rat's nest, and the proprietor wore a long padded kimono.

Their rooms were lit by candles and it was impossible to sleep because someone was singing all night long like a mating cat, and a sudden storm slammed the doors and set the children yelling, while the mosquitoes homed in like dive bombers. Breakfast was a meal of chicken and warm beer and, as they were eating, a young Chinese appeared, looking for Father O'Buhilly. He drove them in an old Packard through villages that were mere clusters of huts, where the peasants lived with their stored grain and their animals and the ancestral shrines they venerated. Farmers were ladling stored night soil from a pit into huge stinking buckets.

''Twill go on to their vegetables and plants,' Father O'Buhilly said. 'They eat the fruit of the soil then return to it what their bodies reject. 'Tis no wonder disease is rife.'

More villages came up, full of the country noises of pigs, babies, hens, gossiping women, yelling men. They were near the river and they could hear the sing-song chant of the coolies carrying cargoes from the boats from the coast of Chungking. A salesman whacked out a rhythmic beat on a block of wood as he walked, a notions dealer cried his wares loudly. The night-soil collector had a different chant, as did the man carrying brassware, his cats' bells, knives, toothpicks and ear-cleaners all dangling from a long pole.

Lee Tse-liu was still in Chungking and they were met by his chief of staff, Colonel Kok Yi-jeng, a tall well-dressed man with a cropped head and a horsehair fly-whisk.

'Trained at Whampoa academy like so many who're close to Chiang,' Johnson said.

It was clear the Chinese officers were passing to Chungking only what Chiang Kai-shek wanted to hear. Towns were being reported captured when they were not, and enemy casualties were clearly being grossly exaggerated. They were celebrating the fact that one of their units had caught a group of Japanese drinking at a stream and killed them all.

Colonel Kok led them in his car towards the battle area, but eventually they had to take to shaggy ponies before heading east to an area where the Japanese had made a foraging expedition across the Yellow Plains, their aircraft strafing the roads, their men sacking and looting. Without guns or aircraft, all the Chinese could do was feed men into the slaughter and where the Japanese had passed there was a black scar of devastation. In their attempts to stop them, the Chinese had cut up the roads so that even the ponies had to be led.

The stories of rape and murder were horrifying. In one area where the Japanese transport system had broken down they had lashed peasants to their carts and used them as beasts of burden and, since they had always beaten their horses and mules to death, they didn't hesitate to do the same to the peasants. In another village, the Chinese had a Japanese straggler who had been found hiding in a wood. He was tied up like a parcel and, expecting to be killed at once, had fastened a notice to his chest begging not to be beheaded.

With a Japanese attack expected any time, troops were moving up in scorching heat under a cloudless sky, snaking along every ditch and bank in long strings of sweating humanity. It was an infantry army and there wasn't a single vehicle and almost no pack animals, so that everything was carried by men, the weapons by the soldiers, the supplies by blue-clad coolies with straw hats. There wasn't a single piece of artillery and the rifles were old, and the yellow-and-brown uniforms threadbare.

'What is it,' Dicken asked. 'A brigade?'

'This,' Kok said, 'is the Thirtieth Division of the Twelfth Route Army.'

'There can't be more than 2,000 men,' Foote said. 'How many do your divisions have?'

'Ten thousand. We are waiting for reinforcements.'

'More likely,' Johnson murmured, 'the remaining eight thousand are dead and Lee's still drawing the money for their rations.'

The trudging soldiers clearly expected nothing but disaster. They were wiry, brown and thin and wore what looked like old German helmets. They all carried two grenades attached to their belts and around their necks long cloth bags full of dry rice kernels, their field rations. Above the straw sandals, their feet were swollen and broken and as they trudged past the sweat rolled down the expressionless faces, while the dust rose as the heat gripped the entire countryside in glistening waves that lifted from the paddy fields.

The mission followed the column into a village only to find the villagers had already left and the soldiers were engaged in tearing down doors to make their fires and seizing what pigs, chickens and vegetables had been left behind. The regimental officers were earnest men whom Colonel Kok treated as if they were servants.

They spent the night in what was claimed to be a hotel, but the walls were papered with sheets from American tabloids of a decade back, still proclaiming in deep black headlines the latest New York and Chicago sensations. Among them were slogans written on red paper calling for resistance, which had been pasted up by government employees. When Foote demanded to see the Chinese hospitals, Kok blinked, startled.

'Hospitals are the same the whole world over,' he said.

'Nevertheless, I guess we'll see them.'

They were in an area where there had been recent fighting and a stream of sick and wounded was heading on foot towards the rear, the men struggling desperately along on their own two feet because there was no transport. They were a pitiful group, limping, dragging themselves up the slopes by clutching rocks and trees, leaning on sticks, their eyes blank and empty. It was rare to see a stretcher, and the whole column smelled of wounds and decay and was surrounded by the flies that settled in a heaving mass on every pus-filled wound.

The hospital was a one-storey building of stucco and teak where the medical care was primitive, and many of the wounded had been days en route. The rooms were full of patients, lying on straw three to a blanket, many of them in a coma or raving, but there were no beds or mattresses and sick and wounded lay side by side. The smell of gas-gangrene made the stomach heave and the crowded rooms were loud with flies. None of the wounded had been washed and there were no anaesthetics, while the instruments for the operations were blunt and unserviceable. Bandages and lint didn't exist, and some of the men had followed their village practice of stuffing their wounds with straw, strips of uniform, leaves, or the intestines of freshly-killed chickens. They all seemed to be suffering from disease and most of them seemed to know there was no hope for them.

'China,' the officer in command, a man who had trained in San Francisco, told them, 'has one doctor to every 45,000 men. And some of us are nothing more than pharmacists.'

Father O'Buhilly, a crucified look on his face, led them out to their ponies.

'Supplies are being sent,' Foote growled. 'Where do they go to?'

'The followers of old Dogleg don't go short of anything, me boy,' the priest said dryly. 'And their women use the petrol that's brought in for ambulances for their cars. So why not the medicines for their headaches?'

Four

They ate at a roadhouse, and the following day at a nearby airfield came across two ancient Gladiators and five old Russian Tupolev bombers with strange undercarriages and noses that looked like inverted conservatories. They all looked shabby and their crews said they hadn't been used in action for years. They were being prepared to fly back to the safety of Chungking.

In the afternoon, they came to a wide, slow-flowing river, which Father O'Buhilly said was a feeder to the Yangtze. It was almost part of the marshy fields that surrounded it, an area of willows and tall reeds, of ferries and boats, and men and women bent over their rice shoots. Changjao was on the edge of this system of inter-connecting pools, lakes and rivers. Part of it had been destroyed by Japanese bombers, to leave a havoc of plaster and laths round a ruined pagoda.

'There's no defence,' Father O'Buhilly explained. 'The barrels of the anti-aircraft guns have worn smooth with use. But we've organised a system of air raid warnings. When the first warning comes, a paper lantern's strung up where everybody can see it, to indicate the airplanes are two hours away. Two lanterns mean they're close. When they're dropped it's an immediate alert. A long paper stocking's the signal for the "all clear". When the airplanes are within fifty miles, the switch at the power station's pulled and the town becomes dead. Lights go out and everything stops. If a policeman sees a light, he simply shoots at it.'

Bustling about, pointing, directing, giving commands, he showed them into a single room with four cots and a charcoal brazier, the floor thick with dust. As they dropped their gear on to the beds, he returned, ushering them outside, and led them along a narrow path through the rice fields. Ahead, strings of peasants in single file burdened with household goods were heading for safety. Here and there was a barrow, pushed by a man, his wife hauling at the rope in front, a child sitting on top. Sometimes a woman rode a mule, side-saddle like an unhappy Madonna, and old women hobbled along on bound feet or rode on the shoulders of strong sons who watched the sky with wary black eyes. Young unaccompanied men walked at a quicker pace, unburdened by families.

Eventually they reached the river and at once it became obvious that every business that existed in the area was being moved. Machinery was being loaded into boats and covered with leaves and branches.

'It's been done before,' Father O'Buhilly explained. 'From Nanking. From Shanghai. At Hankow they moved the whole power station piece by piece.'

Everything detachable was being taken down and packed in boxes, and machinery was being carried on to waiting steamers, rowing boats and junks. Two enormous iron frames, which looked like the supports of a dozen looms, were being moved by manpower alone towards an enormous newly-built pontoon floating at the water's edge. With shrill cries, like ants moving grain, the Chinese were edging them aboard inch by inch, while another horde of men was plaiting ropes and lashing the pontoons behind steamers, to be towed through the rapids further upriver.

'Everything's going,' Father O'Buhilly said. 'When the Japanese attack their punch will land in empty air. The factories will be rebuilt at Yuking with bamboo beams instead of iron girders, and blast furnaces will be supplied with coal carried in baskets. Schools are going, refugees, restaurant keepers, priests, sing-song girls, little merchants. If they can't get aboard a junk or a sampan they'll go by rickshaw or cart or on their own two feet.'

A herd of cattle was being chivvied on to a second huge pontoon, and on another people were piling tables, chairs, sewing machines, coops of chickens, a horse. On yet another there was an enormous steam roller, a scar down the bank showing where it had been lowered, with dozens of Chinese on ropes acting as a brake.

There was a mist like a sheet over the river so that a ruined pagoda stuck out above it like an immense phallic symbol, bottomless and floating on the white vapour. What they had thought at first was empty countryside was alive with people, appearing, disappearing, and reappearing from the banks and among the reeds. The men who were to take the rafts downstream were rigging enormous jury rudders and sea anchors to heave their vast log islands round the bends. Even as they watched, one of them pushed off, firecrackers going in celebration, fizzing and sparkling so that the excited Chinese laughed and began to jump up and down. On board was a group of drummers encouraged by a cheer leader on the stern.

Trains of pack ponies, ears and tails flapping against the flies, trotted along the top of the brown mudbank, laden with strange pieces of wood or metal from some small factory, and more rafts were arriving, some of them carrying sheerlegs for hoisting up their unwieldy cargoes. The din was tremendous with shouting men, screaming women, wailing children, bleating goats, and always the clink and clank of metal as too-large parts were further dismantled to make handling easier.

A column of Chinese troops went past, long files of small blank-faced -men without discipline or fixed pace. The padding of their straw-sandalled feet lifted the dry earth in clouds so that they looked like a huge serpentine of dust. Their officer rode ahead on a bony horse and they were followed by coolies carrying ammunition boxes and sacks of rice. The company kitchen, a single soot-blackened cauldron carried by two men, brought up the rear, then several small pack guns on mules and a cart carrying more sacks of rice on which sick men were lying.

'You're seeing China on the move,' Father O'Buhilly said grimly. 'They're all going to Yuking. About half of them will arrive, the soldiers doing rather better than the civilians. But they'll die too eventually because they drink from the paddy fields which they've manured with night soil and they use their first aid kits to clean their rifles.'

Father O'Buhilly's hospital was in what had once been a country house. It had a walled garden with a circular moon gate and there were still black-lacquered furniture and silk wall hangings inside. It consisted of three narrow wards with beds in corridors and smaller rooms, even in large cupboards. Most of the patients were suffering from bomb injuries, and there was one doctor, a gloomy

Russian, who had fled to China during the Revolution, a defeated melancholy man whose clock had stopped in 1917. He was assisted by a young Chinese mission convert who was loudly telling the patients in English, 'Leave it to Jesus. Jesus will look after you.'

'You'll be needin' somethin' to eat, I'm thinkin',' Father O'Buhilly observed. 'I'll see you get it.'

He spoke quietly in Szechwanese to a young Chinese assistant who indicated the door. 'This way, please, sirs and gentlemen.'

As the others moved away, Dicken gripped O'Buhilly's arm. 'Father, I've seen your patients. I've seen China on the move. I've seen the miracles. But I didn't come *just* for that.'

Father O'Buhilly smiled gently. 'I know, my son,' he said. 'But y'had to know first so that you'll appreciate anythin' she might say to you.'

'Anything she might say? What will she say?'

'That remains to be seen. But you'd surely rather see her on her own, would you not, than in the company of half a dozen others?' He looked at his watch. 'She'll be in her office at this moment. And 'tis no better place there is to talk to her. It's at the back of the building where you won't be interrupted.'

He led the way to a small room at the end of a corridor. Through the open door Dicken saw a Chinese child, its body bandaged, playing with a wooden doll. A Chinese woman was listening to someone he couldn't see, nodding her head. As he started forward, Father O'Buhilly held his arm.

'Let her finish her business,' he said.

Eventually, the Chinese woman nodded and picked up the child. As she passed, Father O'Buhilly moved backwards quietly, leaving Dicken alone, his heart thumping. It was as if he were a schoolboy about to meet a terrifying headmaster over some misdemeanour.

Marie-Gabrielle was standing in a corner, writing in a book. For some reason he had expected her to be wearing uniform like all the nurses he'd ever seen, with starched white skirt and cap. Instead she wore blue cotton trousers and a robe of flowered material. Her face had fined off but she was slim and tall, straight-backed, achingly beautiful, and surrounded by a strange immense calm.

He remained in the doorway, still unseen, wondering how to start a conversation that had been interrupted fourteen years before. Even when he cleared his throat she didn't seem to be aware of him and he finally stepped into the room, suddenly sick with apprehension.

As she turned and her eyes fell on him, she stood motionless for a moment like a statue, the book she'd been writing in still in her hand. Her expression didn't change.

'Dicken,' she said quietly.

With deliberation, she put down the book on the desk and the pen alongside it, then she crossed to him. Half expecting to take her in his arms, he was startled when she held out her hand.

'I don't believe it,' she said. 'I can't believe it.'

-

It was more difficult than he'd expected. She was curiously aloof, her expression unchanged, still caught by that strange calm that seemed to surround her.

'I'll get you tea,' she said, and they talked idly until a Chinese woman brought in a teapot and tiny Chinese cups.

'I suppose you've been busy,' she said, as though she were choosing her words carefully. 'Fighting the war.'

'A little bit,' he said, unhappily aware that the interview was not taking the course he'd expected.

'And now you're here to help against the Japanese?'

'I've been sent to find out something about what's going on, that's all. How the Chinese are doing and what Chiang is doing.'

'The people who run the country from Chungking never come to places like this,' she said sharply. 'They even hate this part of China. They're the intellectuals and they say it's a peasants' war because if we lose a few million peasants, what does it matter? There are plenty more.'

Her anger startled him. It was nothing more than he'd heard a dozen times already, from Americans, British, the Chinese themselves, from Johnson, from Father O'Buhilly; but coming from Marie-Gabrielle, true as he felt it to be, it seemed harsh and accusatory.

'I didn't come here just now to talk of Chiang,' he said slowly and quietly. 'I came to see you.'

There was a long silence while she studied him. Her eyes were steady and he felt strangely embarrassed under her gaze.

'I spent years trying to find you. Years, Marie-Gabrielle. My wife's dead. She was probably dead all the time we were together in Rezhanistan. I discovered within hours of you disappearing. I tried to find you.'

'It's too late, Dicken.' Somehow, in the way she spoke, he sensed that she was listening to him now instead of talking to him. But her calmness worried him. He remembered her as a child, gregarious, happy, swinging on his arm, telling him tall tales, promising to marry him when she was old enough, and in Rezhanistan as a nineteen-year-old girl, vitally alive, still certain there was no one else in the world for her but him. This quiet, reserved, expressionless woman, so unlike the Marie-Gabrielle he remembered, unnerved him a little.

'What did you want of me?' she asked.

'To see you. After Rezhanistan, there was no one I wanted more.'

Her eyes flickered and he seemed to sense a spark of interest. 'That was a long time ago,' she said. 'A very long time ago.'

'Rezhanistan was a long time after Italy where I first met you.' He was suddenly desperate, feeling it required more advocacy than he possessed, to convince her that this new meeting had started an unexpected hope in his breast. 'Nearly eleven years after. You hadn't changed then.'

'I hadn't been to China then.'

'You can't spend your whole life looking after Chinese.'

'Other people have. Many of them. What were you hoping for? Marriage, Dicken?'

It came out bluntly and he was caught wrong-footed, clumsy, searching for the right words to say.

'Other people get married,' he said. 'I went the other day to the wedding of an American pilot who was marrying a nurse.'

'Do you want to marry me?'

In that moment he knew he did. Nothing had been further from his thoughts when he'd agreed to come with Father O'Buhilly. All he'd thought of then was seeing her again, explaining why he'd never found her, trying to make right things that he'd sensed were wrong, to correct the feeling he felt she might have had that he'd betrayed her after getting her out of besieged Rezhanistan. But now he knew that all along at the back of his mind was the hope that she wouldn't have forgotten the promise she'd made as a child that she'd marry him when she was old enough.

'Yes,' he said. 'I do.'

She smiled at last. It was a warm smile and for the first time he felt at ease before her. 'Then, I'm sorry, Dicken, but no.'

'Why not?'

Her cheeks went pink. 'Do I have to explain? Do I have to give a reason?'

The words shook him and disappointment made him bitter. 'My God,' he said, 'you sound like my wife!'

Immediately, her expression changed again and the tartness went out of her voice. Reaching across the desk, she put her hand on his. Turning his palm upwards, he gripped her fingers.

'I didn't mean to, Dicken,' she said. 'I hadn't realised how important it was.' Her eyes searched his face. '*Is* it important? *Really* important?'

'Yes.'

'Not just because you're lonely and hurt because your wife didn't turn out as you expected her to?'

'No.'

She withdrew her hand and sat staring at her fingers for a moment. 'I'm touched, Dicken,' she said. 'I really am. I had no idea.'

'I don't think I had either,' Dicken admitted. 'But when I saw you I knew at once that was what I wanted.'

'What a pity it comes so late.' She sighed. 'I can't leave these people, Dicken. They depend on me.'

He didn't know what to say because he suspected she was right.

'We're moving upriver. Everything here goes tomorrow. Any women who're left behind will be raped when the Japanese come. I tell them to go but they're peasants and their husbands and fathers insist on hanging on because they have a scrap of earth that won't even feed them. The men will be shot and the women taken off for Japanese brothels. That's what always happens. Eventually I shall set up a new hospital in Yuking.' Once again she touched his hand. 'There are other girls in China,' she went on gently. 'American girls. Pretty girls who'll know how to live in a Western city when the war's over.'

'They aren't you!'

As he spoke he knew why he'd never remarried after his wife's death. All the time, through all the years, he'd known at the back of his mind, the idea unspoken, even almost unthought, that he'd hoped to meet her again.

She gave a little smile. 'Some men don't even bother to get married. Men who left their wives in Canton or Shanghai acquired mistresses. They even have families. In a way this war is the making of China. Wealthy children from the coast have grown up speaking the Szechanwese dialect, and men from Shanghai are marrying Cantonese girls, even though their parents wouldn't have understood each other. People who wore smart Western suits and people who wear peasant blue have suddenly realised they're the same people. When Chiang's gone, they'll become a united nation.'

'Christ—' Dicken's anger suddenly burst out '—I didn't come here for a political homily! I don't want a mistress! I want a wife! You! I've reached high rank now. God knows, it hasn't been easy. You remember I talked of Diplock. Well, he's gone now – dead. He's no longer in the way. I could go even higher. I'd like you to go with me.'

She gave him one of her cool smiles, almost as if she were teasing him. 'I no longer have the social manners to fit in with a high-ranking British officer, Dicken,' she said. 'I've lived too long among peasants. It puts me beyond your reach.'

Five

Throughout the meal Marie-Gabrielle was calm and quiet addressing them all, not favouring Dicken more than the others, appearing even to show more interest in Babington, who was much her own age and, like Dicken, had shared the siege of the Legation in Rezhanistan four-teen years before.

Foote was lost in admiration. 'That's a wonderful woman,' he said. 'I just can't imagine her wasted in this backwater.'

When they returned to Chungking the following day, Marie-Gabrielle didn't even bother to see them off. Father O'Buhilly probed gently but Dicken answered him shortly, in no mood to discuss his feelings with anybody.

The priest sighed. 'She didn't want you, boy?' he asked.

Dicken swung round. 'Who said anything about anybody wanting anybody?'

The priest shook his head sadly. 'It was written all over your face. I've seen too much of life not to recognise it.'

It was pointless trying to dissemble. 'No, Father,' Dicken said flatly. 'She didn't want me.'

The priest's great fist rested on his shoulder. 'The Via Crucis was never meant to be easy, boy. An', after all, 'tis no harder to get to Yuking, where she'll be going, than it is to get to Changjao.'

Chungking was covered with a pall of rain. The river was rising and the fog made the slimy alleyways down the hill tunnels of dim greyness.

The rooms where they lived became filled with a misty miasma of chill and they took to wearing their coats throughout the day and sleeping with them on their beds at night. Fires sprang up at the corners of the streets and it became nothing unusual to stumble over a corpse when you went out of doors.

A raw wind was coming down from Siberia and people began to appear in fur-lined coats. Rickshaws with hoods splashed past soldiers in blue quilted uniforms marked with mud, their sandals thin in the sleet-driven puddles.

A sense of purposelessness prevailed. General Loomis grew more short-tempered and his mood spread to everybody else. They were all aware that what was being lifted over the Hump with such loss to brave young Americans was being squandered. Only a few benefited and it was clear that Chiang had no intention of launching an offensive, preferring to let the Americans and the British defeat the Japanese in other theatres while he waited in comfort to draw his share of the spoils at the peace conference.

The visit to Changjao had left Dicken more lonely than ever before. Until he'd seen Marie-Gabrielle again, he hadn't noticed how empty his life had been and the sight of her had made him wonder what he was living for. Johnson was carrying on a heavy affair with an American nurse and even Babington, despite being married, never failed to miss the parties that were held.

A few people who dreamed of bombing Japan were busy building airstrips – at Chungking, Kunming,

Kweiyang and Changsha – and Chinese men, women and children were digging them out almost with their bare hands. Whole villages were being torn down and irrigation systems which had existed for hundreds of years destroyed. But there was always an uneasy feeling that before they came into operation, the Japanese would mount a major campaign to overrun them.

The old Tupolev bombers that they'd seen at the airfield near Changjao were now back in Chungking and the Chinese pilots had been given Ilyushins, which were more modern, even if only slightly so, so that the American pilots were flying the Tupolevs to keep their hands in and to get away from boring desk jobs. Everybody was at it, and there were all sorts of machines – two Gladiators, an ancient DH9 from the days when Chiang had struggled to power, even an old Hawker Hart that was used for ferrying; an old thoroughbred reduced to a cabhorse.

The Japanese attack they'd been expecting started at the end of the winter. Japanese divisions had been moved south from Manchuria where they'd passed the war in idleness, and it burst on the Chinese like a thunderclap and roared across South China, destroying one newly-built airfield after another. Trying to find out what was happening, Dicken and Foote headed north with Johnson and Babington and a Chinese interpreter. The key areas were the gorges of the Yangtze, the bend of the Yellow River, the flanks of Yunnan in the south-west, and the rice bowl in the east. The Japanese had started their probing attacks near Yuking and General Lee was gathering his troops in a wide arc round the river, clusters of men with rusting machine guns and old rifles facing' heavy artillery. Johnson hadn't much faith in them holding.

By the time they reached Changjao Father O'Buhilly had disappeared and the little hospital was filled with exhausted Chinese boys in brown uniforms. Around them the army was in retreat and it didn't take long to find out that the defences had consisted chiefly of two old French 75s with 200 shells between them, a few mortars with no more than twenty bombs each and only 2000 rifles between 14,000 men.

As they passed through the area of the fighting, they saw Chinese soldiers in yellow uniforms spreadeagled on the ground close to the road. Shell holes and bomb craters gaped red in the earth, and among the houses blackened by fire soldiers were carrying a coffin slung on yellow ropes between them. On the river more bodies were floating but not moving with the current because their clothing was caught in the barbed wire that had been erected in the shallows.

There were a few blood-soaked flags in one of the courtyards with captured machine guns, rifles and scattered documents. Among them was a white horse, a splendid animal wearing Japanese accoutrements, which was shell-shocked and whinneying and kept making furious little spurts about the courtyard. In a corner was its owner, dead, his teeth still tightly clenched over a clip of cartridges, his hands bloody and broken. A Chinese soldier who couldn't have been more than thirteen explained. 'He was holding his revolver so tightly, we had to cut his fingers off to get it.'

Despite the casualties they had inflicted, Lee's army was already disintegrating and looting the rice dumps, men staggering off with leaking sacks across their shoulders, indifferent to the outcome of the battle in the prospect of filling their empty bellies.

They had raided the shops in Changjao for food and wine and were setting fire to the petrol stores. Even as the mission drove in, a tremendous explosion shook the earth and roofs lifted in the blast as gold and white flames capped by black oily smoke leapt into the sky. A shed full of ammunition caught fire and tracer bullets began to whiz upwards in red and white arcs like something out of a Disney film.

People caught by the explosion lay with their backs against wrecked buildings, stripped of their clothes, their flesh tattooed with gravel and sand, a few still alive, their blood-caked mouths opening and shutting, their hands clenching and unclenching while refugees plodded by indifferently. Among them an old man had collapsed and his family were heaping straw over the body, while a woman, whose foot had been run over by a cart, had bound the bleeding limb and was hobbling on. A farmer carried his gurgling, laughing baby in a basket strung from a shoulder stave, its weight balanced at the other end with his household goods. Crowds were already gathering at the railway station and had lit fires to warm them as they waited. Most of them were starving and a horse that had fallen dead of exhaustion was being fought over, the carcass already stripped into red slivers.

Near the railway line they found an airfield where two Ilyushins were being prepared for a flight to the safety of Chungking. One of the Chinese pilots agreed to take Dicken up to see the front, and he and Babington climbed into the old bomber which lifted off in a hair-raising take-off that barely cleared the trees at the end of the field.

The countryside was white with early morning frost and in the distance they saw Japanese columns moving forward, circling the Chinese troops in the two great arcs of a pincer movement. The sun was like a fiery red ball in the grey autumn sky. When they landed and reported what they had seen to Colonel Kok, Lee's Chief of Staff, he smiled and informed them that it was his intention to leave the troops where they were to absorb the Japanese thrust.

'They'll be wiped out,' Dicken snapped.

'Victories have to be bought with the blood of soldiers.'

'They could pull back. China's big enough. Where's General Lee?'

'General Lee is in Chungking. The Generalissimo is holding a banquet to be followed by a conference. His generals have been instructed to attend.' Kok smiled coolly. 'We have everything under control. General Lee left precise instructions what to do if the situation deteriorated. He has an excellent plan.'

No matter what Dicken suggested he was met by total indifference and the same blank expression.

'Let's get back to Chungking,' Foote growled. 'Let the general handle it.'

But General Loomis was in a desperate mood, his brows black with anger. 'It's useless, Judge,' he said. 'Stilwell's started throwing his weight behind the Communists now and those guys in Washington are changing their minds. I wish to bejesus I could throw the whole goddam thing up and go home. I wouldn't mind even shooting a Chiang general or two before I went. They're talking now of modernising the Chinese army with the good old US as usual picking up the tab.' He lit a cigar and drew a few desperate puffs at it. 'It'll never work. Stilwell would have to be in charge, and Chiang would never agree to that.'

–

The hopelessness of the situation bore in on them all, depressing them as much as the cold that permeated everything. Occasionally letters arrived by hand from Father O'Buhilly. The Japanese were going through the Chinese armies like a knife through butter. Sick and ill-trained, their weapons faulty, their transport falling to pieces, there were already signs of panic. When soldiers had seized the peasants' oxen to carry their supplies, the peasants had armed themselves with shotguns, knives and pitchforks and started disarming them, first in ones and twos, then in whole companies, until there was nothing at all to face the Japanese.

Then unexpectedly, the priest himself turned up. He was swathed in a huge fur coat and a fur hat with ear muffs, and round his throat was a vast red muffler. He was coldly angry.

'We need help,' he said. 'Whatever help you can give us.' His tone was unfriendly, almost hostile. 'Everybody in Chungking's sittin' on his fat backside and north of Changjao people have died in thousands.'

'Hunger, Father?'

'Not hunger. Murder.'

For a moment the priest shook with rage and seemed unable to get his words out. When they came they were almost incoherent.

'Lee,' he said. 'General Lee. Men, women and children. It was the river.'

253

Dicken dug out a bottle of rye and poured some into a glass. 'Here,' he said. 'Drink that.' Finding a cigarette, he lit it and handed it over. 'Now, get your breath. Sit still and tell me what's happened.'

It was some time before the priest could bring himself to speak. 'You'll be knowin' already,' he said, 'that the Yellow River is known as China's sorrow. With its tributaries it carries more silt than any other waterway in the world, and as the riverbed rises the peasants livin' along the banks are continually raisin' the dykes to prevent it overflowin'. They don't always succeed.'

He begged another cigarette and silently Dicken poured more whisky. 'It's been goin' on for centuries. A struggle between the river and the people. Near Yuking it's twenty-four feet higher than the plain and Lee's soldiers dynamited a hole in the southern bank to stop the Japanese.' He spoke slowly, almost as if the words hurt him. 'It flooded miles of country, drowned thousands in their sleep and left thousands more starvin'. The river was high and I heard the roar as it escaped. Four towns and five hundred villages are under water and all next year's crops will be ruined as well because the soil's washed away.' The priest choked. 'It'll take years to repair the dykes. 'Twas one of the most callous acts in history and it was done because Chiang didn't want to commit his armies, which he wants to guard him against the Communists, and Lee didn't want to lose the loot he's been collectin' for years.'

Dicken swung round to snatch up a map which he spread on the table. 'Go on,' he said. 'Where?'

Father O'Buhilly fished under all the clothing he was wearing to produce a pair of spectacles. They were bent and one of the lenses was cracked but he peered through them at the map and jabbed with a finger as thick as a banana. 'There,' he said.

'And you need help?'

Father O'Buhilly shook his head slowly from one side to the other. 'That was only me anger. There *is* no help. Nothin' can be done for them. All we can do is rescue the babies. Surely God in His infinite mercy will allow us to do that. Surely the little ones have a right to life.'

'How're you going to get them out, Father?' Dicken asked. 'If the country's flooded, you can't use vehicles. Is there anywhere we can fly them out from?'

The priest's head jerked up, and his eyes shone. He indicated his glass. 'We've had two, boy. Why not complete the Holy Trinity?' As he swallowed, he smiled for the first time. 'Bless you, my son. I knew I could rely on you to think of somethin'. Yes, there is a patch of flat land at Sushan. It sticks out from the road like a tongue into the floods. Planes have landed there before. Lee used it on the few occasions when he joined his troops.'

'If he can, Father, we can.'

'Heaven's blessin's on you, me boy.'

'Let's have young Babington in on this. Perhaps even Walt Foote. They're all on your side.'

When Babington arrived, Dicken sent him for Foote, who brought Johnson with him, and they all crowded round the map.

'All I'm askin',' Father O'Buhilly said, 'is for the little ones to be saved.'

Dicken looked at Johnson. 'Can we raise an aeroplane?' he asked.

'Sir,' Johnson said. 'Right here in China there aren't any airplanes nobody wants.'

'What about those old Tupolevs? They can't be used against the Japanese. They probably can't be used for this even, but it might persuade the war correspondents to get a story out to the rest of the world. If they did, we might get something better.'

'Do we have anybody who knows how to fly these goddam Tupolevs?' Foote asked.

'I'll fly one,' Johnson said. 'I've flown one already. George Moreno'll fly another. He's a buddy of mine. And he'll know other guys. They'll be glad to do something instead of sitting on their asses here.'

'What about petrol and ground crews?'

'I'll get 'em,' Foote promised. 'The general will swallow this whole. The poor guy's eating his heart out at not being able to do anything worthwhile.'

Six

The Chinese were avoiding any mention of the disaster and the commander at the airfield was nervous about using his aeroplanes without permission, so that it took hours of arguing to persuade him.

He still remained uncertain that the old Tupolevs could land, despite everything that Father O'Buhilly said, but in the end he produced the ancient Hawker Hart and offered it to Dicken to fly in to find a landing area.

There was a saying among airmen that an aeroplane that looked good was usually good to fly, and the Hart was no exception. She had been built as a light day bomber, converted because of her high performance to a two-seater fighter and finally developed through a number of variants. In Sweden, where she had been used as a dive bomber with such success that even the RAF had been aroused by the techniques, she had maintained a diving angle of 80-85 degrees, what the US Marines had called 'When we say down, we mean *straight* down.'

She still looked a thoroughbred, despite the fact that the canvas wings and fuselage were covered with sewn-up tears and there were oil smears on the cowling. Though the guns had been removed, the heavy armadillo turret was still in place. In 1932 she had been considered an excellent machine, elegant, clean and capable of carrying

500lb of bombs beneath the wings and fuselage. At the moment she didn't look capable even of getting off the ground. But when they checked the old Kestrel engine it still seemed to work and Dicken looked at Babington.

'You've flown with me in some bloody funny aeroplanes, Bab,' he said. 'Are you willing to have a go in this?'

Babington studied the automatic turret. 'We used to say that with that thing the gunner had more control of the aircraft than the pilot. And the trouble with them was that when the aircraft banked, they ran away and you found yourself hanging head down, staring at nothing.'

The old machine struggled into the sky over the peaks of the hills and within half an hour they could see the broad expanse of water where the river had overflowed. Descending near Changjao, they saw ruined villages and the drifting wreckage of houses and barns. The riverbank showed a gaping hole through which the water was still flowing in a trickle.

They found a raised road from Changjao and followed it northwards, eventually seeing what appeared to be a large island, flat and almost treeless, lifting just above the water level. At one end was a group of buildings, one of them larger than the rest, fluttering above it a white flag with a red cross in the centre.

With no idea what the ground was like, Dicken flew low over the patch of isolated land, looking for a suitable landing strip. Eventually he found what appeared to be a large field surrounded by paddles and, with no idea what the surface was like, lifted the nose and let the machine drift in. She settled gently and ran barely twenty yards before she came to a stop.

Immediately, from the group of buildings people started to run towards them. As they climbed down, the crowd surrounded the machine, chattering in their high-pitched dialect. Eventually they parted and Dicken saw Marie-Gabrielle approaching. Her face was alight with hope but when she saw him her face became bleak, shut-in and wary.

'Oh,' she said. 'It's you. I haven't changed my mind.'

'I didn't come to ask you to,' Dicken said shortly. 'Father O'Buhilly asked for help. I've come to bring it. I gather you've got a lot of children here.'

She frowned at his tone, and gestured to the buildings behind her. 'Around five hundred.'

'We're hoping to fly them out.'

'They'll need adults to help.'

'We can take a few. Even you, if you choose to go. Foote's organising transport to Chungking. Let's have a look at the driest part of this place.'

She led the way, her robe flapping in the wind, her feet lumps of muddy clay. At the other end of the stretch of land the ground was higher and better drained, and seemed hard.

'It's rock underneath,' she said. 'That's why it's never been cultivated. If it had been reasonable soil – or for that matter *un*reasonable – they'd have grown something.'

For an hour or more Dicken and Babington walked backwards and forwards, every now and then thrusting a stick into the earth where it seemed dangerously soft. Standing at the end of the field they were able to plot a landing area with only a small clump of trees and a line of brushwood in the way.

'Can we get those moved?' Dicken asked. 'We'll also need the rocks lifting and the holes filled in.'

'It can be done.' Marie-Gabrielle still sounded wary. 'There are enough people here and most of them have tools. Those who haven't, have their hands.'

Within minutes, the field was swarming with men and women. The first of the trees was down in a quarter of an hour and stones and rubble were being pushed into the hole it left. More people were hacking at the brush and a long column of women was bringing baskets of soil to fill other holes. More blue-clad figures were pushing barrows and chopping at the earth, yellow ants with strange medieval tools, hacking yard by yard at the length of the strip they had chosen. A shallow ditch that ran across it was filled, the men shovelling to the sound of a pre-arranged rhythm, and by late afternoon they could see the strip taking shape.

–

Foote hadn't been idle. By the time Dicken returned, he had the general's promise of help and had collected cartons of American canned and packeted food.

'He said "Thank God there's something useful we can do at last,"' Foote grinned. 'He's right behind us and the war correspondents see it as a good story. We've contacted the nurses at the US hospital and they're ready. The US ground crew chief's on our side, too. There'll be no Liberators or anything like that but we've got two of the Tups ready and there'll probably be a third tomorrow.'

The first Tupolev took off early the following morning, piloted by Johnson, followed soon afterwards by the other, piloted by his friend, the dark-haired spaniel-eyed pilot called Moreno. They were five-to six-seat heavy bombers with four BMW engines, old and out of date, their best performance – which they hadn't achieved for years – in the region of 124 miles per hour, their ceiling only 10,000 feet, their range no more than 620 miles. They had undercarriages like inverted tripods, each side with two wheels, and their noses looked like gazebos. With Father O'Buhilly in the rear cockpit of the Hart, a scarf wound round his fur cap and crammed down low behind the armadillo shield, Dicken was already waiting in the air, and the Tupolevs lined up behind him.

Babington had been left behind at Sushan to light smudge fires to give the wind direction and Dicken slipped down and landed, quickly turning off the airstrip out of the way of the first of the bombers. The big machine floated in behind him, its propellers turning slowly, bounced gently, settled, and rolled to a stop. Immediately, dozens of people marshalled by Babington formed up round it and dragged it out of the way so the second could land.

The Chinese were yelling and chattering in their high-pitched sing-song voices, some of them so excited they were standing on their hands and turning somersaults. Then, suddenly, the uproar died. One of the men pointed. Their heads turned and, as they did so, a car appeared from behind the buildings. It was followed by a second and a third. They were full of Chinese officers and Dicken recognised the man alongside the driver of the first car as Colonel Kok. He faced Dicken, smiling.

'How clever of you to think of aeroplanes,' he said. 'It will save us a long and dreary journey by road.'

'These aircraft are for the rescue of children,' Dicken snapped.

Kok gestured. 'Children can't save China, and those are Chinese aircraft. Have you my government's permission to use them for this purpose?'

The authorities in Chungking had maintained only a sullen silence, but Dicken lied that it had, and he saw Father O'Buhilly lift his hand, two fingers raised, in a gesture of absolution. Just beyond him, Johnson, his cap with its broken visor crushed on the back of his head, stood with Moreno and their co-pilots, their faces angry.

Kok obviously didn't believe Dicken. 'I need those aeroplanes for myself and my staff,' he said. 'Step aside.'

As the Chinese began to move forward, Dicken yanked his revolver from its holster and shoved the muzzle against his head. The click as he pulled the hammer back was loud in the silence and he saw Marie-Gabrielle's hand go to her throat. One of the Chinese reached for his weapon.

'He'd better not use that thing,' Dicken said. 'If he does, you'll sure as hell die as well.'

Kok's eyes swivelled but he didn't move his head. He gestured to the officer, whose hand dropped to his side.

'Tell your men to throw down their weapons, Colonel. If one of them makes a move, you're dead. Very dead. This is a .38 and they make a mess at this range.'

For a long time Kok stood stock-still, then he spoke in Chinese. The officers turned from the aircraft and grouped themselves by the cars.

'Now their weapons.'

As the officers threw down their weapons, Dicken gestured. 'Pick 'em up, Bab.'

Helped by the other airmen, Babington started to collect the revolvers and swords and Dicken saw that Marie-Gabrielle was helping too.

'Now get back in your cars,' he said. 'When this is over you'll find your weapons where you dropped them. Go.'

As the cars vanished, the first children were brought from the buildings and were pushed into the aircraft. Immediately the singing started, high-pitched and monotonous, and they could hear it even as the engines revved up and the Tupolev began to taxi down the field. As it soared over Dicken's head, trailing a plume of grey smoke, they were already pushing children into the second machine.

–

The airlift went on all day. During the afternoon, when they were beginning to wonder if they could get more than they had expected out of the island, the incoming machine brought Foote.

'Old Dogleg's creating trouble,' he said, his face grim. 'He claims we're using petrol to save useless lives. He says his army needs the Tupolevs and he wants to know why we refused to lift out Lee's staff. The general's handling him.'

'I hope he can go on handling him just a bit longer,' Dicken said. 'We've got most of the kids out. If we can just hang on a little longer, we can get the sick out too.'

The Tupolevs continued to come in at two-hourly intervals until dark. The last one brought Foote again.

'We can keep going tomorrow,' he said. 'But the general's in a wrangle with Chiang who's mad enough to bite the heads off nails. That goddam Kok signalled him from some place down the road. I reckon you're finished, boy.'

As Foote flew off again, Dicken walked towards the hospital. Father O'Buhilly was just ushering the remaining children in to a sparse meal.

'You've got to leave tomorrow, Father,' Dicken said.

The priest turned. 'This is where I live, boy,' he pointed out gently.

'Not any more, Father.'

The priest led him into the little room where he slept. It was as bare as every room Dicken ever remembered him occupying, nothing but a bed, a table, an upright chair, and a shelf where he kept his missal, his breviary, his New Testament, and the works of a few favourite saints.

'What happened?' he asked.

'Chiang's raising hell and claiming the Tupolevs back. Foote thinks General Loomis can stave him off until tomorrow night. But it's the end for me. I'm held responsible. They'll also hold you responsible. You'll never be able to carry on here when it's over.'

The priest shook his head slowly. 'Sure, I've never believed in hell,' he said, 'but I'd like to, if only to see people like Chiang and Lee and Colonel Kok there.' He nodded. 'Very well. I'm ready to go. What about Marie-Gabrielle?'

'She'll have to go too.'

'Who's going to tell her?'

'I will.'

Father O'Buhilly sighed. 'I've prayed for you both.'

'Perhaps,' Dicken said, 'God's a bit hard of hearing.'

–

Marie-Gabrielle looked up as Dicken appeared in the doorway of her office. Somehow, he sensed a warmer attitude towards him and wondered how she would react to his news.

'I'm grateful, Dicken,' she said. 'You haven't changed. I always thought you were brave and honest. You still are.'

'I'm not all that honest,' he admitted. 'I've known something for some time that I haven't dared tell you. *You've* got to go, too.'

She frowned and he hurried on to explain. 'Father O'Buhilly's also got to go. I'm in trouble, it seems, but I think this place will be in worse trouble. You'll never be allowed to stay. I'm sorry.'

'Where can I go? I haven't got anywhere.'

'You have if you want it.'

She gave him a quick glance and was silent for a moment before she spoke. 'I've lived here too long.'

'They can use nurses at the American hospital in Chungking. They'd even fly you to India if you wished, and there's one sure way of making them. They're going to declare me *persona non grata*. If I had a wife she'd doubtless have to be flown out, too.'

The sustaining anger seemed to drain from her body. Her shoulders sagged wearily and there was something forlorn in the way her hands hung limply at her side. For a long time she didn't speak; when she did her words came unhappily.

'It was years after Rezhanistan,' she said, 'when I learned your wife was dead, and then I had no idea where you were or how to find you. I decided by that time you must have remarried.'

'Well, I didn't. Marry me, Marie-Gabrielle.'

'I'm Catholic.'

'I don't care if you're a Turk, a Mormon, a Rosicrucian or even a bloody fire-worshipper.'

For the first time she smiled and, taking a step forward, she put her cheek against his. His arms went round her and they clung to each other, laughing at themselves. Then she pushed him away gently. 'But it makes no difference, Dicken,' she said quietly. 'We're both too old.'

–

Father O'Buhilly left in the first machine the following day, sitting in the cockpit alongside Moreno. The machine that flew in two hours later was a different one with a different pilot and contained Foote.

'The general reckons he can hold off old Dogleg until we're finished,' he said. 'There's just one thing—' his face grew hard '—Moreno's engines cut on landing just as we left. It didn't burn, though, and they seemed to be gettin' everybody out.'

Even as Foote flew out, Johnson returned. 'You heard about Georgie Moreno?' he asked.

'He crashed.'

'Yeah. All the kids were saved, though. A few of 'em were burned but none of 'em bad. She broke in two and those Chinese teachers got 'em out fast.'

'And Moreno?'

Johnson shook his head. 'Not Georgie.' He paused. 'Nor Father O'Buhilly.'

Seven

The celebrations among the foreign element in Chungking at outwitting Chiang and his generals were muted for Dicken by the disappearance into an American hospital from which she never seemed to emerge of Marie-Gabrielle. Several times he called, trying to see her, but there were always excuses – she was off duty, she had gone somewhere with one of the American nurses, she was too busy – so that it wasn't hard to form the opinion that she was dodging him. With the death of Father O'Buhilly, it left him empty of feeling and with the certainty that his time in China was growing short. He wasn't wrong.

Hatto arrived from India, angry that he had managed to combat all Diplock's evil influences throughout Dicken's career only for him to ruin everything as he reached high rank by getting involved in the taboo subject of Chinese politics.

'Officers of your rank aren't asked to leave an ally's country,' he said. 'What the hell happened?'

Foote came into the explanations and Hatto listened carefully. He seemed to appreciate what had occurred and when he had visited General Loomis he was in no doubt.

'Don't worry,' he said. 'We'll fight it. The general's on our side.'

As he flew back to India, Dicken, expecting his orders to leave almost hourly, was surprised to find they didn't come, and he could only put it down to the changing attitudes. Suddenly the Communists, because they were fighting and Chiang was not, were being regarded as an unexpected ally.

'Those wise guys in Washington are turning somersaults,' General Loomis announced. 'And as always, they don't do the thing by halves. They're beginning to see the Communists now as Jeffersonian democrats, and there are plans that when the Japanese throw their hands in at the end of the war, their weapons will go straight to them so they can kick out old Dogleg. I hope to bejesus they're right because I have a feeling we'll have put one bogey down only to raise another.'

It was still bitterly cold and the walls of the offices and rooms in Chungking seemed to drip moisture. However, with their incredible energy, the Americans were beginning to make themselves comfortable, and it was a comfort which they generously spread to the other Allied missions. Then, towards the end of the winter, American correspondents scenting a scoop north of Chengshan came back with horrific stories of famine. Lee's blowing in of the dykes near Yuking had forced people nearer to Chengshan and the flooded fields gave no hope of crops. A relief effort had been started but it was marked by lethargy and inefficiency, and tax collectors were still trying to wring money out of the wretched people, while soldiers were rounding up men so weak they could hardly walk to collect fodder for their horses.

'Lee's retreating with the whole of his goddam army,' Foote said. 'He's pulling out with all his men. He has a convoy of vehicles a mile long.' His hand moved across the map on his desk. 'Here. Moving south with the refugees between him and the enemy.'

The story of disaster left the Chungking government unruffled, and with their usual emotional generosity it was the Americans who organised the convoys of lorries north. In one of them was a group of American nurses, medical officers and missionaries in fur caps, parkas and heavy boots, and among them was Marie-Gabrielle.

As the lorries disappeared Dicken left once more with Foote, Johnson and Babington in one of the old Tupolevs. As they landed at Chengshan, peasant families were already sprawled in acres waiting for trains to take them to safety in the west. Many had come in old and battered trains that had sneaked past the Japanese artillery in the night, riding on flat cars and in boxcars and ancient carriages, bracing themselves on the roofs in the freezing cold so that fingers became numb and they fell off to the track, but most had come under their own power, by cart or barrow or on foot.

The Americans were quick to set up radio stations, tents and marquees and organise soup kitchens. As the starving people queued up, all round the airfield were thousands more, here and there little food shops conspic-uous in the growing darkness by the blue flames of their stoves and the smell of frying.

Several times Dicken saw Marie-Gabrielle, bulky in padded clothing, near the tents of the American hospital, but he was never able to get her on her own. He was convinced by now that she was avoiding him but he could never be sure whether it was because she distrusted him or because she distrusted herself.

In an attempt to round up refugees, Dicken drove with Babington into the town in a lorry. There had been a fire that had gutted booths and godowns and their wreckage was strewn across the cobblestones in a litter of smashed earthenware and frayed flapping cane matting. The wind lifted drifts of yellow paper, fragments of cloth and loose straw and chaff, and a red streamer twirled where it had caught on a projection.

The city's population had been cut to a quarter of its normal numbers. Bombed, shelled and occupied in the past by the Japanese, the place could offer no comfort to the starving hordes. Buildings were empty shells, devoid of roofs, and the people who appeared from doorways, tottering on their feet and spreading their hands to ask for food, seemed like ghosts.

Lying alongside a doorway was a girl in her teens, her body only half-covered, as though someone had snatched away her outer garments for their own use. Her lips were black, exposing white even teeth, her hair frozen into the mud and snow of the roadway. Further on they found other bodies, an old woman beneath a table in a doorway, an old man, a child, its legs and arms like sticks. The whole town stank of urine and human filth and of the people who shivered in the cold, their grey and blue rags stirred by the bitter wind. Over the hordes of wretched people, steaming breath rose in clouds, and their eyes were like dark holes in expressionless masks. More people lay in the gutters. One or two who were still alive were lifted into the lorries to be taken to the hospital tents, but most were already dead. A woman in rags clutching a baby rose as they stopped alongside her; but as she did so the baby fell from her trembling hands into the snow and started to cry pitifully.

As snow began to fall, deadening the footsteps, the town became a tomb peopled by desperate grey-faced ghosts. In the evening, the hordes of starving people round the open kitchens of the food shops, their eyes watching every morsel as it was cooked and eaten, suddenly and unexpectedly made a rush. Pots were upset and hands snatched what they could reach in a desperate silence, as if their owners had no energy for speaking. As they hurried away, children followed them.

'K'o lien! K'o lien! Mercy! Mercy!'

The members of the mission had filled their pockets with food from the American forces canteen and as they tried to give it away, the children snatched at it, their tear-stained faces smudgy and lost, small shrunken scarecrows with pus-filled slits for eyes. Starvation had made their hair dry and brittle, hunger had given them bloated bellies, their skins were chapped and raw, and their voices had shrunk to an unhappy muling.

The neighbouring villages were even worse. There the silence was terrifying. The countryside was bare and the streets deserted, doors and windows flapping open, and echoing with emptiness. Fields had been stripped and peasants living on peanut husks were searching the heaps of refuse for rejected scraps of edible material. Some even crammed earth into their mouths to fill their empty bellies, and people like spectres were skimming the green scum from pools for food.

A dog digging at the turned earth had exposed a body and they found the corpse of a woman clutching the cold ground. She had once been pretty but now her body was grey-blue, a thin rain moulding her clothes to the lines of her frame. Here and there, however, hardier characters were still trying, with clubs in their hands, to guard their spring wheat, knowing that if it was stolen, they would be joining the hungry mob. And even now the Chinese instinct for trading was at work, and people had chipped bark from trees and pounded it for food, which they were selling with leaves and a scrap of sauce.

By the time they returned the hospital tents had become like scenes from Doré's pictures of hell. Marie-Gabrielle, her face haunted, was feeding two children who had been brought in. Desperate with hunger, their parents had tied them to a tree so they couldn't follow as they searched for food. Another family, she said, had been sent by their mother to search for food and when they had returned had found her dead, the baby still at her breast.

'We've even heard of parents killing their children rather than see them starve,' she said in shocked tones. 'And of whole families committing suicide. And cannibalism! Cannibalism! The whole thing's too big!'

Tears streamed down her face as she spoke. 'I think I'm tired of despair,' she said.

'It could be,' Dicken said bluntly, 'that you're just tired.'

The following day the enormous throng of misery heaved and began to move. Small groups began to set off across the plain, like the broken remnants of a string of beads, bunched together, their heads down against the wind. Two people who couldn't keep up lay in the snow sobbing their desolation.

'Jesus,' Foote said bitterly. 'I always thought of the Chinese as a lively lot. Misery's made these poor bastards mute.'

The silent horde passed the airfield slowly, shuffling past in a soundless hush that was broken only by the scrape of feet and the squeak of carts. They walked mechanically, concentrating on getting one foot in front of the other. A man pushed a barrow, the figure lying on it covered with a blanket, the naked feet covered with goose-flesh, the limp head wobbling. Fathers dragged carts, mothers pulled at ropes, their eyes unseeing, their backs to the cold wind and the destroyed land.

The old Russian bombers ferried American supplies and medicaments but it was like trying to hold back the flood. Even the old Hart was brought into service, with Dicken and Babington flying from one bare, empty patch of land to another to inform the Americans where the refugees were gathering.

Then, with Foote heading south to raise more supplies, Babington, who had been north, travelling on a pony with a Chinese interpreter, risking his life among peasants more than willing to kill anyone with transport, brought back a new story.

'That column of Lee's, sir,' he said. 'It doesn't contain weapons or supplies. No soldiers. No officers. Not even a snot-nosed little boy bugler. It's the loot he's gathered round him over the last four years. I was in Chingku when it stopped and I saw the lorries. They're stuffed with furniture, carpets, chests and God knows what. He's using his troops to push the refugees between him and the Japanese.'

–

There was still snow on the summits of the mountains as the Hart lifted off and the land between looked bare

273

and bleak and empty. The refugees were all moving in the direction of Chungking along a wide road that wound round the hills, a long stream of human beings, with here and there an ox, a donkey, a mule or an odd cart, thousands of blue-clad figures trying to struggle to safety. As they flew low over them, a few waved but for the most part they continued to plod on indifferently, their eyes on the road.

Just ahead of them the road divided so that the junction looked like an upside-down Y. The Japanese were coming down the main leg from the north, a mass of lorries in a briskly-moving column. Among them Dicken could see guns and carts carrying machine guns. Then, swinging south, one eye on the swarm of refugees coming down the western arm of the Y, he saw that on the other arm troops were stationed across the road, behind them a string of lorries that he recognised as General Lee's. They were facing north, their weapons directed towards the junction of the arms of the Y. Behind them was a bridge over a steep gorge. It was Lee's intention to fire on the refugees to force them north into the path of the advancing Japanese.

When they returned to the airstrip Foote was holding a signal flimsy.

'You're for home, Buster,' he said bluntly to Dicken. 'The general couldn't hold off Chiang any longer. You and Stilwell both. You go as soon as your relief can fly in. He's on his way now with Willie Hatto who's coming to protest. The general fought as long as he could but old Dogleg had all the aces.'

Dicken frowned and explained what they'd seen.

'There's nothing we can do,' Foote argued.

'We can blow that bloody bridge out,' Dicken said. 'One good bomb on it and Lee's lorries will be stranded and so will the Japanese, because *they're* using wheels as well.'

'What about the refugees?'

'Nothing will stop *them*. They'll go into the gorge or over the hills. They'll manhandle their barrows and carts and lead their animals.'

'Okay. But who's going to drop the goddam bomb?'

'I am.'

'What from, for Christ's sake?'

Dicken slapped the canvas side of the Hart. It sounded like a drum. 'This,' he said.

Eight

'For God's sake,' Dicken said fiercely. 'You must remember Udet, Walt!'

Foote frowned. 'Sure I remember Udet. He used to pick up handkerchieves with his wingtip. He was always doing the American air shows. He made films. He shot himself in 1941.'

'There was more to Udet than that,' Dicken said. 'He was the best seat-of-the-pants pilot I ever met. He was the man who persuaded the Luftwaffe to go in for dive bombing.'

'Well, go on. What the hell's Udet to do with this?'

'You know where he got his dive bomber idea? From United States Marines dropping flourbag bombs into small whitewashed circles. I was with him when he saw it done. He bought a couple of Curtisses and took them back to Berlin and Goering went overboard for them. And, because they could build two or three Stukas as cheaply as one four-engined job, they put everything they'd got into them. It probably lost the war for them.'

Foote was staring at him, bewildered.

'It's not new,' Dicken urged. 'Some bloke called Bonney did it as long ago as 1915 with a little Moissant against the rebels in Mexico. He carried home-made bombs fired by rifle cartridges.'

Foote came to life. 'This isn't 1915.' He indicated the Hart. 'And that isn't a dive bomber.'

'It's been used as one.'

'Adapted. Stressed for the job. That isn't.'

'It'll have to do. The Swedes dived them vertically and were getting sixty-seven per cent success. One of your countrymen claimed a hundred per cent.'

'The bastard was probably boasting. And it was in a Curtiss F8C. And without opposition.'

'There won't be opposition.'

'Don't kid yourself, Dicko,' Foote rapped. 'There'll be opposition. A hell of an opposition. Lee won't let someone rob him of his loot without putting up a fight. Besides, with a big bomb underneath, that old contraption'll be like a hummingbird trying to carry a walnut around. He wouldn't get off the ground and neither will you.'

'We've got to take a chance,' Dicken insisted. 'Can you fly me a couple of big ones up here, together with a bomb rack and a couple of riggers to fit it underneath this old has-been?'

'You'll never get away with it.'

Dicken shrugged, thinking of Marie-Gabrielle. 'I'm an old has-been too, Walt. It won't matter much.'

–

The bombs, the bomb rack and the fitters arrived within eight hours. Johnson, who flew them in with one of the Tupolevs, was puzzled.

'Who the hell are we going to bomb?' he asked.

When Foote told him, he gave Dicken a quick look. 'Sooner you than me,' he said.

'I'll need a bit of back-up,' Dicken said. 'If I'm hit I'll head south and follow the road. God knows how far I'll get – canvas aeroplanes don't stand up to cannon fire much – but it'd be nice to know somebody's coming to meet me.'

'We'll be there,' Johnson said. 'And I'll be over the top of you. I've brought more than one bomb.'

As they all disappeared to check the Hart and its bomb fittings, Marie-Gabrielle arrived. She looked tired but her eyes were glowing with anger. Dicken was in the tent studying the map when she appeared, and she went into the attack at once.

'They tell me you're going to try to kill yourself,' she said. 'Why? Why?'

'You could say it's because I don't like Lee. But I also don't like the thought of those refugees being pushed into the path of the Japanese.'

'You'd do this for them?'

'You're not the only one with a touch of compassion.'

She gave him a strange look, her eyes shining. 'You can't do it.'

'Does it matter?'

'It always mattered.'

He stared at her, feeling a stir of panic. He was suddenly in desperate need of some bedrock truths from her as armour in his confusion.

'*I* tried hard to prove it did,' he said. 'But you never showed much damned interest.'

'I was wrong.'

He stared at her, a sudden knot of hope in his stomach. 'What made you change your mind?'

'Many things. This particularly.'

'Foote says I've got to go home. I've had orders.'

'I'll go with you.'

'Do you mean that?'

'I'd expect any children to be brought up as Catholics.'

He grinned. It was as good as a surrender. 'Making conditions isn't the way to enter a compact of this sort,' he said gently.

'I'd want children.'

'Well, I'm a bit long in the tooth these days but—' Dicken smiled again '—I expect I could manage one or two.'

She held out her hands and, as he took them, she flung her arms round him. The wind against the tent was like the claws of a tiny furred animal scratching vainly at a wall for freedom. Then he heard her whisper close to his ear.

'Don't go, Dicken.'

He held her at arm's length and looked at her. 'What's happened to all that compassion? All that eagerness to do something for your flock?'

She shook her head and he saw tears on her cheek. 'Damn my flock!'

He put his arms round her again. 'I'm afraid you've transferred your compassion to me,' he said. 'I can't damn your flock.'

'What happens if you don't come back?'

'In that case,' he said soberly, 'you'll have to learn to live with it. A lot of people have had to do that in this war.'

—

She was watching as he climbed into the Hart. The big bomb was hanging beneath, a menacing shape, painted a

279

dull grey that was the same colour as the sky. A Tomahawk had just landed. The pilot, who had flown north from one of the overrun airfields in the south, appeared alongside the Hart. He wore a grin that seemed to spread from ear to eat

'This here's Ratowicz,' Johnson said. 'He says he'll help, too.'

Ratowicz's grin grew wider. 'Sure, I'll help,' he said. 'I'll come down from the opposite side. I know what to do. We used to practise with four planes attacking at once in cloverleaf pattern to confuse the defences.'

As the chocks were dragged away and he opened the throttle, Dicken saw that Marie-Gabrielle had now taken up a position just ahead, a forlorn figure that suddenly started waving frantically.

He climbed to 10,000 feet, the old Hart responding like the thoroughbred it was. Glancing upwards, he saw Johnson leading the old Tupolevs, their silhouettes black against the sky, behind them, higher still, the Tomahawk.

The mountains were like a tumbled green and grey tablecloth cut into peaks and valleys and the air was the misty blue that only an airman knew. As it always did, it tugged at his heart and made him feel privileged that he should catch the touch of the sun before it reached down to humbler fellow mortals, and he suddenly wondered if this were to be the last time he'd ever look on it.

Seeing the road, he dropped down to get a better view. The refugees had almost reached the junction and he could see Lee's troops waiting with machine guns and knew he had to succeed. Even if the Hart hadn't been designed as a dive bomber, it had been used as one and could go down like a lift, and it was up to him to do the rest. He offered up a silent prayer that it wouldn't fly out of its wings. Father O'Buhilly would have approved. He never minded letting God know what was expected of Him.

Let me do this properly, he begged, and suddenly he found it wasn't merely to stop the Japanese or save a horde of helpless people, but to exact some measure of vengeance against the man who had humiliated him as a prisoner years before. If only for Father O'Buhilly who had shared it with him. Memory was a strange thing and old miseries flooded back unexpectedly. In the same way that stupid words came from the past to embarrass, old humiliations brought the scalding desire for revenge.

He dropped down further and realised suddenly that because of a kink in the road that Lee's men held, the bridge ran almost north and south and, with the wind blowing from the south, he would have to make his approach over the Japanese column to drop his bomb along the main span.

As he flew north to turn into the upright of the upturned Y, he thought of Marie-Gabrielle and what she'd said. Suddenly he felt that what he was attempting was the job of a young man, and he found he was afraid, especially now that at last she had shown he meant something to her. For a moment, he held the bank, circling, unable to bring himself to make the decision, but he'd always been a man who'd faced unpleasant facts squarely and, levelling off, he turned into his dive path.

The Japanese had seen him now and he saw their guns begin to fire. Shells exploded close by, then as he dropped lower, tracer came floating gently towards him, growing faster and faster until it whizzed past. Other weapons opened up and he saw the men below him firing their rifles in groups under the orders of their officers. The Hart shuddered and dipped and he could hear the wind screaming.

More tracer came up at him, like coloured golf balls, and he could feel whacks against the fuselage and see rents appearing in the wings. The Hart was already a mass of holes when he felt a burning sensation in his leg. Glancing down, he saw his flying boot bore a neat pattern of what looked like buttonholes, but it was only as the blood started flowing that he realised he'd been hit.

The Hart was shaking badly now, her fabric tattered like an old blanket. She was rotating gently round her own axis but the movement could be controlled and he used one of the projections above the engine in front of him as a sight. Out of the corner of his eye he could see Ratowicz going down from the opposite direction, lower than he was, and the fire faltering as the men below couldn't make up their minds whom to fire at. Then he was over the Japanese column, still almost vertical, his eyes all the time on the wooden bridge. The refugees were starting to scatter across the slopes on either side of the road and he saw Lee's officers running as it dawned on them what he was intending.

As they slapped at their men, a fresh fusillade came up at him. Something hit him in the side that seemed to paralyse his leg but, by concentrating, thinking of nothing else, he found he could make it work. The thin line of the bridge grew larger and larger until it seemed to fill the whole of his vision and he could see the faces of Lee's men staring up at him. As he pulled the release, he felt the bomb drop away and the old plane lifted as it was freed of its weight. Heaving back on the stick, he almost blacked out as the nose rose, and the blood sank to his heels as the machine shuddered in protest. There was a bang beneath him somewhere and for a moment he thought the wings had collapsed, but the machine continued to fly. He felt it hit again and again. The Germans had discovered in 1940 that their Stukas were vulnerable as they pulled out of their dives and the old Hart was no Stuka.

Then out of the corner of his eye he saw an aeroplane approaching from his left. Ratowicz, he thought. Coming in to help. Then he realised it wasn't Ratowicz. It was a machine he'd never seen before and it had red meatballs painted on its wings and fuselage.

Christ! He jerked his head round. It was a Japanese! Where the hell had that come from? Just when he'd thought he'd made it, too!

He put the Hart into a tight turn as the Japanese came in and it missed its pass. Holding the turn, his head pulled round until his neck ached. He watched it come in again. There was no use fleeing because if he did the Japanese would have him at once. His only hope was the Hart's manoeuvrability.

He had not managed to regain any height and they were close to the slope of the hills. The Japanese machine shot past again, its guns going, and fear caught Dicken by the throat and stopped him breathing. Covered with sweat, sticky and clammy under his clothes, he suddenly realised that he was also being shot at by a machine gun placed in a tower on the side of the hill, and he turned in alarm.

The Japanese aircraft came round again, screaming past him, just missing the tower as it pulled up. Holding the

Hart in its turn through all the tracer that was coming at him, unable to think of anything else to do, Dicken was looking desperately for some avenue of escape, some twisting valley he might dive down where the Japanese with his greater speed wouldn't dare follow.

Now he was between the Japanese aircraft and the machine gun on the hill. The tracer was passing just above him when he suddenly saw the chance he'd been wanting and edged closer to the slope. He heard the bullets from the tower hitting the Hart, then the Japanese aeroplane came screaming in once more. As the Hart turned under him, the Japanese pilot tried to follow but he lost height in his bank and touched the slope with his wingtip. The machine wobbled, lifted and finally hit the machine gun post. It cut the tower in half, and the wooden frame flew into the air so that the cluster of men on it collapsed into space. The machine crashed just beyond, cartwheeling end over end to smash through a group of little houses with a terrific flash, the engine rolling out in a whirlwind of flames and fragments that flew into the sky.

Pulling the stick back, Dicken found his stomach contracting in a wave of nausea. The advantage of flying alone, he thought wearily, was that you could be sick with fear without anyone seeing.

Just ahead of him was a steep hill and for a moment he thought he was going to hit it. But the Hart just managed to stagger over it and, turning, aware that his leg was growing stiff, he swung back over the bridge. It had vanished and he could see a huge column of smoke lifting from where it had stood. The line of soldiers had scattered and as he turned away he saw the refugees, warned of danger by the firing, swarming over the slopes and beginning to slither into the gorge, to wade the chest-high river and scramble up the other side.

He was feeling suddenly old and tired and his whole body was hurting. The Hart was just staggering along now, the engine missing badly, and he could see the ground through a huge hole in the floor beneath him. Rapidly losing flying speed, he followed the road south, trying to keep the aeroplane above stalling speed. Then he saw the hills flattening out and a string of lorries approaching.

As the engine stopped suddenly, the propeller jerked upright and stayed there and he knew he hadn't more than a minute or two left. He could see a patch of flat land just ahead of him and decided to put the machine down there. As he banked, trying to make his final approach, he saw men running from the lorries, but the Hart was finished and he couldn't bring her round, and as he saw the grass change from a green blur to separate blades, he lifted the nose. Unexpectedly she ground-looped and stood on her wingtip so that he banged his face on the front of the cockpit, then the machine was still, rocking slightly, lopsided, shattered, one wing crumpled and broken.

For a moment he was too dazed to move, then he realised he could hear a faint hissing sound and saw smoke in front of him. Forcing himself back to consciousness, he slammed at his safety belt and began to heave himself from the cockpit. He fell to his knees on the grass, vomiting violently, and, as he stood up to run, his legs gave way underneath him.

-

He came to in the back of a lorry. His leg was swathed in bandages and he couldn't see out of one eye. As he tried to move, he realised his clothes had been cut away and there were more bandages round his waist.

'Christ,' he murmured. 'What have they done to me?'

Even as the thought crossed his mind, he felt the lorry stop and heard the squeak of brakes. Then he heard the tailgate open and people scrambling in. It was growing dark but he could just see Foote's face above him, with Babington's, and, surprisingly, Hatto's.

'The boys have just landed,' Foote said. 'Johnny Johnson dropped his bomb smack on the head of the Japanese column. Ratowicz hit the side of the gorge and brought it down on top of them.'

'What about Lee?'

Foote grinned. 'His troops bolted and when the refugees realised what was in the lorries they pounced on them. They came away carrying food and clothes, even gramophones and radios. I guess he's lost the lot.'

'"Vengeance is mine,"' Dicken murmured. '"I will repay, saith the Lord."' If Father O'Buhilly couldn't be there to say it, he would say it for him.

Then he realised someone was holding his hand and, turning his head, he saw Marie-Gabrielle alongside him, dressed in a khaki field uniform. He thought she was the calmest, most beautiful thing he'd ever seen.

'Am I badly hurt?' he asked.

'Yes,' she admitted. 'You are.'

'Am I going to die?'

'No.' She spoke with such intensity that he believed her.

Hatto leaned forward. 'We'll fly you out in a few days,' he promised. 'You'll be in India in no time. This time there's no argument. You've got to go. Lee's hopping mad and ready to shoot you, so you'd better.'

Dicken's fingers tightened on Marie-Gabrielle's. 'I'll need someone to look after me,' he pointed out.

'I'm coming too,' Marie-Gabrielle said.

'Will they let you?'

'They insist.'

'The war'll be finished before you're around much again,' Hatto said. 'We've just heard. In Europe the show's over.'

'I hope the audience was satisfied,' Dicken mumbled.

'The actors weren't too bad.'

'Pity the lions ate the trainer.'

Hatto laughed. 'Calls for a gloat dance,' he said. 'The three of us.'

'Later,' Dicken murmured. 'When I feel more like it.'